GREAT WAR
1898
A BIG STICK

JACK MOORE

BOOK 3

Century Dawn

We know that on New Year's Eve of 1900 in the last few moments of the 19th century, the soon to be vice president of the United States of America was not celebrating the arrival of the 20th. There were libations and celebrations nearby and we know this by the same method that we are sure that Theodore Roosevelt did not feel compelled to join in. At the time, when most people were in the streets and waiting for the bells to chime atop Independence Hall, the former colonel was sitting in his hotel room in Philadelphia, writing about exactly how he felt. Roosevelt firmly believed that there was little cause to celebrate. He wrote in his journal that he did not bear any ill will towards those who thought the occasion should be marked with revelry, and he remarked that he could hear them from the window of his room, yet Roosevelt was consumed with the greater issues facing not only his nation but the entire world.

Roosevelt's frustrations were not due to the greater war that the world now found itself embroiled in. If his writings are to be taken seriously then it is quite clear that he thought the war was quite necessary. Like so many in the United States, since their defeat at the hands of the Confederate States, they felt much was wrong with the world and Roosevelt seemed to echo the sentiments of his fellow countrymen when he said, "As much as it pains me to say, only fire will purge this evil from our midst."

The axe that Roosevelt had to grind was only apparent when he discussed the prosecution of the war. This seemed to tear at his very soul because it is clear from his writings that he believed his nation not only capable of winning the conflict, but of fixing the world in general. It was a very optimistic appraisal and a tall order considering the position that the United States occupied in 1898 when the current war began. Despite the fact that no one doubted the emerging power of the US, even after the loss of its southern states, the nation was still regarded by the great European powers as an agrarian, regional, and somewhat backwater experiment in democracy that had failed. Ironically, this was as true of American allies and enemies alike.

While it was quite obvious that France and Russia had greatly depended on the US during the war, they never saw the aid provided by the Americans as anything substantial. Their attitude had been that the American contributions were little more than conveniences and that they, France and Russia, could still prosecute this war without American aid if need be. This was not some vague attitude either. America's allies said as much and were quite open with their opinions.

As much as this infuriated Roosevelt, who had now begun to involve himself in foreign affairs in a way that he never had before, he could understand why his nation had not yet won the respect that he believed it so richly deserved. So far, America's only real venture to demonstrate its ability, to project its will beyond its own borders, had been what Roosevelt had termed a sightseeing expedition in China. Despite how crucial this region was considered economically for the European powers, it was still a backwater, much as North America was. The US adventure also required the participation of the Russians, and without that help, American operations in the Pacific rim were impossible.

America's most important alliance, with the Boulanger Regime of France, was an unofficial partnership and cooperation between the two powers was always matters of convenience. The multiple treaties between the US and the Czar of Russia were formal, but it was clear who the senior partner was, and this was not the United States. If this was how her friends saw her then Roosevelt was under no illusions about America's enemies.

Roosevelt had come to a conclusion and apparently it was as he wrote all of this down. He decided that they could afford to scoff at his nation because their enemies, who were namely Britain, Germany, and Austria-Hungry were well beyond America's grasp. The US could hurt them by means of hitting their possessions and puppets, such as Canada, Mexico, and the Confederate States of America, but anything else was currently not an option. Roosevelt could not bring himself to understand why no one had even thought to try.

It might seem overly ambitious, but then again Theodore Roosevelt had never let such a thing stand in his way before. After all, just a little over two years ago he was a minor functionary in the administration of President Elihu Root. He had gone from that to Lieutenant Colonel, then full Colonel, and in twenty-two days he would become the Vice President of the United States. If that were possible then why was it not possible for his nation to not only join the ranks of the great powers, but be the most powerful of them all?

Roosevelt did not see this as impossible as so many around him might have thought.

Of course, there were many obstacles to be overcome if this were to ever happen. It might seem to many now, and it did to many then, that Roosevelt was an overzealous, crusading, simplistic, idealist, but I would hope that his accomplishments would prove this not to be the case. That is not to say that he was not any of the afore mentioned, it is just to say that Theodore was far more. He saw both his position and that of America very realistically.

Roosevelt understood that despite the fact that he was about to become Elihu Root's vice president, Root had little use for him besides having that toothy grin on an election poster. Roosevelt knew that the Root administration was not about to let him walk in and start dictating policy any more than Great Britain was about to surrender her fleet. Despite this, he believed that he could make both of those situations a reality and he was willing to try.

We cannot be sure, but if his journal entry of that night is correct, and this is truly when Theodore decided on a new and bold crusade, then not long after midnight on the first day of the new century it must have seemed as if it were cursed from the start. It was barely twelve minutes after midnight when the first sounds of war visited Philadelphia since the British had occupied the city during the America Revolution of a century past. The not too distant explosions that shook the very room that the future Vice President was sitting in were not from artillery or ships. Roosevelt was well aware that Philadelphia was safe from such attacks. He was no stranger to the sounds of war at this point and he was also aware of the new weapons being employed by his nation's enemies. That's why Roosevelt knew the attack could come from only one direction, the sky.

The raid on Philadelphia, in the very starting minutes of the new century, was by the Confederate States First Air Flotilla which consisted of seventeen airships, all of whom were now on their very first combat mission. This was the first service seen by any such vehicles built by the CSA since the CSS Thunder had raided Cincinnati just under a year earlier. These new zeppelins were very different from the Thunder which had delivered a small group of soldiers on what today we would call a special operations mission. These airships were larger faster and built to do only one thing, drop bombs from the sky. That is what caused the explosions that Roosevelt heard on that night and this raid was not unique. It was in coordination with the allies of the Confederacy, all of which were hitting targets on three different continents on the same day.

Several hours earlier in Europe, Germany had launched her newest 'sky trains' that were also on their very first combat missions. They carried monikers such as Wunderzeppelin and Das Uberzeppelin. Starting with the LZ-54 and followed by every subsequent airship, they were aircraft of truly monumental size and scope. Each craft had multiple gondolas, most of which supported a single engine and two crewmen per engine to keep the propellers spinning. The LZ-54 had eighteen engines and some of the later models would have over twenty. It allowed them to fly faster at higher altitudes, and with more stability than any of the previous models. Even more important than that was that they could fly much further. All of France was now easily within range of the German air fleet as were cities such as the Russian capital of St Petersburg.

The battle of the Ionian Sea had proven once and for all that the Zeppelins had practical uses. They certainly had limits, but their detractors found that they no longer had an argument against them. These clouds of war were not just useless toys. It also changed the minds of many of the benefactors of the airship as well. The first bombing campaign against France had been largely a failure and this was how the Zeppelins had come to be in the service of the navy. Now with such a decisive victory under their belt, even men like Admiral Tirpitz had begun to wonder if maybe that first land bombing campaign had simply not been executed or supported properly. The desperation to end the war was certainly enough to convince the Germans to give a land bombing campaign another try, hence the LZ-54 and her sister airships.

The only allied power not completely on board with this new strategy was the British Empire. While the operations in the Ionian Sea were enough to convince the Salisbury Cabinet that airships were worth pursuing, and vigorously at that, the needs of the British were quite different from that of Germany and the CSA. No matter how many troops that Britain sent to the Balkans, her war was still mainly one at sea. Commerce raiding was still the number one concern in Britain and the Zeppelins were seen as a means to protect vital merchant convoys and sea lanes. This is why British efforts to bomb the enemy into submission were halfhearted at best. Her new airships, nowhere near as large or complex as those of her allies, would not participate fully in the bombardment of France or the US. They would limit their land targets to naval bases and enemy ports such as Brest on the Brittany peninsula. Most of her airships would begin joining her far-flung fleets in an effort to decisively tip the balance of the naval war.

It is very hard to say if any of the leaders of the allied powers understood what was happening on that night. Some of them hinted in their letters and journals, although it has to be stated that many of these sources were from many years later when the authors were afforded the clarity of hindsight. That is why I believe that on that first night of the new century, the leadership of all the nations were quite unaware of the milestone that had been reached and even passed. They had just crossed a line that they had reached in very small steps. This might explain why no one ever understood that it had, indeed been crossed.

On the very first night of the very new century, war was no longer something that happened on distant battlefields, prosecuted and limited to professional soldiers and sailors all of whom had some idea of what they were getting into and were normally there because it was their job. Now everyone was going to know war, whether they chose to or not. The past conflicts that were governed by at least some rules, whose gross brutality was moderated by some attempts at civilized behavior, were now gone. The limits once endorsed, by the very men who did the killing, would be no more. Desperation had combined with technology to produce a conflict like no other in history. Soon, the devastation, just like the war itself, would become totally encompassing and nothing would be out of bounds.

Failing Assessments

The strategic bombing campaigns, that were largely aimed at France and the United States, were an attempt to convince the civilians populations of the high cost of war. In that respect they were terror raids, plain and simple. To be fair to the governments of the Confederate States and of Imperial Germany, they did do their best to restrict the target lists to the military and industrial. In the case of Joe Wheeler's administration in Richmond, the limits of Zeppelin technology were simply avoided in discussions and a lot of nodding and winking was going on. In the case of Kaiser Wilhelm, he absolutely forbade attacks on civilian targets and was quite resolute that his orders be followed on the matter. The German high command, fully understanding the limits of their airships, got around this problem by simply lying to their monarch.

The fact was that navigation and bomb sighting was not up to the task of what is called, in the modern world, surgical strikes. It is true that the airship crews were sent out to find and destroy military or economic targets. That was true of the attack on Philadelphia, witnessed by Roosevelt, in the early hours of New Year's Day. The Confederate target on that night was the naval yards and the support structure around it. They easily spotted the city from up high due to the celebrations and the many lights that were on for that purpose. Unfortunately, that was all they really could see, the lights. They dropped their bombs when they thought they were over the target, as per their navigational estimates. The pilots of the Confederate Air Forces were completely wrong.

What the Confederate flight crews did figure out, from the lighting beneath them, was the location of the Delaware River. Naturally, and in contrast to the land, the river was not lit, and they had a good view of the outline, however not a single bomb fell on the naval yards or even in the city of Philadelphia. Most of their bombs landed on the eastern shore of the river in Gloucester City. Not a single military facility, or even factory, was hit. Most of the destruction was limited to civilian homes. Three days later this fact was well known to the crews who were given the best possible intelligence, all courtesy of William Randolph Hearst and his newspaper empire, that wrote about and fanned the details of the attack for all that it was worth.

After the next set of raids on Cleveland, Pittsburg, and Indianapolis, the enflamed rhetoric from the newspapers abruptly ceased. That was because someone at Fort Lincoln had finally figured out that the newspapers were giving the Confederates something that any bombing campaign needed, bomb damage assessments. This squashing of news stories was only the first of many countermeasures against the raids that were in the pike. They were also one of the easiest.

One thing is very clear about the raids in North America. The US Army was caught completely off guard. Just the fact that it took them weeks to realize that the newspapers needed to be censured is a clear indication of this, and also it would appear as if they had no plans at all to deal with the problem. One would think that since they had already been subjected to the raid on Cincinnati, during the previous year, that someone might have considered such a move by the CSA, yet this was apparently not the case. There was definitely panic at Fort Lincoln.

Ultimately, the US would have to adopt something that their allies had already developed. It does not speak well of the US Army on this subject when you consider the lethargic attitude of the French military in dealing with the airships, yet somehow the French had managed to produce a viable countermeasure before any serious raids had begun on their cities. Fortunately for the US, the conversion of an artillery piece to anti-aircraft gun was a fairly straightforward process even if the Americans ignored some hard-won lessons that the French had already been taught.

One might consider that the main reason the US Army did not take the airships seriously was because they did not think them that big of a threat. From a technical standpoint their risk assessment seemed to be valid enough in that even the large scale raids were not producing any significant damage to the wartime infrastructure but the military planners suffered from some very fundamental in the box thinking errors in that they had never considered the fact that their civilian population would suddenly be in harm's way, or at least not to this degree. They had failed to consider that fact and had to come to grips with the primary purpose of having a military, to protect the civil population.

Of course, the rapid deployment of anti-aircraft batteries did little to solve this problem and in fact it made it worse. The airships were now forced to fly at higher altitudes, and this made their already haphazard aim even more so. This did manage to give more protection to critical industry, rail lines, and military targets since now their chances of being hit were the same as anyone else's, even if they were the primary targets of the raids. What this meant was that more bombs were going to fall on what the army was calling, in their official reports 'noncritical targets.' A translation for this euphemism would be civilian's homes and businesses. This much was understandable, but it was also not the only problem being caused by the countermeasures.

An intense survey of documentation made after the war seems to give serious credence to the claim that most of the damage done from the raids was not caused by Confederate bombs. Strangely enough, the best reports on this matter did not come from the army, but rather a collage of insurance claims filed at the time. The army reports on the matter were at best vague in their assessments since they seemed to have an interest in keeping these incidents as such. The insurance companies were an entirely different matter since most policies exclude wartime damage from their coverage and quite a few people did their best to claim that their properties were damaged in other ways. This meant that the insurance companies went out of their way to prove otherwise and more than a few of these claims wound up in court.

The overwhelming opinion of the insurance adjusters was that most of the damage that they were seeing was not being caused by the Confederate bombs. They were, however, being caused by falling debris that was the result of artillery ordinance being fired at the Zeppelins. This might have become something of an issue at the time, but as these cases wound their way through the courts the US Government stepped in and offered aid to people who were left destitute by the attacks. Most of the court cases vanished and the story remained silent until well after the war.

In this matter, the US Army cannot be held completely accountable for the problem. The civilian populace of the US shares some blame here as well. It did not take long before it was realized that cities needed to be blacked out at night. Indeed, someone seems to have thought of it the very night of the Confederate raid on Philadelphia. There were several police reports filed the next morning, claiming that a man on horseback was riding through the streets of Camden and shooting out porch lights with a revolver. While this incident seems anecdotal at best it does illustrate a problem that would plague the US for the rest of the war. People simply would not conform to the mass of regulations and city ordinances requiring black outs in urban areas. Apparently, being lined up in a Confederate bombsight was not enough of a threat to convince a large number of people to put up new curtains or simply unplug their lamp.

In their defense, this was an entirely new situation that had never been faced before. It is quite clear, from a host of private correspondence, that people really had no idea what to make of these attacks. The ranges of attitudes about them were across the board and you had people who thought it all 'humbug' and then others who were buying 'bomb nets' for the roof of their home. In this much the Confederate war plan seems to have failed because it is quite clear they were hoping for a mass panic in the US and it never materialized. I think it is safe to say that these attacks seemed so fantastical for the time that they hardly felt real, even when explosions were going off across the street from your house.

To the credit of the US Military however it was only the army that was unprepared. The Navy was an entirely different matter. They had paid attention to what happened to the French and Italian fleets in the Ionian Sea. They quickly realized the threat this new technology would pose to their blockade of Canada and began preparing countermeasures almost before the smoke cleared in the Mediterranean Theater. That is quite possibly why they would even precede the French in claiming first blood and be the first to intentionally shoot down an airship.

Since mounting new weapon systems on a ship is relatively easy as it is done all the time, and the Navy already had weapons capable of shooting high enough to 'bust a balloon,' it was not so hard for them to convert several destroyers to exclusively be anti-aircraft platforms. It was also not very long before they encountered their first British airship at the mouth of the St Lawrence Seaway. The sudden and violent attack by the DD-405 must have come as something of a shock to the crew of the HMS Tully. The fire they received was not only reaching their altitude but was extremely accurate. The Tully exploded in midair and nothing larger than the size of a breadbox reached the water.

Like most military technologies, the new airship war became a game of measure and countermeasure. Each side would try new things and their opponents would find a counter, causing the cycle to repeat itself. The ultimate result, that the Entente came to realize very quickly, was that the only way to stay in this game was to have an air fleet of your own. Before the end of 1901 this would be the case and every major belligerent would be deploying their own Zeppelins and bombing each other's cities. The real issue remained, and this was true for both sides. While they could all effect the bombing raids, they had no real way of stopping them. The Zeppelins would always reach their targets even if the damage they did once there was minimal at best. Still, little things eventually add up to be big things and this had more than a few key people worried. That was how it all got started.

The Gardener

Since the war began in November of 98, the US Army had learned a lot about fighting on the Tennessee Front. This front was considered one of the more critical by Fort Lincoln of any south of the Canadian border since the basic plan for dealing with the CSA was to drive down the Mississippi Valley all the way to the gulf. Unfortunately for the US Army, the Confederacy was not only well aware of this plan but had taken more than adequate steps in defending the western part of the state. Naturally, as we all know, this included planting the invasive weed kudzu, which proved to be so effective that Confederate soldiers came to be known by that name.

Even as US troops drove Johnny Kudzu south of the border there was no way they could drive the weed with them. The US soon found that the weed not only helped break up attacks at the front, but it also made occupying territory just plain difficult. The typical scenario was that a US forward base, such as supply depots and field hospitals, would move onto a patch of ground that looked relatively clear, usually because the ground had been fought over recently and the artillery had destroyed most vegetation. As it turned out, to the army's chagrin, this only made the ground more inviting to kudzu, which now found that even the meager competition from local plants was gone. Within weeks the weed would be back and within a month it would overgrow everything that the army had set up if a legion of soldiers were not devoted to hacking it back on a daily basis.

The Confederates did not suffer from this problem since they depended on the weed to camouflage their block houses, rifle pits, and sniper positions, of which it did all too well. This is how the US Army's 361st Combat Engineer Battalion found itself with the one and only dedicated mission of eradicated the kudzu. It was a tedious and thankless job and made the men of the 361st the butt of a good many jokes by other soldiers, particularly when the moniker 'The Lost Battalion' finally stuck with them sometime in 1899. It was apparently a reference to a joke about how the unlucky engineers were getting lost in the weeds and unfortunately for them it was not far from the literal truth.

Prior to the summer of 1900, the 361st would be the limit of Fort Lincoln's willingness to devote resources to combating kudzu. As they saw it, the weed was a regional problem and hence the responsibility of XVIII and IX Corps to deal with. Neither unit had the resources to do very much and indeed reports written by their staff indicated that they were of the opinion there was nothing they really could do. US troops learned to use kudzu in a similar fashion as Confederate troops, but the weed was only really beneficial if you were on the defensive. The US Army was tasked with the mission of overwhelming Fort Bragg and capturing Memphis, hardly a defensive operation.

The Lost Battalion attempted every possible solution that was known at the time for fighting pesky plants. They burned field after field only to discover that the roots were safely underground, and the ash made for excellent fertilizer. Then came attempts to get at the roots with explosives. They left nice craters, which turned into little lakes, that thirsty kudzu seemed to be quite fond of. They were also making the rear areas look like the front lines and the Corps commanders put a stop to the blasting. The truth was, the 361st simply did not have enough explosives to get every single root system anyway so their early efforts always led them right back to lines of men with giant hacking blades.

Then came some unexpected help from the least likely of places. Charles Lee Reece was a chemist and longtime college professor that found himself working back in industry once the war began. The pay was far better, and Reece commented that he actually felt like he was doing something important. Specifically, he took a position with the DuPont corporation who at the time specialized almost exclusively in making smokeless gun powder, which was considered a very crucial military technology. It was in this capacity that he had visited the Tennessee Front on any number of occasions and how he came into contact with The Lost Battalion.

After an embarrassing incident in which Reece had mistaken the soldiers as military prisoners because of their appearance and their job, he became somewhat interested in how this could happen. When he was educated on the subject of kudzu, something he had virtually ignored up until this point, he realized he could be of service. Once returning to Wilmington he quickly tasked several of his chemists to begin researching the subject of using chemicals to kill weeds. Reece had been vaguely aware that this was being tested in Europe and he was pleased to discover that the US Army Corps of Engineers had actually tried it in the United States.

Not understanding how the military bureaucracy worked, Reece was a little confused as to why the army had not thought to try a chemical approach to removing the weed when they had been treating invasive plant life in waterways for nearly a decade. Then he discovered that, while technically speaking the CoE was a part of the Army, they had little to do with the actual military organization and were primarily civilian. Not wanting to deal with the bureaucracy any more than he had to and knowing that DuPont had the capability to produce as much Sodium Arsenite as was needed, Reece took it upon himself to proceed with a field test on no-one's authority but his own.

The Lost Battalion had no objections when Reece showed up and explained what he wished to do. Their subsequent attempts at treating the plants with the chemical had mixed results but for the time being they were certainly better results than anything tried before. The 361st went full steam ahead with their new defoliant and only then did they discover some side effects. There had been no indications that physical ailments would be a problem or at least not during the trial runs when only limited amounts were being carefully handled.

When Reece was called back to Tennessee, he quickly discovered that the soldiers had largely ignored his instructions on handling the Sodium Arsenite. Many were suffering from blisters, problems with vision, nausea, and a host of symptoms that the army doctors were at a loss to diagnose. Reece did not doubt it was his defoliate and at that point he might have given up, but Reece did not see a disaster here. What he saw was an opportunity.

Reece began to ponder the idea of using his defoliate on Confederate soldiers and not just plants. He had big ideas of clearing both the kudzu and the enemy off the battlefield at the same time. The only problem that he saw with his idea was that Sodium Arsenite was simply not strong enough to do the job. It was only making men sick and even then required prolonged exposure. When Reece returned to his labs, he set up yet another research project and only then did he learn that his idea was not exactly new.

Many chemists had been proposing the idea of using chemicals as weapons for many years. There proved to be more than an adequate selection of chemicals to use which were readily available and very cheap. Most of the substances in question were a biproduct of routine industrial processes, many done at DuPont, and were simply disposed of. The idea had apparently struck some politicians, worldwide, as a good one while others were horrified by it. There had even been serious talk amongst diplomats of banning the weapons even though they did not yet exist.

Reece was of the opinion that now with a war raging across the globe no one would be talking about getting rid of a new, and potentially game changing, weapon. In the first few months of 1900 he turned his academic fact-finding mission into an actual testing project. By early 1900 he had amassed a small stockpile of a variety of gasses including chlorine and bromide. All that Reece was lacking was a means of delivering these weapons to the enemy. This is where Reece ran into his biggest problem.

The military, and in particular Chief of Staff General Shafter, was simply not interested in the project and by some accounts he was typical of most soldiers who were horrified by the idea and dismissed it out of hand. This did not stop Reece nor DuPont, who began pulling strings on Capitol Hill and eventually even in the White House where John Hay was made aware of the project. Hay thought the idea had some merits but apparently not enough to authorize any full-scale development and deployment. Hay did however authorize a small budget that greenlit the development of an artillery shell that could deliver the gas.

It would be in the shadows that Reece would work until not long after the Confederate Airships struck at Chicago on January 20th, 1901. Root's inauguration to his second term was only two days away and it was clear to all that the CSA was letting Root know they could hit him anywhere he went. Chicago had been selected to be the city where the inauguration would take place, and while the administration denied it, the reason for this selection was largely because they thought the city safe.

Root's anger over the matter put John Hay in something of a predicament since he had assured everyone that the airships could not reach that far north. Root demanded action because no matter how small the damage was, it was making them look weak at a critical moment. Samuel Langley's airplane seemed little more than a pipedream at that moment and Root wanted his own big stick. That's when Hay presented his president with the news of the little project going on down in Delaware. Hay had calculated the timing of this news with the diplomatic skill he was so famous for. Root was enthused and Reece would get the big budget he wanted along with almost a blank check on any resources he needed. By March, DuPont would be turning out chemical artillery shells by the train carload.

A Crack in Time

In the annals of human history, there are a few select moments of time where so many events are compressed, that suddenly it is the future that one can see instead of the past. The very first month of the very first year of the twentieth century was most definitely one of those focal points. Even more ironic is how it is all centered around a single day. Maybe this is clear to us now due to hindsight, but the strange coincidence that occurred on the 22nd of January of that year most certainly did seem to those at the time as if a torch had been passed from a vanishing era to yet another.

In Chicago, President Elihu Root and his running mate, Theodore Roosevelt, were sworn into office. Root was now officially on his second term and by the very act, his reinstatement was a message that nothing had changed, and that America was still in the war. Even if no one knew it at the time, it was also not as important as was Roosevelt's swearing in, which was treated as something to be disposed of. For someone who was quite famous for his speeches even at this point, Theodore would not utter a single word to the gathered crowds. He would stand in a line of men, looking not any different from the others, for most of the ceremony.

One has to understand that this was very typical for vice presidents of the United States. The position was something of a black hole for politicians and so much so that many of Theodore's friends had urged him not to accept the nomination. Going all the way back to the very first Vice President, John Adams, it was quickly discovered how easily this position could be ignored. Unlike John Adams, very few Vice Presidents would ascend to the next logical step of commander and chief. That position was usually reserved for the Secretary of State, and in the past even the primary function of the Vice President was called into question when the first President had died in office. It had resulted in a constitutional crisis because many did not believe the Vice President should lose the status of 'vice.'

While the constitutional issue of presidential succession was largely resolved in 1901, no one gave it much thought because it had been a very rare occasion that a president died in office. On that day, in January of 1901, Root appeared to be the poster boy of good health. He gave a three-hour speech with a tireless energy that normally his Vice President was famous for. What the people in the crowd were unaware of was that this was one of two speeches that Root had prepared for this day. The first one, the one he thought he would be forced to use, was a much shorter speech and not because Root had any mercy for the crowd who braved the cold on that day.

What was not commonly known by the public, and even many inside the administration, was that US military intelligence had managed to get a close eye on the Confederate airships that were stationed in northern Alabama. They were also equally successful at getting out raid warnings via a successful spy ring that was well imbedded in the state government of Tennessee. The information that they passed along on that day was never more crucial to Root, who had expected those Zeppelins to show up in the sky of Chicago while he was on the stump, however the strange fact was that the Confederate Air Force had been ordered to stand down on this day.

Root never pondered why and simply thanked his blessings and went with his longer speech. He would not find out what the connection was until later that night when the news reached a Chicago ballroom that the leader of America's most hated enemy had died earlier in the day. Oddly enough, during one of the many inaugural balls, for the President of an enemy country, Queen Victoria was given five minutes of silence to memorialize her passing. Even now after all the blood, the people in Chicago, and America in general, still understood on an almost subconscious level that while they might be living in a rival nation they were still living in an era that would be named for the woman who had just died. No matter what you felt about the British, Victoria's death was a moment that transcended national rivalries and was most certainly a bookmark of human history. The war only made this moment more heartfelt.

It is strange how so much, that was not very important in the material sense, was leaving such a heavy mark on the impressions of so many at the time. While it was well known in the circles of governments across the globe, that Victoria was merely a figurehead, her presence had most certainly captured the imaginations of the people far and wide, and made everyone, even those who lived in rival nations, feel a sense of stability. The subsequent events only went to demonstrate how true this was. It also showed how desperate people were becoming and by extension it made their governments even more so because they knew the hard part was yet to come.

This seems a bit of historical irony when you consider how irrelevant Victoria had become in her own government and even in the context of how she redefined the very throne that she occupied. In many ways it is easy to surmise that Victoria was more loved in death than she ever was in life, and one can go right back to her very first days on the throne and see this. She was but a teenager when she was crowned, and her age had been one of the chief reasons that opponents of the monarchy had attempted to dispose of the institution entirely. The compromise left Victoria as head of state, but in name only. She never truly tried to change this situation and, seemed perfectly happy to be the 'moral center' of Great Britain.

Even that part of her job changed entirely when in December of 1861 her husband died unexpectedly at the age of 42. The truth was that Albert had been ill for some time but downplayed this fact, especially to his wife. Victoria and Albert were hopelessly in love, something very uncommon amongst monarchs of the age, and as a testimony to their unofficial power, had made loving one's spouse a standard when it had never really been before. Albert's death also exposed a problem with this particular custom, and it is quite possibly why monarchs had never treated marriage as anything more than a business arrangement before that time. This problem was that Victoria was heartbroken and remained in mourning the rest of her life. The subsequent effects on politics and culture would show itself but only be realized years later and then mostly by historians that are rarely listened too.

The events surrounding Victoria's death are a good case in point. It was Victoria's custom after the passing of Albert, to spend the winter on the Isle of Wight at her estate known as the Osborne House. While the estates look palatial by any standard, the fact was that her family hated it and constantly begged her to spend the Christmas season at Buckingham Palace. This was so true that one of Victoria's last requests was that Osborne House remain in the Windsor family. This caused something of a predicament for her son, Edward, who tried to pawn the place off on any number of relatives, all of whom refused.

There was the added problem that it was not only her family that had requested she spend her winter somewhere else. When the war began, the Isle of Wight seemed rather exposed to the Royal Navy because, after all, France was just right across the channel and they had already seized the Channel Islands of Jersey and Guernsey. It was greatly feared that Victoria's presence on the coast would be a tempting target for President Boulanger. Of course, the truth is this was mostly wartime paranoia. We now know that Boulanger had absolutely no interest in Queen Victoria or the Isle of Wight. Jersey and Guernsey were right off the coast of Brittany which, to the French at least, made them a security problem. The Isle of Wight was seriously defended, within sight of England, and beyond its worth to even raid.

Still the Queen's presence at her estate always meant that the Royal Navy had to siphon off resources to increase the security of the island for her annual pilgrimage. While there was not even an unofficial mention of it, one can surmise that there was nothing but relief in Plymouth at having been relieved of this responsibility. The same could not be said of their King and his unforeseen responsibility of disposing of an estate that not a single royal would have anything to do with. Oddly enough, the one man who was willing to claim title to

Osborne, was also kneeling beside Victoria as she passed. He was her eldest grandson, and unlike Victoria, he was a monarch in the true sense of the word. He was the Kaiser of the Second German Empire, and his name was Wilhelm.

At the time of Victoria's passing, it is hardly imaginable that Wilhelm had given much thought about owning another estate. It is quite possible that his reasons were personal. He had spent much time there as a child and adored his Grandmother even if she privately did not return the favor. Victoria would often comment in private about her grandson, and it seems that her opinion of the boy was that he was very much a 'boorish bully.' Yet he was the one holding her hand when she died, and it would be Wilhelm that would go very much forward with the memorialization of his grandmother, even exceeding her English family.

The passing of the estate was also one of the very first concrete changes brought about by Victoria's death. By the end of the year the grounds would be mostly occupied by visiting German military officers, most of whom were advisors sent from the Kriegsmarine to coordinate operations with the Royal Navy. By the end of the war it would become a military headquarters, responsible for all operations in the channel that involved the navies of both nations. After the war it would become a permanent symbol of Anglo-German military cooperation.

This would not be the last real change brought about by Victoria's death. In fact, this would be one of the smallest. The most visible change was only days away, even if it would take years before anyone realized that Victoria's death had anything to do with it. It would be quite literally a silent change despite being well publicized at the time. It would terrify the collective general officers, their staffs, and the politicians of every nation. It would be easily fixable from their point of view, but it was the very first and very unexpected sign of what they all knew was coming. Ultimately, they all knew that they could fight the symptoms but, in the end, they were powerless to stop it.

The Message

Given the extensive library that now bears his name in Tennessee, it is hardly imaginable that this would be the first time that Cordell Hull shows up on the historical record. It is not entirely true since I have discovered at least one newspaper article where his name does appear in a list of graduates from the prominent McTyeire Law School, in Nashville. This obviously predates even the mention he received once passing the State Bar Exam a year later and has been claimed by some to be his entry on the stage of public affairs. I have to admit that the significance of either of these articles is at best a footnote in history since it was Hull's action in January of 1901 that was his first real notice by anyone.

This would not be an act of war, as everyone knows, since it was later the subject of a movie that was, ironically, filmed in California. It is well known that exceptions to the rule are what make headlines in newspapers and with that being the case what Hull did on the morning of the twenty-third was most definitely an exception because it was an act of peace. Hull would later go on to note that his participation in this matter was not an act of divine providence nor any particular skill. He was, by luck, simply at his battalion headquarters when the orders arrived and was picked for no other reason than he was standing around and looking as if he had nothing to do. Hull would go on to explain that this was true insofar as he had been patiently waiting his turn to report to his battalion commander on an unrelated issue for which he had been summoned. Naturally, the movie would show none of this.

It would also seem as if word of Hull's mission had beaten him back to the trenches because, in Hull's own words, everyone seemed to be jumping in anticipation of his return. As is often the case with the military rumor mill, many of the men in Hull's company thought this was the end of the war. Hull noted smiles and pats on the back as his company First Sergeant tied a big white flag to the stick that Hull would carry across no man's land. The enemy soldiers on the other side held their fire and strangely enough, they seemed to also have some clue that he was coming.

This is where the Hollywood version drastically departs from reality. Contrary to popular opinion, Hull was not the only

Confederate Officer marching out to meet his counterpart on that day. This scene was playing itself out up and down the lines of a fifteen-hundred-mile-long front and was hardly unique, nor was this the first time. Both sides had cause to communicate with each other from time to time and it was quite often that a flag of truce would present itself. What was unique about this instance was that the flags were going up, front wide, all at the same time.

This might note some importance to the request being made by the Confederacy. It might also be important to note that not a single officer over the rank of Captain was presenting the request to the United States. For that matter, not a single respondent was anything more than what the Confederates were using as their messenger boy. It would seem that the Lieutenant Colonels were not particularly interested in getting their hands dirty on this matter but, in reality, they were simply following a protocol that had developed along the front.

This detail is also important if, for no other reason, than to set the historical record straight. The movie was very wrong on many points, and while it was dramatic, the man that Hull talked with on that day was not a young recently graduated second lieutenant from West Point, by the name of George C. Marshall. The man was, in fact, the commander of E company, 10th Ohio Infantry (Reserve), and his name was Captain William McFarland. At the time that Hull and McFarland conversed, Marshall was still at West Point and would not graduate for another six months. It would seem clear that the movie chose to replace McFarland due to later events involving both Marshall and Hull but there is no truth to the story. McFarland would go on to win the Medal of Honor but unfortunately it would be a posthumous award.

The most unique factor in Hull's mission was not anything that Hull did himself. Something that is not shown in the movie was the fact that Hull did not talk with McFarland alone. The Ohio Captain was followed out into no man's land by someone who was no man, even if Hull did not quite recognize this at the time. Elizabeth Cochrane was dressed much the same as any US soldier would be with the exception of the rifle. Both Hull and McFarland carried only their flags since that was the custom for these meetings, so Hull thought that this thirty-six-year-old woman reporter, who went by the pen name Nellie Bly, was some kind of aid.

What Nelly was armed with was something that, for the time, was very hi tech. It was so new in fact that Hull had no idea what it was. As Hull wrote in his journal, he first thought that it was a weapon, and then after seeing it in detail thought it might be a box of cigarettes, and after that he had no clue until Bly asked if she might get a picture of the two men together. The item in question was an instant camera from the Eastman Corporation and they were becoming very common on the US side of the line. Hull was distracted from what he described as this 'impossible camera' when he realized he was talking with a woman. Still, he agreed to let her take several photographs, one of which became somewhat famous and has survived to this day as the negative is preserved in the vault of the Eastman Corporation's museum.

Of course, the fanfare surrounding this incident is largely due to later events and the significance we place on this meeting today. At the time, Hull delivered his message to McFarland and there was little fanfare besides Bly's pictures. Both men would meet a second time several hours later when a reply from Chicago, where Elihu Root was recovering from his Inauguration, was cabled back to the front.

It is often said that this was the first major decision of the Root Administration's second term. He agreed to the Confederate request which he stated in his cable as being the "spirit of a true gentleman." There would be a general ceasefire between the forces of the United and Confederate States beginning at noon on that day and lasting until noon of the next.

This temporary halt to the killing was allegedly in response to the death of Queen Victoria, and while it is true that this prompted the ceasefire, one has to note that both sides were very tired of war at this point. It was also winter in the northern hemisphere and offensive operations were at a virtual standstill for the time being, so the general staffs were more than willing to go along with a halt in hostilities if for no other reason than to just catch their collective breaths. They had no idea what kind of jar had just been opened.

At that moment, in Germany, Canada, and Poland, similar flags of truce were going out into the fields between the combatants and similar requests were being made to the forces of the Entente. Again, in contrast to the film, there is no evidence that this was a coordinated effort on the part of the allies. It seems to have been an idea who literally fit the category of the 'time has come." This is significant because one has to consider the true meaning here. If these requests had initially come from men like Balfour, Waldersee, Wilhelm, Franz Joseph, Porter Alexander, or others who were in charge of the strategic picture then you could make a case that this was indeed a request for memorializing the passing of a Queen that had true global influence. What seems to be more likely here is that many who were much closer to the fighting were looking for any excuse to stop. Again, this conclusion is the result of hindsight, but it seems logical.

The fact that their superiors, those mentioned above, went along with what became an almost universal truce, seems like it is a case of 'what could it possibly hurt?' Despite later portrayals, it would seem that the initial response from national leaders was that this was of little consequence. At the time, there was no way they could have known what kinds of problems it would cause nor did they seem to realize exactly what it truly meant until much later. The movie started out by showing the leadership as cautious, reactionary, and quite antagonistic, but this was not the case. Those were attitudes developed later and not for the afore mentioned reasons. What caused the leadership of the world to eventually reel from this truce was most obviously plain and simple fear.

Vacation

The truce that followed the death of Queen Victoria is somewhat ironic and quite possibly even a contradiction between reality and perception. This might even serve to explain exactly why the powers that be in 1901 took the events of this single twenty-four-hour period as an ominous warning. Some might explain the truce as an outburst of nostalgia for 'the good old days' which had only recently vanished quite sudden and violently in the literal flash of an eye. It could be that the soldiers on the front lines had simply reached their breaking points. Then again, maybe they had all finally figured out what they were fighting for - nothing. I believe that it was most likely all of the above and more.

One of the most interesting aspects of the truce was how long it took to come to public light. It was certainly no military secret and was widely reported when it happened but no matter how many people were fighting the war, the simple fact is that most people were nowhere near the front. They were all used to seeing fantastical headlines on a daily basis and this was just one in an endless stream, not the first nor the last. Most civilians simply missed the significance of an almost universal truce and the details of that truce were never truly reported for what they were. That might go a long way towards explaining why this small chapter of the war was forgotten about for almost sixty years before the movie industry took it out of context and used it as political fodder for more contemporary political issues.

It may have been just one day, and in comparison to the war as a whole, seemingly small. Not only did the civilian populations miss its significance but so did the very men that made this day noteworthy. The soldiers on the front lines of the world were too busy to put the entire incident into context. Judging by the sampling of any number of soldiers' correspondence, they only saw the truce in the same terms that they saw the war, that being the small stretch of ground in front of them. The men who did understand what was happening were the exact same ones that apparently went out of their way to bury this incident. They were also quite successful in that it took us almost six decades to dig it back up.

Most of the stories that come from the frontlines seem almost anecdotal when put into context. Indeed, it is hard to argue that they were anything but small, only those small things added up. When the guns went silent, men began to slowly dribble out of their trenches and into no man's land. In places like North America where on both fronts the antagonists all spoke the same language, this happened nearly the instant the truce took effect. The guys who did most of the fighting and dying all began to quickly trade goods with one another. This was followed by laughter, handshakes and not long after any number of sporting events broke out. Soldiers began randomly wandering in and out of each other's trenches, sharing alcohol, and there was even one instance of sharing recipes from back home.

This was even true in places where the opposing armies did not share a common language. German and French soldiers mingled just outside of Metz and the party that erupted began taking on an organization of its own. Austrians and Russians, Serbs and English, Boers and Indians, even Chinese and Chinese, all joined in the peace. The South African and

Asian theaters are particularly important to note because there was no great love for Victoria in either of those theaters, yet the fighting stopped. The only place we do not have any reported change was in Alaska where despite the fact that it was high winter, raids went right on year-round and even increased during the cold season. One can easily explain the Alaskan situation when you realize that most of the combatants there had simply not heard of the truce until it was long over with.

Again, the leadership of the time seems to have failed to grasp a very fundamental difference between the majority of the soldiers who were fighting this war and those men they commanded during peacetime. The number crunching had certainly led to some odd attitudes that would take nearly a century of conflict before anyone could grasp this. The men in the trenches might have had enough military training to function but they were still at their core civilians in uniform. This breed of solider has only three basic goals after they encounter their first battle. Those are to stay alive, stay comfortable, and count the days till they can go home. All of that certainly showed itself during the truce.

It was not something that their officers, who were leading from way behind the lines, seemed to grasp and I can only surmise that this had a great deal to do with their alarm. On that day, their armies simply stopped following orders. That went right down the line and was just as true for the commands from officers at the front as it was for those pushing pins on maps. What is interesting to note is how from a historical point of view this truce seems to have been completely ignored at the national leadership level. We do have journal entries from many men, including John Hay who paid lip service to the humanity of the situation but little else. The lack of any other writing on the matter is the interesting part.

Fortunately, Theodore Roosevelt was his usual blunt self. He was quite often too honest for his own good and this included words that he very well knew were for posterity. Unfortunately, even if he was now the Vice President, he was not included in the inner working of the administration that he now served. What Roosevelt did note about this day was that it disturbed a great many people in the administration, all of whom were still in Chicago when it happened. One could not have known this when reading the words of men like Root and Hay. Yet it is easy to understand why.

The collective national leaderships of every nation, whether they be at Ten Downing, The Sedan, The White House, and so forth, all knew of the looming problems that at the time Roosevelt was barely even aware of. The men that handled the economies, the distribution systems and national policy in general all knew the numbers by now. Everything was coming unglued and the only thing holding it together was oddly enough the very thing that was tearing it apart, the war. One has to wonder if they were not sitting around waiting for the clock to wind down, the truce to end, and wondering if the war would even start back.

I have been accused of painting this situation with the brush of doom and gloom. Many do not accept my conclusions and I can understand this on some levels. This event, once it became well known at the pop culture level, was something of an emotional landmark. It is seldom analyzed in context given how long it took before anyone truly realized that it had even happened. Once this information is plugged in to the war in general, and not seen in the microcosm for which it is usually portrayed, one gets a very different picture and can understand why it must have alarmed the leaders of the world, and why they did not see peace, but rather anarchy. In this light, the truce does not seem to represent peace as much as it does the impossible quagmire the world found itself in and that there was no longer any way to go back.

What evidence do we have of this? The very second that the truce ended, the artillery on both sides of the line began hurling a rain of shells down on the other. It still stands as the single largest artillery bombardment in history and it went on for three days nonstop. While the men in the trenches were used to such large bombardments they were normally followed with an enemy advance and this time, that did not happen. It was almost as if by an unspoken consensus the leaders of both sides decided to cooperate in an act that would collectively punish their armies for having disobeyed orders during the truce. While I believe there was more to the bombardment, I also think that it had to be in the back of the minds of the men who ordered it.

The Imperial Divide

The biggest waves created by this one-day truce was not as hard felt anywhere more than in London. This might seem odd seeing as how the British Isles were the one place on earth where direct consequences of the fighting were virtually nonexistent. The reason this is true is because of the indirect consequences of what some in the Salisbury Cabinet were seeing as an army wide mutiny. This is the kind of thing that is far more important to an empire with an army that mostly consisted of colonial troops, some of which had questionable loyalty to the empire. When seen in this light, and when you consider that of all the belligerents the British Empire was the most status quo power, then you can begin to understand the concerns of men like Balfour and Chamberlin.

One might consider that India, the crown jewel of the British economic empire, would have been the first source of trouble, but strangely India remained largely passive about their overlords. Considering the cultural and ethnic divides, this might seem strange but taking a closer look at the situation puts it very much in perspective and the lack of any real opposition movement in India is completely understandable. The war had very little effect on India in any real sense and in fact the changes that came about tended to be positive.

India was a land that was very divided by its own choice. It had not ruled itself in centuries and for most Indians this was seen as perfectly normal. India had contributed troops to the conflict but a quick look at the journals of many serving British officials reveal that the ethnic concerns prevented large scale recruitment. Direct military support from within India came from the more traditional segments of the population that had been providing the bulk of the India Trading Company's troops for at least two centuries. Even most of those troops were used for the security of India and little else.

If anything, life for the average Indian improved during the war. There was almost no fighting around India, and where the British had reservations about using most of her population for military purposes, they had no qualms at all in using Indians as a labor force. Emigration for these purposes to places like South Africa had been common before the war and hostilities only expanded both the number of emigrants and destinations. All the while in

India itself not only could the country feed itself from local sources, but suddenly new jobs and industries were growing as a result of the war.

It was not that India lacked an independence movement, they most certainly had one, but this idea seemed to mostly be rooted in the Indian business and community leaders. If these men, most of whom were English educated, had one overriding virtue it was patience. The war was enriching them and laying a modern infrastructure that they fully understood would strengthen their hand with the British after the war. They were apparently willing to wait. As for your average Indian, who had yet to be really introduced to the idea of nationalism, the idea that was embraced by their local leaders seemed almost absurd. It was certainly not as pressing a matter as problems with other Indians.

That is why it is with great irony that Britain's problems with her commonwealth would start in the very nations that spoke the same language and of whom most of their inhabitants shared the same color of skin. Strangely enough it would also start in areas that had remained virtually untouched by the war and would not really start until a few years after the commencement of hostilities. Again, this seems counter intuitive, but also again, a close examination reveals that it is perfectly logical. Britain did have considerable support for the commonwealth in most of her Imperial holdings. This is understandable when you consider that most of these lands enjoyed varying amounts of self-rule.

The supporters of the commonwealth did not hesitate to rush to the banner of war in 1898, but by 1901 most of these men were on the front lines, dead, or had changed their minds about their support. The opposition to the British Empire had not been so eager to get involved in the war and many of these men were the ones who stayed home. With the supporters gone and with at least some democracy, many of them got elected to offices and began to immediately oppose the war. When the legal route did not work, and many agitators were hoping for just that, labor strikes and passive sabotage followed. This would cause the Salisbury cabinet any number of headaches in Australia and New Zealand.

None of the problems down under would become so critical as the developing problems in Canada. Strangely enough, none of them would sneak up so thoroughly on the London government either. The main reason for this seems to be the simple fact that before the war Canada was a very quiet and non-controversial place. It was strategic, and economically important to Britain, but careful control of immigration and the right mix of self-rule and imperialism seems to have worked well, or at least on the surface. Not a single British cabinet, in the years before the war, seems to have dug too deeply into the situation. The reason for this is actually quite simple. Things always ran rather smoothly in Canada and why fix what is not broken? What the British did not realize at the time, was that not only were the seeds of discontent being sown in Canada, but Imperial policy was one of its biggest contributors.

There was nothing very sinister or conspiratorial about some of these imperial policies and no way that anyone could have foreseen the results. In fact, some of the policies were both needed and beneficial, while at the same time creating side effects that would only matter if certain things were to happen. No one has that kind of clarity of vision about the future. One such policy, quite possibly the single most instrumental, was the reform of the Canadian education situation. I say reform because the laws that were implemented all called themselves reform acts, and for the most part they were. The side effects were another matter.

What was not talked about in regard to the education system was what kind of system it was, who invented it, and why. After the Fenian raids that occurred in the aftermath of the American 61, London woke up to the needs of defending her North American possessions. Naturally more Imperial troops were a starting point, but in the event of general war with the United States, the difficulty of transporting an entire army across the Atlantic was recognized and that was including the assumption of naval supremacy by the Royal Navy. With that in mind, it was realized that the bulk of the early defenses would have to be the responsibility of the people who lived in North America.

This is why the education system was eventually, and completely, revamped to a model that was first introduced in Prussia and then later all of Germany. Eventually all of the major powers would copy this system once its true purpose was recognized. While these school systems did teach the classical curriculum of literacy, philosophy, and math, they did something far more. Prussia was presented with the unique problem of making all German speaking people feel more like

Germans and less like the little patchwork quilt of states they truly were. There was also the additional goal of militarizing their entire population to deal with the threat of Russia and France. All of this could get a needed boost if everyone was indoctrinated early on.

That's not to say that these schools taught military arts because most did not. What they did do was get kids used to considering themselves a part of a greater nation and not just a small community. They also got them used to the idea of standing in line, sitting in neat orderly rows, eating generic food, and following simple orders like stand and sit. They also stressed learning by the repeat and remember system, which in the military is called drill, drill, and drill. All of these are basic military skills, that if you do not have to teach in basic training shaves months off the time required to whip raw recruits into at least passable soldiers.

This system was slowly introduced in Canada from the late seventies into the early nineties, and by the time of the war, most Canadians from middle age on down had been exposed to the system to at least some degree. For males, the training only continued after school as every able man was required to do at least some military time, even if letters home bear out that most never believed they would have to fight. What all of this did was more than just create a wartime Canadian military, it created a common culture that transcended class, culture, and even language barriers. It made every Canadian feel as if they belonged to a real country and not just an imperial commonwealth. No one in London seemed to have noticed and you can't really blame them because until the war began to drag out no one in Canada seemed to have either.

Since 1867, technically and legally, Canada had been an independent nation. The reality on the ground was an entirely different matter. War planners at Pall Mall fully understood the strategic and economic importance of Canada. With a hostile US sitting below one of the longest borders in the world, it was quickly decided in London that Canada could not be trusted with real independence. As a result of this unspoken policy, despite the fact that Canada had its own head of state and elected assembly, the real decisions about national policy were all being made by the Governor General, which was a position that was manned by an appointee from Britain. If there was any disagreement between the

Governor General and elected officials of Canada, it was usually the Governor General who got his way and he only answered to people in London, usually the Foreign Secretary.

Until the war this had not really been much of a problem. Canada was fortunate to have been assigned some talented individuals in this office who were usually eager to work with the local government as opposed to offending it. The man in charge in 1901 was no exception, no matter how much he has been vilified ever since. The fact was that Gilbert-Elliot-Murray Kynynmound, the 4th Earl of Minto, was a reasonable choice for the position given the circumstances under which he took office.

Minto had already lived in Canada before he was appointed Governor General. He was a military man with several campaigns under his belt and more importantly, he had already served as the military secretary of a former Governor General. Minto helped organize and build Canada's military infrastructure and there were few who knew it better than he. Minto was familiar with the political landscape of Canada and for the most part well-liked by local power brokers. He had been assigned to the position with the specter of war looming in the near future and took office shortly after it began.

With this in mind, one would think that Canada was in good hands and that was the sentiment at Ten Downing. What the Salisbury cabinet did not seem to realize was that Minto's very qualifications would be his undoing. His single biggest problem was that, while he was a veteran soldier, most of his time had been spent working staff jobs where he merely advised and then handled the technical details of issuing orders. Minto was most certainly in no way qualified to command an entire field army let alone manage an entire theater of war yet that is exactly what he tried to do.

Minto had the kind of personality that was advantageous to working on a military staff, attention detail and micromanaging, but not quite suited to running an entire front and having to make the calls that are needed in a timely manner. When working as a staff officer he was always outspoken and made sure his opinions were heard, even if they were not always followed. As a commander he rarely listened to any of his subordinates and usually made it clear that since he had once held their jobs, he knew them better than they did.

This did not win Minto any friends and as the war went on there were fewer and fewer who cared to deal with him. This was very true of the official Front Commander, Major General Redvers Buller, who had been sent to Canada on the very same ship as Minto. Buller was fully of the impression that Minto was going to run the government and that Buller would be in charge of military operations. Once at their posts, Minto made it very clear that he was in charge of everything. Bullers, who lacked any real desire to deal in politics, simply went along with Minto. Bullers' resentment would only increase, and this was agitated by Minto's relationship with the other principle military figure on the scene, the Canadian General William Otter.

Minto had known Otter since he served as Military Secretary and the two men at least got along. Minto, having been friends with Lord Roberts, started out on shaky ground with Bullers since Roberts and Bullers had been professional rivals for decades. When Minto would even think about seeking military advice, he most often went to Otter who was in theory at least the junior of Bullers as well as being a colonial. Most of this infighting was confined to the upper echelon of the British war effort in

Canada but it helped set a tone that the situation would only make worse as the war began turning against the allies. These small cracks would slowly become canyons.

One has to also remember that these three men all shared common ideals and goals. They were of the same faction and they could not get along. This does not bode well for the theater since the real opposition in Canada was more political, and even cultural, and not military. It was in the political that Minto would almost fail completely, because while military men might disagree, even dislike each other, at the end of the day there is a command structure and orders will be followed. In the world of politics, no such thing exists and here, quite often, the world of the radical can work its way into the mainstream and particularly in times of war. Radical was a word that was quite often used in the prewar era to describe a certain man by the name of Henri Bourassa.

The Continental Divide

If you graduated from a high school in the United States and you took a history class that progressed beyond the basics, then you are likely to have heard at least a mention of Henri Bourassa. You were probably told that he was a patriot of Quebec and that he had always favored independence. As much as it might draw fire from fellow historians, I do not believe there is much evidence of this and in Canada, where Bourassa is even mentioned less than in the United States, the story is quite different. The truth is that Bourassa was a radical, but you have to put that into the context of his time. He seems to have been a man that was guided by certain ideals but past that he made some very common-sense choices when confronted with actual issues. There have even been accusations that the man was a paid asset of the United States Government but again there is not really any evidence of this. There were agitators in Quebec who were, but it would appear as if they had largely failed in their mission. Bourassa was educated in the United States but his association with the US seems to have gone no further and while all of the official papers concerning spies have not been found, I believe this would be a case of deeds and not words. If you examine Bourassa's actions, there is plenty of evidence that he had as little use for the United States as he did for the British Empire.

Books could be written about the things that Bourassa was not, and in fact many have. That does not really tell us what he actually thought. He was certainly a man that loved politics. He was elected mayor of his hometown at the tender young age of twenty-two. He followed that by spending multiple terms in both the elected legislatures of Canada and Quebec. On more than one occasion he said he was done with the pursuit of politics, only to run in the next election. This is all well-known and documented but it makes a profound statement about Bourassa's intentions. He seemed more than content to work within the system even if sometimes he definitely opposed it.

Even before the war Bourassa had shown himself a radical. He had originally aligned with the liberals but eventually had a falling out with their nominal leader, Wilfrid Laurier, and ran for office as an independent from that day forward. The war only drove the supporters of these two factions even further apart but in 1901 Laurier was the Prime Minister and Bourassa was no longer in office. On the surface this would seem to indicate that Laurier had won the battle for the heart and soul of their party but when you take a closer look it was far more complicated than that, and indeed this was a good example of Canadian politics of the era, all in one microcosm.

Before the Confederation, the Fenian Raids, the British garrisons, the transcontinental railroads, or even the war, Canada was a nation that was trying to find itself. Originally it was settled as a collection of French colonies and while these were not as extensive as their English counterparts to the south, several well-established cities had sprung up. The colonies changed hands at the end of the Seven Years War and Great Britain virtually owned the continent for several years until the American Revolution. This forced Great Britain to rethink its policies in Quebec and Nova Scotia. Up until that point, if the local populations did not revolt then Britain virtually ignored the area. They made sure there would be no such uprising by winning over the catholic priests who were the de facto leaders of the region.

The newly independent Americans made this policy dangerous and the war had all but proved that. Britain began shipping in immigrants to settle deeper into the interior for fear that eventually the Americans would do so and claim this land instead. The British policy of containing the US directly conflicted with the American policy of expansion and the result was another war by 1812. This war ended in a draw that made both sides realize that the military option was going to get them nowhere and that they had more to gain in trade than conquest. By the 1840's the US and Britain had worked out their territorial differences and even signed a treaty that both sides could live with. While the treaty was far from perfect, and there were still border conflicts, the treaty was largely a success until the American War of 1861.

When the Americans sponsored the Fenian Raids which were largely a retaliation for the British recognition of the Confederate States, this told the British government that a demilitarized Canada would no longer be practical. While we have examined the effects it had on Great Britain, it is safe to say that they were nowhere near as profound as the impact on the Canadian people. Not only were they being asked to contribute to this defense and per capita far more than anyone in Britain would, they were also being asked to help pay for it as well.

This is the atmosphere that men like Henri Bourassa emerged from and when taken into context one can understand his overall goals. He was not so much fighting against the empire as he was the social ramifications of living in a country that's entire existence was now dedicated to the pursuit of fighting a war. One can appreciate the irony of this in that before the American 61, Great Britain had gone out of its way to avoid the mistakes that led to the American Revolution, but the very existence of the American nation had now caused them to repeat those mistakes all over again. It was a vicious cycle that Britain found itself trapped in. This only fueled the arguments of men like Bourassa of whom he was certainly the most prophetic.

While the Imperial policies had laid the groundwork for the emerging nation it was the war itself that would be the cement that made it very real. As noted before most Canadians took the changes with a grain of salt and many could see the utility in these polices and had no argument that the United States was a genuine threat. None of them really believed that the war would ever come since the good majority of them enjoyed amicable relations with their southern neighbors despite world politics, much of which might as well have been happening on another planet as far as they were concerned.

This changed with the first US soldiers that crossed the Canadian border.

While it might appear to many that Canada, with its long border and wide-open spaces, is not very defendable against an attack from the south, this is something of an illusion. The fact is that most of those wide-open spaces were wilderness at the time and there was no infrastructure to support the large armies that were required to mount offensive operations. The actual passable regions were few, narrow, and in areas like Ontario and Quebec, were actually easily defended with well trained and dedicated troops, something that Canada had. There was also the St Lawrence seaway which was wide and swift. If holding back the enemy proved impossible to the south of this line then this body of water, which was practically a miniature ocean, was the most formidable of obstacles.

In 1901 the Anglo/Canadian forces had managed to hold the American advance well to the south of their final fallback position. It was critical that they do so, because not only did they receive critical imports from the seaway, but two of their most important manufacturing centers, Montreal and Quebec City, were sitting right on it. By 1901 the weakness in this defense had already shown itself but proved to be less of a weakness than the US Army had hoped for.

The Americans had managed to cross the river in one place, across from Watertown, New York. They found that they could advance no further from this point, mainly due to the rugged terrain and the nearly impossible task of concentrating enough troops in the bridge head to break out, however, the serious effects of this crossing did not require going any further north. River traffic to the great lakes were effectively cut from the very start of the war. It was an expensive operation for the Americans, but one that proved worth the high cost in lives. It had serious ramifications on the front further south.

The southern region of Ontario is a peninsular that is created by the Great Lakes. The geography makes the region extremely difficult to defend, yet the Canadians managed and with very little help from the British Army. They did manage to slow the American advance to a crawl, but it was an advance none the less. By 1901 the city of Toronto, the major target in the region, had been surrounded and lain siege to but was still in allied hands. The severing of river traffic from Montreal had serious consequences for the people who had decided to ride out the siege. The Canadians were still managing to get supplies in but it was never enough to replace the consumption rate. Civilians were the first to feel the pinch.

It was at Toronto that the first division in the Imperial British command structure was seen. Governor General Minto saw the situation from a soldier's view, one that was looking at the wider picture, and he determined rather quickly that Toronto could not be defended and by this time was not even worth the cost. Oddly enough and probably a first, General Bullers was in complete agreement. This agreement from two former antagonists was a sign of things to come and nowhere near as surprising as another alliance that was forming. Henri Bourassa was the first to begin clamoring about the British plan to abandon Toronto. This surprised many in that the largely English-speaking city was normally beyond Bourassa's scope of concern. It was not nearly as surprising as when both General Otter and Prime Minister Laurier openly agreed with the man who had been a political thorn in their side for decades.

Minto has been often portrayed as being livid at the impudence of the 'colonials' in their open revolt to his decision. Even a light study of the records, that we have, prove this to be completely false. A lot of things can be said of Minto, but one thing is genuinely true in that he did love the land he was ruling, even if he did so at the behest of a foreign nation. Judging by his writings, he did not see Otter or Laurier in the light of 'colonial subjects.' He viewed them more as comrades in arms. Their sudden revolt did not anger him, he was more puzzled and curious than anything else.

Minto's actions to resolve this problem drew much fire in London, primarily from Joseph Chamberlin. Indeed, many have been critical of his resolution ever since and I think this unfair. I think Minto realized that he had no choice but to concede to the Canadian demands in this matter. He called Otter and Laurier into council with him. This was not so controversial due to the fact that it routinely happened. Where many drew the line with Minto was his decision to meet with Bourassa, who was also present. This actually says more about Bourassa than it does Minto in that the francophone held no office at the time, but it is clear by his presence at these meetings that he had now shown himself in command of a great deal of support inside of Canada. It was the kind of support that obviously transcended his traditional bases of power and even included elements of the English-speaking community as well.

Future historians would portray Minto as bowing to the demands of usurpers but again this is unfair. The simple fact is that Minto's power was completely based on the presence of British troops and in the area around Toronto, there were none. Any way that Minto went, he was going to have to deal with some rather nasty consequences and it was Laurier who recognized this and drove his points home. The loss of Toronto would be a serious blow to Canadian morale, and for that reason alone it had to be defended to the last. It was really the only point that was made in these meetings, and while Minto disagreed, his other options were far more devastating. He could not afford a showdown with any of these men. He had to have known that he would loose and show the entire nation that the crown's own representative was now a paper tiger.

One must keep in mind that this first sign of a crack between crown and colony was before the British War Office decided to commit the bulk of their forces to the Balkans and not Canada. The planners at Pall Mall made their decision based on the most pragmatic of reasons and due to this they cannot really be faulted. What the military planners, working under Woseley, were not really aware of were the political impacts. They were military men after all, and not particularly concerned with the realm of the political in the first place. They were just trying to win a war. There was no way they could have known the ramifications of this decision and in particular from a commonwealth member that had shown itself to be loyal to a fault.

Unfortunately for Minto, he seems to have been all too aware of the ramifications and he said as much in multiple communications with not only Chamberlin and the Foreign Office but with Balfour and even the ailing Salisbury. Minto's warnings were falling on deaf ears, however. While it seems that both Chamberlin and Balfour were both aware of the impact, they seemed to lack the imagination to realize what could happen as a result. It is the kind of lack of vision that comes with not being on the ground and wearing jaded glasses that are colored with the tint of a bygone era. Unfortunately for the world, as far as national leaders went, they were far from alone.

The Center Does Not Hold

There are many who place a great deal of blame on the Salisbury Cabinet for the deterioration of the situation in Canada. Naturally, most of this is laid at the feet of Henry Balfour and Joseph Chamberlin, but one must point out that a great deal of this only holds true when placing the Canadian theater of war in a microcosm and ignoring the entire world war that was going on. By the spring of 1901 there was a great deal more to worry about and some of it made the Canadian situation look tame. It is true that the Salisbury government had known for some time, and probably sooner than any other national government, that the war on international shipping was going to begin causing severe shortages of consumer goods. This did not just mean a lack of creature comforts either. Food was about to become a problem.

While food shortages often drum up images of long bread lines and people sitting around with ribs that seem to be bursting from their sides, these are usually the most dramatic examples and quite often the exceptions to the real problems created by food shortages. The simple fact is that such shortages effect different regions in different ways and the sum accumulation of problems often appear as other things entirely, and at least in the public mindset they are not related to the actual problem. This was never clearer than in the case of Britain in 1901.

The fact is that the cabinet had taken steps to protect their populations, both at home and in the commonwealth, from the coming disaster. It can easily be argued that the measures that originated from the office of Joseph Chamberlin were some of the more successful. Many in Britain never realized that the problems they faced were directly a result of the break down in international shipping and the decreased quantity of food that was making it to ports in the British Isles. People were getting food for the entire war, which is usually the mark of a rich country, and Britain was that, but the quality and diversity of food declined and was very noticeable. It was in fact so noticeable that looking over newspapers of the period it is easy to see. Articles with recipes for dishes that were designed to make palatable meals out of table scraps were common. There were also any number of articles about people growing food in tiny plots behind their urban homes.

Oddly enough, the single largest government initiative to relieve the food shortages never showed up in the newspapers. The government had quietly been re-designating the use of land from industrial to agricultural. They did so through very quiet means, usually disguised as the initiative of local officials, and these plots were most often worked as community affairs. In some cases, entire rural estates were converted to farm use and recently unemployed industrial workers were recruited to try a new profession. None of the above-mentioned initiatives were going to solve the food problem, but they went a long way towards buying time for Great Britain.

Such measures were taken in most of the belligerent nations during the war and quite often sold as patriotic duty. The problem was that, like Great Britain, these measures could only be taken in territory that they controlled. While the British Empire might be the largest on Earth it was far from controlling the entire planet and areas outside their dominion were largely left to their own devices, many of which were suffering from food shortages even before the war. They were the first to be hit with the problems created from the lack of international shipping and these problems could change the scoreboard for the combatants. This was never truer than in China.

When someone thinks of famine it is often thought that this is due to an inability to grow enough food. In general, this has been true in the past. The human race, like any other species, has always grown or shrunk in direct proportion to the food supply. As a result, the population has almost always hovered around that line of almost having not enough to eat. The modern world has changed this equation dramatically, and it has been noted by many a sociologist, that our rapid growth in the twentieth century has had a great deal to do with the birth rate trying to catch up with a sudden explosion in our ability to produce food. Strangely enough, the population has never caught up and the surpluses continue. Despite this we still have famine.

Modern famines are never the result of a lack of food production. This was very true in the early twentieth century where the fault lies squarely with the transportation networks and the lack of political will to increase their size so that they could meet the rising need of food stuffs. There are those who put this fault at the feet of those who pay for the building of ships, trains, and other means of transport. This is an unfair assumption since it is quite clear that all of these men were bending over backwards to do the very thing that others accused them of being too cheap to do. There is also the little fact that no one in the late 19th or early 20th century even understood that this was a problem. The science of studying macro scale economics, the base of which is food production and distribution, was in its infancy and yet to realize where the weaknesses actually were.

Modern agricultural processes had already been introduced, largely by the United States, beginning in the late 1880s. By the start of the war, most industrialized nations, and a few who were not, had already taken up the American practices. The world shipping network had yet to catch up with the sudden explosion in agriculture and this left the areas that were still skimming by with older inefficient methods at the mercy of chance. When the war began chipping away at the transportation network, it was too late for the people who were doing things the old way.

This was never truer than in China, where her extremely conservative leaders saw no need to change anything about their agriculture. At least here, they had some merit to their arguments in that China had been successfully feeding herself for thousands of years and doing a much better job of it than anyone else. This is where the clear-cut case of a lack of transportation is most visible. China was still producing surplus food stocks in 1901, but none of it was getting to where it should. China's problems were largely political, and the war was only making this worse.

While China had a unified government in theory under the Manchu Dynasty, that was in name only. For most of the 19th century the country had been racked with political descent, rebellion and foreign invasion. All of this served to fracture a weak regime and China's territorial governors had more control over their areas than did Cixi, the Dowager Empress. When Cixi decided to fight it out with all of the foreign powers, most of the Chinese governors decided to let her do it alone. Even many of her core supporters, such as General Jung-Lo, sat by and watched her lose.

Once the Americans occupied Peking, any influence that Cixi had on her top officials was gone. Unfortunately for the Americans, the man they replaced her with, the Gangxu Emperor, had no more influence than did Cixi. Each governor went their own way and many, such as Zhang Zhidong, were openly cooperating with American enemies, most notably the British in Hong Kong. This meant that the internal borders of China suddenly became roadblocks and food transportation began to dwindle. None of the Chinese leaders had taken any precautions to prevent a famine because apparently none of them even thought it a possibility.

When a few natural disasters combined with the war, there was outright starvation in many Chinese urban centers. The unrest that it caused did not stop at the borders of imperial provinces like the food stuffs that were rotting on the river docks. The result of this unrest manifested itself in a very Chinese kind of way. The host of urban legends, superstitions, and a collage of religious beliefs began to flood the local markets. This rich diversity of human superstition began to merge into a cohesive belief system that was all its own.

This new religion was paranoid, xenophobic and exaggerated the very real problems that the average Chinese were facing. It not only incorporated the problems created by the war but had a firm foundation in the prewar erosion of Chinese culture that was already moving at full steam prior to the conflict. It blamed everyone for these problems except usually those who were most responsible, and this new belief system demanded action.

The going fad in China at the time was the 'secret society.' This kind of organization, somewhat comparable to European groups like the Masons, looked exciting to many young, hungry, and unemployed Chinese males who otherwise felt powerless. Not only did these groups offer solutions but they looked good doing it. You see, the average Chinaman found their rulers to be as distant from them as the European invaders and so far, they had seen nothing from the dynasty that would fix many of their problems. In fact, many of these secret societies were as anti-Manchu as they were anti anyone else. Most of these groups also began to coalesce into a single organization and oddly enough, it was not political, military, academic, or any other organ of society that is normally charged with the administration of civilization. When China's leaders failed to take care of the problems, who did the Chinese people turn to? It was their entertainers, and in this case a group called the Order of the Harmonious Fist.

The Un-Orthodox Solution

The shortages were not just felt by the allies or the assorted neutrals, most of whom like China were all now in various levels of undeclared war with either side. The Triple Entente had more than its fair share of problems as well. The United States was probably the least effected of anyone by the various shortages but was not unscathed. Despite the fact that most of the citizens of the North American belligerents, both Allied and Entente, suffered the least of anyone they still felt a pinch in the form of skyrocketing food prices. Many a historian have tried to place the blame for this on a multitude of factors, but when one examines the evidence that we have, there seems to be only one reason for the rising food costs in North America. It seems that individual grocers, dry goods stores, and market dealers raised their prices for no other reason than they knew they could.

The US and Canadian Governments attempted to combat this with laws, but the merchants quickly found ways around this. One grocer even went so far as to demand that a customer buy his dog with a barrel of flour. The flour was marked with the government price while the dog went for an outrageous sum. Once the customer got home with his needed flour, and his unwanted dog, the animal was trained to run away and come back to the grocery store. This kind of gouging was across the board, and in places like Mexico many merchants simply refused to sell their goods unless they could do so at the prices they set. In the Confederacy, with each state trying its own approaches, the attempts at combating food prices were an unqualified mess and led to a black market of goods that were quickly competing with legitimate businesses who found they could not keep up. More than a few major retailers filed for bankruptcy under these systems.

While problems in the US were very real and impacting people's lives in a noticeable way, what all of the civilians of North America had was an unshakable resolve that this was 'abnormal' and that, sooner or later, the 'normal way' would eventually return. This helped stifle much unrest but in places like Russia, this was not the case. Just like in China, Russia was a land that seemed homogenous to the foreign observer, but this was only an illusion. There were even many native Russian speaking peoples who pledged their loyalties to their region before that of Czar Nicholas. That was not even counting the social problems that were being created by a rapidly industrializing economy that was being overseen by a ruler that was not only trying to rule his people in an old feudal styled agrarian manner but seemed to not even realize the changes were happening.

Russia was also a very large place, and while that seems obvious to anyone who looks at a map, such a precursory examination is only scratching the tip of the iceberg. While Russia had made many strides in the road to modernization there were still large tracks of the country, most of it in fact, that was still living in almost stone age conditions. There were also many areas where people did not speak Russian, did not fancy living under the Czar, and lacked a modern infrastructure on top of it. Georgia was one such place.

This region had always been considered problematic by St Petersburg. In 1901 it was being ruled by the Czar as the Tiflis Governate. The name says everything in that since the conquest of the region, the Russian Empire was doing their best to 'Russianize' their subjects and would not even call the people what they were. Even birth certificates were issued with a Russian name and not their real one. The

Orthodox Church was pushed in the region and one of their primary duties was to make sure that everyone spoke Russian. It was a war of ethnic conversion and one that was not too popular with the population.

Ironically, the single biggest resistance to this system would come out of the very institution that had been supplanted to make it happen. In this case it was a single individual whose Georgian name was Ioseb Besarionus dze Jughasvilli. He was the son of a cobbler and a very religious mother. His father had many lapses with alcoholism, was reportedly abusive and seems to have lost his business because he could not control his temper. Jughasvilli grew up in an environment of perpetual turmoil, and like Theodore Roosevelt, was a sickly child on top of this. His mother sought to get him out of this environment and packed the boy off to religious school as soon as she could. He would remain in this world for many years.

By the second year of the war, Ioseb had managed to avoid service in the army due to his enrollment in seminary. He had also done everything required to become an Orthodox Priest. When it was time to take his final exams, for reasons known only to Ioseb, he simply did not show up. What we do know, as reported by many of his classmates, is that Ioseb was both a lackluster student and something of a rouge scholar. While the boy did not excel in academics, he was a voracious reader. Ioseb had become exposed to many of the ideas that were floating around at the time, and somewhere in that jumble of ideologies, he seems to have been transformed into a diehard Georgian Nationalist.

It is easy to surmise that Ioseb was the product of a turbulent childhood, and by that reasoning, it is a logical assumption that he grabbed on to whatever ideology got to him first. There was no stronger pull than that which was going on in the streets of Tiflis. There had been no fighting in Georgia, but the war was being felt here in many ways and had been since the outbreak of hostilities. Not only was food getting expensive, but as the casualty lists grew the Russian Government was pressuring their regional governors for more soldiers. Many of the troops slaughtered by Winston Churchill in and around Belgrade were in fact from this region.

Horror stories from the army camps and from the front had long since reached Georgia. While there are no official accounts one only has to look at the writings of Jughasvilli to find all that you need to know. Many a historian take his journals and correspondence with a grain of salt and with good reason, however in this case it would seem that Ioseb only had to tell the truth. More than a few young Georgian men had already fled to the mountains in order to avoid being conscripted into the army. Despite popular lore, most of these men were city dwellers and had no idea how to take care of themselves in the wilderness. Once Ioseb was expelled he quickly found himself on a list of draftees, so he too fled to the hills and showed the others how to survive.

That is not to say that Ioseb Jughasvilli knew any more about living off the land than the others. He was a city boy and knew no more about hunting and gathering than those who were around him. What Ioseb did have was a superior vocabulary and an arsenal of rhetoric. It was something that these starving individuals gladly consumed and before long Ioseb had effective control of most of the emerging groups in his area. Another strength that Ioseb had, at least in this task, was that he did not consider himself above killing anyone who might be a threat and even in some very public and horrible ways.

These multiple groups of young Georgians, like in China, would slowly merge and had a near endless sea of replacements as the war went on. Once Ioseb became their undisputed leader, he was left with the dilemma of how to make good on his promises. Ioseb had no way to feed, shelter or clothe these people except by the method that he was most comfortable with. The almost Orthodox priest turned to stealing what was required.

In the beginning, Ioseb was very indiscriminate about who he would take from. He obviously chose his targets by the method of whether or not the victim had what he needed. As time went on, he definitely changed his strategy after it became clear that such raids were counterproductive in that it destroyed potential allies who would later prove to be useful. It was this realization that separated Ioseb from any number of bandit leaders that were now showing up in wilderness areas around the world. It would transform his 'bandit kingdom' into a revolution of sorts, and groups such as this, would plague the world for years to come, long after the war had ended.

The Golden Rules

It is with a strange sense of irony that the one place you might think effected the most by the dwindling movement of supplies would be the place where they were always scarce to begin with, that being the furthest end of the Russian Empire. It is true that materially speaking Alaska was poor in the prewar era, however that is not to say they were dirt poor, and in fact it was just the opposite, they were very literally dirt rich. Not only was the populace of Alaska used to feeding themselves before the war began, but suddenly the export of gold came to a screeching halt because the powers that be did not want these ships being captured or sunk.

Even before the conflict, the Russian authorities had a very inefficient system in regulating the removal of the gold from the upper Yukon valley. Claim jumping, normally a euphemism for murder and theft, was quite common before the war and oddly enough it did not get worse under wartime conditions. Prospectors in Alaska were already well armed and on guard for such things, so the additional violence which usually targeted things other than gold, caused an actual decline in such activities. The other reason for this was because suddenly gold was widely available and easily obtained by less violent methods.

With a halt to most international shipments, gold began piling up in Alaska and everyone suddenly had bags of the dust, or giant nuggets, that could have bought them a mansion in San Francisco or Vladivostok. That is not to say that everyone was rich because at the time a huge nugget that was worth thousands of dollars in the rest of the world was barely enough to get a drink in a Ketchikan Saloon. This might sound like hyperinflation and one might suspect that it would be the result of an ever-smaller store of goods, but that was anything but the case. Since the beginning of the war, the amount of goods that were trickling into the Alaskan ports were growing by substantial and very noticeable amounts.

This might sound as if it is contradictory to the law of supply and demand but only if you do not realize what the demand truly was. The gold market outside of Alaska had never been higher. Contrary to popular myth, war does not stimulate economies and more often than not they bankrupt the nations waging them so the demand for gold was at a premium by 1901.

The demand in Alaska was the act of getting that gold shipped to somewhere that it was actually valuable because the supply in Alaska far exceeded its need. In fact, the only thing that really made it hold any value at all in the Russian colony, was the fact that everyone knew the war would eventually end.

For most people, the idea that if they held on to their stockpiles until the end of the war, when they could leave the harsh conditions of the wilderness behind them and retire in some comfortable place, was enough. It also bred some strange sights and behaviors. It was very typical during the war for housewives to have in their kitchen a jar of flour, a jar of honey, and a jar of gold dust. So many people were burying gold under their cabins that even today finding lost gold in Alaska is a major recreational hobby. Tourists actually pay to dig holes around the wrecked sights of old cabins that have been picked over for decades. Despite this sit and wait attitude, it was not enough for some.

If banditry was making a comeback in some places that had long since been cleared of such activities, Alaska again was the exception because those kinds of behaviors had been the norm in the colony since long before the war. It was the real law on this frontier, and it bred a good number of people who were more than prepared for the harshness and violence that war breeds. It was very Darwinian in that many men such as Wyatt Earp, Seth Bulloch, and Vladimir Ulyanov had long since proven their ruthlessness, ambition and wit. Those who could not see far ahead had long since been weeded out or subjugated to lesser roles in the organizations that would spring up during the war. These growing factions in Alaska (and Northwest Canada as well) were singular of purpose and mind. Their primary goal was not to wage war for the benefit of some far-off government and in fact it was not to wage war at all. They only wanted to get the gold out of Alaska as fast as they could.

Look at what people do and not what they say. This is a golden rule that will explain much of the confusion about the war in Alaska. Despite the relative ease in obtaining huge sums of gold during the war, that was not to say there was no shortage of violence and quite often this violence was wrapped in a flag and sold to others as an act of patriotism. More often than not, the people behind this violence had no qualms about which flag they used and quite often traded them as their needs fit. In the beginning, the violence was most often due to personal reasons when people with long standing feuds saw the perfect opportunity to right some kind of wrong. Eventually these personal vendettas became more organized and directed for purposes that had more to do with business, even if the violence itself became more ruthless.

It was men like Wyatt Earp who understood that senseless killing could be made into killing for cause and created his own bandit kingdom, much like Ioseb Jughasvilli in Georgia. There were profound differences though. Neither Earp nor any of the other Alaskan power brokers ever targeted the Russian Government, or at least in the beginning. The authorities were near powerless anyway and had no real orders to stop Earp. Bribes and the occasional accident took care of any official that became too interested in the gold smuggling. Oddly enough, if that was true of Russian officials the same can be said of those in Canada. Despite the reputation that Earp had on the Canadian side of the border, that of being their arch enemy, he had little problem in dealing with British sources and there is plenty of evidence that he did.

The same can be said of Ulyanov and Bulloch. All three men seemed to have become convinced of the same idea and quite possibly they did it together over beers. The time to get the gold out was while the war was still on. Not only were the markets at their peak but after the war there was every chance that the government would no longer be so ineffective and might try and come back and take that gold for themselves. To put it simply, these men understood another golden rule, which was and still is that time is money.

This is relevant to the war in that it governed the course of campaigns in this most remote of theaters. While much has been made in popular legend after the war about various 'battles' along the frontier, a closer examination of these 'engagements' seems to suggest that they had more to do with factional disputes amongst smugglers than military strategy. It's very hard to get an exact picture because the participants in these incidents were rarely soldiers, kept no records and their personal accounts vary so widely that it is sometimes hard to know if the witnesses are actually talking about the same incident or not.

Ironically, one of our best sources on the 'Great Northern War' is also an illustration of the problem of figuring out exactly what happened. Jack London wrote much on his experiences in Alaska during the war, and as I have noted before, he eventually had a falling out with Wyatt Earp and returned home to San Francisco. The reason why this source material is both priceless and problematic is because it is one of the few sources we have that is even remotely reliable and London romanticized the picture he paints for us. This romantic view has since entered pop culture, been the inspiration for many movies and novels, and has clouded many crucial details about the war in Alaska.

After many decades we have now cleared up at least some of the fog of war and managed to dispense with many myths. This is largely due to the fact that one such battle, that was apparently the result of a dispute over smuggling routes, would go on to change the course of the war in some very profound ways. In fact, you could almost say that the war started and ended on the Alaskan/Canadian frontier.

The Nature of The Beast

If the trouble in North America was manageable and in China bad, the place that wins the gold medal for the most suffering was a region that actually did produce more than enough food stuffs to feed itself. At the same time, it utterly failed to do so, that is if you could go so far as to say that there was even an attempt. In South Africa by 1901, famine was just one more weapon being used to kill, and at least in this it had been an unqualified success. For almost a century, before anyone realized the mineral wealth of the region, cattle had been the biggest game in town. The discovery of gold and diamonds had done nothing to change the status of the cattle industry and this was true of even independent native African states. Here, with the natives it seems to be even more true in that many of these people used cattle as currency. Cows were even used to buy wives. Such was the importance of beef.

The problem with the beef industry is, if you will pardon the pun, the very nature of the beast. For anyone who is familiar with the romanticized tales of the Texan Cowboy, then you have at least heard of cattle rustling. This is one of many common problems with raising cattle and one reason why pigs have always been more popular. Cows require large tracks of land just to maintain a heard of the size required to make them economically feasible to raise. Then you have to get them from the pasture to market and normally these places are separated by vast distances, usually because that entire distance is needed for grazing.

By the 19th century, a lot of the practical problems with raising cattle had been solved by technology. Without artificial refrigeration, the large-scale distribution of beef was nearly impossible. Ships and railcars, built with large iceboxes that depended on both the natural and the artificial kind of freezing, began to enter service in the latter half of the century. Suddenly, the supply of beef could meet the demand because moving frozen steaks was far more practical than herding a live animal, which was the only way it could be done before. It was this technology that suddenly allowed beef to supplant pork in the industrialized nations for the first time in modern history and on a global scale.

This is not to say that all of the problems had been solved. The popular myth of the cattle rustler has a grain of truth to it. It was a problem in Mexico and Texas before the war, where rustlers had an international border to hide behind. In South Africa, with all of its little microstates, the problem was even worse, and this was before the war. As the war went on, the governments responsible for suppressing these lawless activities became powerless or otherwise occupied. With the economic collapse that resulted in a barter economy, theft became common and the first industry to take the hit on the chin was the one that was most exposed, the cattle industry.

Naturally, the wide expanses covered with the sprawling herds were the perfect place to steal one of the single biggest targets of bandits, that being cattle. While the independent raiders were a serious problem these thieves were nothing compared to the officially sanctioned bandits, that being the armies at war. Like the privateers of old, the armies had an official license to go after each other's cattle, and while lacking the resources to launch an offensive against militarily viable targets, they had more than enough resources to do a proper job of cattle rustling. Raids became common and happened deep within the territories of both sides.

There were many who called on the various governments, in the patch work quilt of states that was South Africa, to do something about this menace. The almost unanimous position of these officials was that they were doing something and that something was trying to win the war. In all fairness to those officials, it was impossible to tell if someone who was rustling cattle was doing it for profit or patriotism. Indeed, in retrospect, a good number of raids were done for both reasons, and anytime someone was caught they always claimed to be a soldier on a military expedition since if you were stealing cattle for profit it was a capital offense and a thief would be executed. A soldier was treated as a prisoner of war and spared.

Like everything else in South Africa, the problem of banditry was colored by the ethnic divides in a land where such things could even be deadly in peace time. This was never truer than in a certain section of the British Natal Colony. This particular region was somewhat different from others because up until just a few decades before it had not only been an independent nation but a growing empire in its own right. Outsiders knew this area collectively as Zululand. If the rustling problem had gotten bad and hopelessly entangled with the war in other parts of South Africa, in Zululand it had completely merged.　　After the British destroyed the Zulu kingdom in the early eighties, there had been a great deal of sympathy for the Zulu in Europe and even in the white communities of South Africa. The then king of the Zulu, Cestshwayo, had been brought to Cape Town as a prisoner, but found himself riding into town on a buggy and given a parade as if he were a conquering emperor returning to Rome. These sorts of displays put pressure on the British Government for there were many who had felt the war unjust. Like many wars of this age, the casus belli of the conflict was completely contrived. Unlike others, those involved in creating the conflict had handled the matter rather poorly and the excuse for war looked to be nothing more than that.

While the excuse for the conflict was weak at best, the real reasons for the war were far sounder and they followed the British policy in South Africa, to the letter. The war was not about expansion or conquest, but rather unification of South Africa. It was equally about keeping the Boers away from the ocean. Even more than the Zulu, the Boers were also standing in the way of unification, and by extension the precious railroad that Britain wanted to build from Cape Town to Cairo. One of the things that kept the Boer nations in check was their lack of access to the sea, and Zululand in many ways offered them a port. Even if it was underdeveloped, Zululand had a good coastline and many places that could serve as an excellent harbor.

Despite the romanticized versions of history, that paint the Zulu and Boers as mortal enemies in constant conflict, this is not entirely true. This image was, in my opinion, largely born of 19th century racism where the Boers needed a great and uncivilized enemy with which to play the bad guys in stories that they told their children. While the Boers and Zulu did fight, more often than not they also cooperated with each other seeing as how they had a mutual enemy that was far more deadly. This cooperation, unknowingly, had begun right from the start. The Boers had left the Cape and migrated inland to get away from the British. They did not have to conquer any land to settle because it had already been done for them. By the time of the Great Trek, as it is known by the Boers, Shaka was already on the scene and he had systematically exterminated most of the residents that lived in what would become the Boer republics.

Of course, Shaka had no way of knowing that this land he had emptied would be settled by others who had more firepower than he did. What Shaka did know was that, just like the Boers, he was already having trouble with the British. The irony of this is that without the British, Shaka would have never had an empire to begin with. While Shaka's personality may have forged this once minor band of Bantu into an empire, it had been his advisors, most of whom were educated in Britain, that made it possible. Much like the Japanese, the Zulu's had adopted European technologies and customs that aided their cause and put these things to immediate use.

The Zulu never went as far as the Japanese in their adoption of European ways. They had no problem using European metallurgy, guns, tools, and even adopting the regimental system for their almost universal military service. Again, contrary to the romanticized version, they did not hang on to most of their Bantu customs either. Shaka, and his little clique, either made up their own or heavily modified the existing customs and what they created was entirely unique. Shaka even went so far as to outlawing footwear. He would personally kill anyone he saw wearing it. While some have pointed to this as some primitive African custom, the truth was that this was a fetish that was entirely owned by Shaka. The rest of the Bantu had no problem with shoes, they simply lacked the charisma and sociopathic personality that Shaka used to get his way.

It was these strange customs, created by Shaka and his advisors, that set the Zulu empire on a collision course with the British. They would have been anyway because of the unification policy, but the custom of not allowing warriors to marry until after they had seen battle was speeding up the crisis. To put it bluntly, guys want sex and if they have to kill someone to get it, they will. While the Zulu's enjoyed an early string of successes in the 1879 war, one that captivated imaginations worldwide, they were ultimately crushed and by 1898 Zululand enjoyed some semi autonomy within the confines of the British colony of Natal. It was far from a perfect situation, however.

Great Britain could not afford to directly occupy Zululand with the number of troops it would require to keep them sufficiently suppressed, so Britain did what Europe had been doing to the rest of their colonies for centuries, that being the act of playing one group off on the other. The Zulus were divided up into over thirty autonomous zones and each was ruled by its own strongman, all of whom had problems with the others. One of these strongmen was the great grandson of Shaka himself. His name was appropriately, Dinazulu, and when the war broke out in 1898, he had been an agitator against the British for decades. He had been such a thorn in the side of the British that on several occasions they had urged other Zulu leaders to invade his territory and remove him.

None of these attempts were successful, so eventually the British had to directly intervene. They tossed Dinazulu in jail at one point, but this did nothing to quell him since he still had considerable support in and outside of Zululand. Dinazulu also had other cards to play and one of them was at the time considered an odd one if you did not understand the politics of South Africa. You see, Dinazulu also had one particular ally who happened to have a skin color that was several shades lighter than his own. He was a Boer by the name of Louis Botha.

These two men had a history that went way back, and it is reported that they were even personal friends. Botha actually raised a Boer Commando to help Dinazulu thwart the British backed invasion of his territory in 1884. By the time that the Boer states went to war with the British, both men were actively conspiring to lead a general Zulu uprising. It is theorized by some that had the war not began when it did, Botha and Dinazulu would have probably started it a few years later, anyway.

The reason for this is because, even if these two most unlikely of allies were also friends, Botha was also not acting entirely for altruistic reasons. Another British policy, strongly linked with their unification policy, was one of keeping the Boers contained to the interior and as a result landlocked. This policy showed its practicality when the war began because the Boers were cut off completely from their allies. Botha wanted some of Dinzulu's coastal real estate. The Zulu's were not using it and the Boer's needed it. There were two problems. First Dinzulu had to be ruling his land again and the second was another of those strange twists. Botha had more problems with his own people than the British.

While President Kruger could see the utility in Botha's plan, he did not see anything good about Botha. He considered the man ambitious, capable and ruthless which were qualities that Kruger sorely needed in 1898 when this plan was first hatched. The problem was that Kruger also recognized that Botha wanted the Presidency and if he successfully pulled off his Zulu coup, he could very well get it. Kruger used the Jameson raid to fend off Botha's appeals for support in his Zulu adventure. The plan came to nothing. After the Boers were crushed by Kitchner, Kruger began slowly losing support, most of which was shifting in the direction of Botha. By 1901, adequate support had materialized and these two leaders, Botha and Dinzulu, were about to kick off a chain of events that would change world history.

General Revenge

There has been a great deal that has been written about General Georges Boulanger's role in the war. It is so much in fact, that I have not devoted a great many words to this subject. A great deal of the subject matter, written about the President for Life of France, has definitely painted the man as a villain, sometimes buffoonish, and quite often pins the blame for the entire war on him. While there is little doubt that Boulanger shares in the responsibility, to say that he was entirely responsible for the conflict is unfair. The reason this has happened seems quite clear. France grew to hate the man and most of the literature devoted to his role in both war and government, was actually written in England where he was even less popular.

After the fall of the second empire, France was looking for another Napoleon Bonaparte and his descendants and family did not seem to have a replacement handy. Louis Napoleon proved this to many after his defeat at the hands of the Germans in 1870. With this in mind it seems that Georges Boulanger was an obvious choice to be a new Emperor, even if it was not so obvious at the time, and despite the later image that was painted of him.

Boulanger was an aggressive dashing young military officer who had a career that paralleled Napoleon's almost to the letter. He came up in the artillery, served in several small wars in Italy, and then entered politics while advancing his rank in the military at the same time. He was also quite good at winning support on both the left and right of the French political spectrum of the day. In fact, his introduction to politics was made by a man who would later be one of his greatest critics. He was another Georges, considered a leftist radical, with the last name of Clemenceau.

Clemenceau had thought Boulanger a Republican and brought him in to the chaotic political scene in Paris. Boulanger drew a great deal of support from the workers and suburbs of Paris, most of whom were on the left, spanning from Radical Republican to outright communist. It was not long after that when Boulanger became something of an outspoken conservative favoring the Monarchists to a degree. Clemenceau backed away from Boulanger, but at this point it was too late because while Boulanger got new support from the right, but he also managed to hold on to his supporters on the left. A situation developed where no one could afford to offend the man who had feet on both sides of the fence.

One has to wonder how Boulanger managed to pull off this political juggling act and then wonder why he would even want to. The name of the movement that grew around him, along with his nickname, tells most of the how. His followers became known as the Revanche and he was General Revanche. In English, put simply, Boulanger was General Revenge and all of that was directed at Germany. While this might explain how he pulled it off, the why of it became obvious when he took control of the Third Republic. The German issue was the only one that gave him support from the right and left, which was required for him to follow in the footsteps of Napoleon and become the new Emperor.

Oddly enough, Boulanger never quite achieved what he sought. While he definitely became a dictator, he never became one that had a solid grasp of absolute power. While historians now often refer to this period, and Boulanger's government, as the Revanche Period, even Boulanger himself still officially called the French Government the Third Republic. Most everyone else at the time did so as well. Boulanger even insisted on it and I think that has a lot to do with the difference between agitating for power and actually holding the reigns. While Boulanger was rising to power, he could say almost anything he wanted about the Germans. At that time, it did not matter. Once Boulanger controlled France, suddenly the statements that he often shouted, to get him to that position, could start a war that he was not prepared for.

Unfortunately for Boulanger, this was one of the last wise choices he made as the leader of France. That is not to say that his administration was an unqualified disaster, but it seems while Boulanger spent a lot of time figuring out how Napoleon rose to power, he either ignored or did not understand how the man kept it. This was something that even Louis Napoleon had figured out in his term as Emperor. The original Napoleon was a devoted student of Julius Caesar and simply followed his playbook, step by step. In fact, Caesar was simply copying ancient Egyptian Pharaohs who had discovered the formula ages before Europe. Dictators require two things, conquest and new buildings.

On the conquest side, Boulanger did manage to make some gains, however, they seemed pale in comparison to Caesar in Gaul or even Napoleon at Austerlitz. If at any point Boulanger had figured this out it might have gone a great way towards explaining the importance that he had placed on his African railroad venture, the very one that led to the start of the war. He needed a win somewhere because as for throwing up great buildings or creating giant public works programs, he was a complete failure. While Boulanger held the reigns, no substantial public works programs came down the pike. It is true that there were some improvements to the French infrastructure but there was nothing as grand as Napoleon's Arch de Triumph or his legal code. There was nothing to even compare to Louis Napoleon's public works initiatives and when your accomplishments cannot even be compared to a sewer pipe, you might have some problems.

Here is what English historians point to as their evidence that Boulanger intentionally started the war. It was by virtue of the fact that he had the most to gain. While fear of Germany was enough to get General Revenge crowned, it was not enough to allow him to keep the throne, unless he actually started that war. While there is no doubt that Boulanger planned for such a war, that is not saying much when you consider that so did almost everyone else in France. The events that led up to the conflict, I would hope, absolutely demonstrate that the man was as in the dark as everyone else. I would also hope that this demonstrates how Boulanger's actions at the end of the war were far more important than those at the beginning.

By the spring of 1901, the British had a new secret weapon they were using on France. This was not some big gun, cloud of war, or even a wireless lightening detector. This weapon was a rather unassuming and quiet little Frenchman who happened to be a Jew, a former military officer, and had been at the center of an international controversy nearly a decade before. His name was Alfred Dreyfus. He had been accused of spying for the thinnest of reasons and many claimed it was due to his ethnicity. Even after it was clear to French Military Intelligence that he was not the spy, this information was buried, and his trial continued. Even the detractors of Dreyfus quietly felt that the young man had been railroaded and did not deserve Devil's Island. Still, the issues that arose from his very public trial were enough to split France in half.

Those who supported Dreyfus, such as Clemenceau, laid the blame for the fate of the young boy squarely on the doorstep of Boulanger. While it is well documented that he did meddle in the case, the truth is that Boulanger was largely disinterested. He had enough troubles of his own at the time, and even remarked that Dreyfus was a 'minor affair.' Even so, this was not how it appeared to the average man on the streets of Paris. Handbills that were highly inflammatory, very anti Boulanger, and allegedly written by Alfred Dreyfus, began to appear on every lamp post in the city of lights. Even to this day, it is unclear if Dreyfus really even wrote any of these lengthy condemnations of Boulanger and the war. It did not matter.

By this time, everyone knew that Dreyfus had been liberated from Devil's Island, by the Royal Navy. The British had made much fanfare of his arrival in London where the boy was now living in an expatriate community of Frenchman who opposed the Boulanger regime. He was something of a celebrity and exactly how much he actually did to try and remove Boulanger is open to speculation and quite often hotly debated. This point is largely irrelevant. All that Dreyfus needed to do was be there and it made an impact, even if this impact was not what the British propagandists were hoping for.

Georges Clemenceau is a perfect example of why a revolution did not occur in the name of Dreyfus. Every government will produce a number of exiles. In many cases, dictatorial regimes produce exiles who have fled for their lives, or fear of arrest and even execution. Clemenceau had been such an exile, but not from Boulanger. Clemenceau had to flee from his homeland during the reign of Louis Napoleon and he moved to the United States where he ran two newspapers and tutored wealthy children in French. After coming home, in 1871, he remained there and that includes after Boulanger came to power.

That is not to say that the regime did not take its toll. By 1901, Clemenceau was no longer holding political office. Boulanger did not run him out of the government, Clemenceau did so quite voluntarily and went back into the newspaper business where he routinely attacked the French President with daily opinion articles that he personally wrote. Boulanger might have liked to arrest his rival but like with most of the opposition he had, he found his hands tied in the matter. To arrest the dissenters would only weaken his regime since many of them, like Clemenceau, were popular with some of Boulanger's core supporters as well.

Its relevance to the Dreyfus situation is obvious. While there were many who left France in protest of Boulanger's leadership, most of these did so voluntarily. It took a lot of power out of their rhetoric and as a result many in France ignored the exiles and thought them foolish. That is not to say that it did not have an effect. There were other problems bubbling just beneath the surface. They were just starting to be openly discussed when the Dreyfus Bills started appearing on street corners. It was a combination of issues that would begin a factional shift in France and Alfred Dreyfus was just one of many, even if he might have been the straw that broke the camel's back.

Shots Heard Round the World

This particular subject has developed a genre that is very much all its own. This is why I have attempted to keep the scope of the topic limited to its more direct consequences to the war. That was a formidable task, and in many places, I am sure I failed. It is hard to discuss an assassination without at least mentioning some of the conspiracy theories that have sprung up over the years. This is largely because many of them started no sooner than the smoke had cleared and they very much impacted the political climate of the time, public sentiment, and had a direct bearing on the war. Even more important is its impact on our view of the conflict because it is very hard to put the war into context if you believe aliens are controlling world events with the enthusiastic support of a cabal of business interests who meet in the basement of the world bank.

What is certain and uncontroversial is that in late February of 1901, with his inauguration just a little over a month behind him and the US spring offensives scheduled to commence in only weeks, President Elihu Root departed Washington DC via a train on a whistle stop tour that was aimed at improving US morale. While conspiracy theorists love to point out that the US had not suffered any significant disruptions at this time, which to a degree is true that is only if one takes the situation out of context and forgets everything else that was going on. The US had just finished a presidential election that occurred in a time of war. These are not historically the times that people rise up and overthrow their government since technically speaking that is exactly what they had just finished doing. People may have been too tired to take to the streets but that is not to say they were not tired of the war.

While no one could quite put their finger on why, the simple fact was that the US war machine was lagging. There does not seem to be any evidence that it was due to sabotage or outright opposition to the war. It looks to have been more a case of the majority of the populace lacking the enthusiasm they had shown when it first started. Most of them were simply ready for it to be over with so that their lives could get back to 'normal.' Signs of this were everywhere and it is interesting to note that both Confederate spies and the White House were misreading these signs. While it can be easily surmised that Confederate Naval Intelligence was definitely painting this evidence so that their leadership in Richmond could see it with rose colored glasses, since it went to the heart of Confederate War aims, it seems that the White House chose to panic of its own accord. There appears to be no other reason for the sudden change of plans that put Root on that train.

His choice of stops is easily explainable and logical as well, that is if you take the situation into account and do not treat it as an isolated case, such as most conspiracy theorists do. Root was mostly touring factories, induction centers, big farms, and was giving speeches from the back platform of his rail car at nearly every town they stopped. He was most definitely targeting areas based on voting patterns from the last election. That might sound odd when you consider that he was not going to run for reelection, but remember, all of the House of Representatives and a third of the Senate would be up for re-election in just under two years. Given the poor showings that the Republicans had on Capitol Hill in the last election, one can understand a desire to shore up these weak spots.

There is also the simple possibility that Root's motivation for these stops had little to do with the next midterm election. He simply could have been more interested in the verdict of the big show, the war. His desire to win it could be all the motivation that he needed. Some have argued that Root was not that altruistic and my counter to this is simple, you don't have to be. Root was now on his second term and there is little doubt that he was concerned with what history was going to have to say about him. He had to know that his Presidency and this war were going to be irrevocably linked, so he had personal motivations to end it in the next four years and with a favorable outcome for his nation.

The single biggest point of controversy is what would ultimately become his final stop in this tour. There has been much clamoring over the years about his choice of the hospital at Fort

Harrison, Indiana. Many have argued that Root would not wish to associate himself with casualty lists that had become so hated in the US and indeed in every belligerent nation. It has been said that he would have never risked a photograph with soldiers who were missing limbs. While every war had produced such veterans, this one had easily tripled the number, as a precent, of those who would be walking around after minus a vital body part. This was not due to some horrific new weapon, but ironically, due to advances in medicine which were saving more wounded than in previous conflicts. At the time, no one was really aware of this and the disfigured soldier was rapidly becoming a symbol of the war in many countries, including the US.

One can easily dismiss claims that Root's visit to Harrison was some kind of setup. Root had already posed for many photographs with wounded and disfigured veterans. The claim, that he would not do such a thing, only emerged some sixty years after the war, and was made by an author of a book who thought it odd, but like most conspiracy theorists had not bothered to do much research. Most of the pictures of Root and disabled veterans were not the kind of thing that Presidential Libraries like to make public. They had many such portraits, but most were kept filed away and not on display. His stop at the hospital was logical enough, and while this may have been the first, he also had several others on his itinerary, but tragically would never reach them.

The army hospital also serves as a point of conspiracy for the assassin as well. I first introduced us to Frank Zholhus when he was a member of the Ohio Territorial Guard that defended the J. Roebling Bridge from the Confederate attack just a little over a year before his date with infamy. Again, there have been many who claim it suspicious that he was even at the hospital on the day in question, but again I point out this only appears to be the case until the evidence is scrutinized and put into the proper context.

It is true that Zholhus was not seriously wounded during the Cincinnati Raid, but it was enough to require a six-week trip to the hospital, two surgeries, and over a year's worth of observation afterwards. All of this can easily be found in his service record which has been on public display for a half century. This is where conspiracy theorists like to point out that he was a member of the Ohio Militia and not Indiana, hence he should have never been assigned to Fort Harrison in the first place. While this might sound good, one only need to look at the law of the time to understand why he was there. Zholhus was wounded while defending a bridge that crossed state lines. He, like the rest of his unit, was federalized for that duty and oddly enough they fell under the authority of the US Department of Agriculture and not the US Army. There were a lot of bureaucratic reasons why this was the case, but it did qualify Zholhus for any federal compensation including full Veteran's benefits and in this case US Army medical care.

There are those that toss all of that aside and then point out that while Zholhus was living in Indiana, under a doctor's care, there was nothing wrong with him. That is true but, it is also something that we now know more about, after his medical records have been examined and, quite literally, under a microscope. Zholhus did suffer from any number of infections while he was recovering, including a very nasty infection of staphylococcus that he most likely picked up while in the hospital and probably from a physician. Some have used that as evidence that the records have been changed but, staph infections had been known about for twenty years before Zholhus was wounded. The fact that he recovered from it, without antibiotics which were not yet invented, is impressive but, not impossible as there is a twenty percent recovery rate from the strain that we believe he had.

All of the medical evidence that is used to point towards a conspiracy has one common thread. It is people looking over their shoulder with the advantages that hindsight affords, and with many decades of medical advances that take the situation out of context. The irony in this is that it was a medical advance that kept the man in Indianapolis. It was due to a rather strange theory developed by a number of physicians in the 1890s and was rooted in one of the most useful medical advances of all time, the X-ray. I do realize that there are many who think this ludicrous and for them I simply point to the fact that no matter what you think of it, the simple fact is that Zholus was ordered to Indiana and diagnosed long before Root even knew he would be reelected let alone make this good will tour.

What Zholhus was thought to be suffering from was a result of the fact that he was actually x-rayed by a doctor that had little experience with the device and almost no experience in reading the finished product. You have to remember how new x-ray machines were at the time and they were still not so common in Army hospitals. Almost no Army physicians had experience using them, and after the first few pictures, they began to make a common mistake that physicians had been making since the X-ray machine was first introduced. You see doctors learn their anatomy with cadavers that are lying on a table. As a result, the organs are all flattened and positioned in much the way you see in books. The reality is that while we are walking around, they obey the laws of gravity and do not look anything like the way they do in those nice, neat pictures. The first X-ray machines required that you stand up, and when the first organs were viewed in the pictures, the doctors were horrified at what they saw. Many went so far as to write this up as a new disease and many people were placed in these hideous contraptions to help push their organs back into place.

It did not take long before some doctor thought the matter through and realized that what they saw in x-rays was perfectly normal. Still, medicine is a science, and it has competing schools of thought. It is also bound by the same realities as other professions in that a lot of older physicians were not trusting of new devices, or in this case new explanations. Zholhus was one of the first to be x-rayed at the hospital in Cincinnati. He took several subsequent trips to the machine, and apparently the doctors there thought he suffered from this strange deformity of the organs. The hospital at Fort Harrison was for long term care, and hence he was ordered there.

This is not so ominous and given the complications from his wounds, Zholhus was probably lucky that this happened because he did recover from those complications. It is very possible that he would not have had he remained in Ohio. Many have pointed out that he was discharged from the hospital long before he had his run in with the President, but this is not true. In order to free up bed space, Zholhus was discharged from the actual hospital but not his doctor's care. He was one of many who were living in either the barracks or local housing, drawing a soldier's wage, and doing whatever in between doctor's visits. There was nothing ominous about it.

It is also true that Zholhus was not scheduled to see the doctor on the day in question. Many have pointed to this as unusual, but Zholhus had complete access to the hospital any time he wished, had been there numerous times without an appointment, and again this is another case of taking things out of context. The President was going to be there that day and almost everyone that had any connection to the hospital showed up to shake Root's hand. The presence of one Frank Zholhus would not have sent up any red flags at all, and in fact his absence would have looked more suspicious.

Finally, there is the fact that Zholhus had a gun. The thirty-two-caliber revolver that he kept in his pocket is used by conspiracy theorists as the ultimate evidence that this man did not act alone. They point out that there is no way that Zholhus could have gotten so close to the president with the weapon, then produce it just as he clasped hands for a shake and empty all five shots into the President's chest. In fact, many question why Zholhus even had a weapon at all. Both of these facts are easily explainable once the details are examined.

Today we are used to a President that is tightly guarded by professionals that do nothing else. Root's only security that day were two bodyguards that had been hired by the government from the Pinkerton Agency. While both of these guards were top notch for their

125

time, there were no protocols on how to defend against assassins. It was events like this one, that led to the science of defending against such things. The fact that Zholhus got a weapon so close cannot be seen as requiring a conspiracy when you consider what happened to Zholhus in the immediate aftermath. This proves that not only did he get a weapon close to Root, but so did nearly everyone else in the crowd. Doctors removed thirty-seven bullets from the corpse of Zholhus, all the result of hospital patients shooting him, only seconds after he opened fire on Root. The only thing this really tells us is, if you're going to shoot a head of state, do not do it around a crowd of agitated and wounded soldiers.

That takes us back to why he had a gun in the first place, and ultimately, his motives which have been called into question since that day. The fact that he actually died before the President is not just ironic but sadly it means we will never know, for certain, why Frank Zholhus decided to shoot Elihu Root. His ownership of the weapon is not such a big mystery, however. Many of the soldiers in his situation drank heavily and spent a great deal of time in saloons. At the time, the local saloons had a reputation for setting up soldiers to be robbed. This not only explains the weapon Zholhus had but the ones that killed him as well.

This ultimately brings us to motivation. Many have claimed that Zholhus had none. Again, I say this is only if the man is taken out of context. In reviewing his story, it is quite obvious what his motivation was even if we can never prove this conclusively. The man simply had a miserable life, was the victim of one bad turn after another, and had just finished dealing with what should have been a simple medical problem that was made worse by the very system trying to cure him. While such circumstances would not drive the majority of us to kill, it could easily be the case with a man who was on the edge to begin with. When you see this in the context of the times, with national leaders being made the very face of the war, the target for Frank's ills becomes understandable. After all, that was why Root was there in the first place, playing the face of the war. If the extraordinary, and sometimes almost improbable, circumstances that led these two men to that fateful day had not occurred, there is every reason to think that it might have been another shooter, at another stop, at another time.

If Elihu Root was not exactly a cherished leader in his time, his memory as a President certainly became one. While his whistle-stop morale tour had not shown any signs of accomplishing its goals before Indianapolis, his very last day of it at Fort Harrison accomplished everything and more. Root went from being the man who started this accursed war to near sainthood and almost as soon as his heart stopped. You could almost surmise that until the assassination the American public was asking themselves why they were fighting this war. Ironically, Frank Zholhus gave them the strongest reason ever. It has also been suggested that Zholhus was an anarchist and he was trying to start a revolution. Oddly enough he did, only if he were truly an anarchist, it was not the revolution he was intending.

Sagamore Hill

There are more than a few movies about the life of Theodore Roosevelt. A good number of them either start or end on the same day in his life and not surprisingly at the same place. This place being his private home at Sagamore Hill. This is because that particular day was a major event in his life. Oddly enough, it seems to have been more important to everyone else than to Theodore who took the news of the President's death with a sort of pragmatism. Some have criticized the man for his almost lack of emotion about the matter while many of the movies have given him those emotions. The conspiracy people tend to point to this as evidence that he knew it was coming. The main reason for all of this confusion is from the most predictable of sources, and the simple fact is the movies got it wrong.

The most popular narrative is that Thomas Platt, often portrayed as a humble servant and admirer of Roosevelt, rides up to the front door in a carriage and is greeted by many children. This happens just before Roosevelt and his wife Edith emerge, and upon being told the news, Theodore then gives a heartfelt speech on the front steps of his home. About the only thing that this most common scene of cinematic drama got right was that Platt did indeed arrive in a horse drawn carriage. The man was terrified of automobiles.

Platt was not the first to arrive and there was complete confusion at Sagamore Hill when he finally got there. Once the news of the assassination, via the wire services, reached

Platt he knew what had to be done. He was ever the calculating party boss and used the same courier, who had brought him the news, to send a request to the NYPD for help in protecting the man who was about to become President. Platt turned what was already an ordeal into a circus, although in retrospect his actions seem reasonable enough. I don't think Platt anticipated the emotional outpouring, that was on the way, and you also have to remember that Platt was not gifted with hindsight in this matter. He had to consider that Root was not the only target that day.

You also have to address the fact that it was the NYPD who were showing up in force to protect the still Vice President. Sagamore Hill is on Long Island and well outside their jurisdiction, but Theodore was a former Commissioner of the NYPD and a popular one at that. They were not about to allow anyone else to guard him on a day like this. Platt's request reached Captain Henry O'Leary first and apparently he took it upon himself to organize the effort. He did a poor job because the only people that did not seem to know about Platt's request were O'Leary's bosses. Every beat cop in Manhattan was aware of it within the hour, and even after O'Leary left with a five-man detail, beat cops were abandoning their post and rushing out of the city. They would be sporadically showing up at Sagamore Hill well into the next night.

O'Leary's people would be the first to arrive since they were not only using a motorcar, but unlike so many of the other would-be protectors, O'Leary actually knew where Sagamore Hill was. Many of the other policemen, using their own independent initiative, would never reach Roosevelt's home and this included one man who was lost, on a horse in a uniform that many a Long Island resident were unfamiliar with, and mistaken for the vanguard of a Confederate invasion force. Drunken patrons of a Hempstead saloon would chase this unfortunate officer all the way back to his home in Brooklyn where a street fight broke out over the matter.

What Captain O'Leary discovered when he got to Roosevelt's home, and as near as we can tell he was the first 'official' to arrive, was that the news of Root's assassination had already reached the Vice President who, contrary to the movies, was still the Vice President. Several local Oyster Bay residents that personally knew the Roosevelt family, had already heard about the assassination and went directly to Sagamore Hill to spread the news to the man who most obviously needed to know it. Many of them were already loitering on Theodore's front lawn when the NYPD arrived. Even they were not the first to break the news because Roosevelt owned a piece of modern technology, a telephone. This little fact has somehow been completely overlooked by the film industry.

The man who did deliver the news was actually someone that is relatively famous, and at the time a household name. This is ironic in that in every single narrative of this day, he never comes up. He was a newspaper man by the name of Richard Harding Davis, personal friends with Roosevelt, had been with him in Mexico, and was at his paper and near their telegraphs when the news first came in. He promptly went to his phone, and as a result, Roosevelt knew that Root had been shot within twenty minutes of it actually happening. Root would not die for three more days, but it was already known that he was incapacitated by the shooting. When the police, the dignitaries, and the spectators began arriving at Roosevelt's house in force, he had already grieved, but fully understood that he had a job to do.

Roosevelt's first action seems to have been to make another phone call. This has been partly verified by the logs at Fort Lincoln. Roosevelt was trying to reach General Shafter, but the man was currently not there. Roosevelt did speak with the ranking officer on duty who assured him that nothing unusual was going on at either front. This may or may not have satisfied Roosevelt that the assassination was some grand conspiracy by the allies. His following actions suggest this because, at that point, Roosevelt began the process of trying to get a grip on what was soon to be his government.

Here is where the US was very fortunate because despite being left out of the loop by Root, Roosevelt understood the inner workings of his government better than most, and before he ever took office. He knew who was really in control of what, and in a very Roosevelt fashion, he retreated to his private study, away from the circus that was building around his house and picked up his pen. In the likelihood that Elihu Root would not survive, Roosevelt had obviously decided that he would be ready and was determined that the US Government would not suffer any loss of continuity. Theodore also told his wife Edith to begin packing. They would be boarding a train for Washington as soon as it could be arranged. It was at this point that Platt's general characterization in the movies can be shown to be completely false.

It is understandable that Roosevelt wished to get to Washington as soon as possible. Again, you have to remember that no one at this point knew if this was a plot to decapitate the government in a time of war. There were certainly many important people who thought so. The sudden influx of requests on the Pinkertons for bodyguards is a good indication of this. In fact, it seems as if the only entity that did not believe this possibility was the Federal Government itself. There were no plans for such an event and even less action taken. Roosevelt's situation proves this beyond a doubt.

As Vice President, Roosevelt had the authority to requisition a military train for transportation. He never used it and some even ask if he knew that he could. He was used to traveling like anyone else and most of the time he paid for this out of his own pocket. He did submit vouchers to the White House for reimbursement, but that could often take months. Now he was the acting head of state in a time of extreme crisis and a possible target for an assassin's bullet. One would think that the government would arrange his transportation to the seat of power. They not only did nothing, but actively tried to convince the Vice President to remain in New York.

In this particular instance I could say the conspirators are a they, but the power of hindsight allows me to name names. The 'they' in this particular instance seems to have been only two men and Thomas Platt was one of them. The other man, and I am guessing he was the one giving Platt orders, was Secretary of State John Hay. When Roosevelt spoke to Platt at his home about transportation to the capital, Platt assured Roosevelt that it was coming, yet we can find that he did nothing about it at all. What we do know is that one of the first people he talked with via telephone before leaving Manhattan was Hay. The Secretary had good reason to wish to delay Roosevelt and this is why I believe he instructed Platt to do so.

It is also apparent that Roosevelt was aware of this, or at least suspected that Hay was deliberately trying to slow the process down. Roosevelt did not wait for government transport. He also decided to leave his family in Oyster Bay and proceed to Washington on his own. He used the circus like atmosphere that was building around his home and slipped out unnoticed. The only protection the man had was in his coat pocket. It was the Colt Naval revolver he had carried with him in New Mexico. He purchased a train ticket in Manhattan later that night and was in Washington three days later, the train having been delayed any number of times for military traffic.

Some have criticized Roosevelt for this. Root died before he reached the city, and the United States went almost an entire day without a head of state. This was delayed even longer because once in DC Roosevelt did not go directly to the White House. Instead, he began visiting prominent Senators and power brokers for private conversations, none of which were recorded. That is not to say that John Hay was unaware that the Vice President was in town. He had known that Roosvelt was missing since about an hour after the Vice President left Sagamore Hill. It was obvious where the man was going, and once Roosevelt began visiting Washington insiders it did not take long for word of this to reach Hay. It is apparent that the Secretary of State was doing the same thing that Roosevelt was, only Hay had a three-day head start.

This might have set up the board for a nasty power struggle if one of the players had been anyone but Theodore Roosevelt. Hay, like so many others before him, completely underestimated the man. Roosevelt was not interested in fighting for control of Washington with his Secretary of State and was well aware of Hay's intentions. All the while, Hay was preparing for a head on train crash with the soon to be President, not realizing that just like his trip to Washington, Roosevelt had switched tracks. Hay did not seem to understand the situation with the public at large, something that Roosevelt apparently did.

The sympathy, the anger, the indignation over the assassination gave Roosevelt an unusual amount of pull with the voting public and he had figured out how to use it. It would allow him to circumvent the normal power brokers and make appeals directly to the voters. In a working democracy, even powerful men that hold unelected positions of power, can ill afford to ignore the public for too long, particularly in a case like this. Those who have to stand for election are in an even more precarious position. Roosevelt only had to remind them of all this, the senators and industrialists alike, to make these power brokers back down, or to even hitch themselves to his wagon. He apparently began using this strategy the moment he got off the train in Washington.

That was why when Theodore Roosevelt was sworn into office, on the front steps of the capital building, he would have the kind of honeymoon period that most elected officials only dream of. He was the youngest man ever to rise to this office. He was bursting with energy and he had a sudden surge of public support that not only supported him but had confidence that he would lead them to victory. Those who thought they could stand in his way would only come to so much grief. John Hay was not the only political opponent who found themselves in hot water once President Root died. There were others who found themselves the targets of public vengeance as well.

William Randolph Hearst was easily the most visible secondary casualty of the assassination. Despite being a fellow republican, Hearst had been a thorn in the side of the Root administration from the start. His man, Ambrose Bierce, had accompanied Roosevelt into Mexico looking for a juicy story to embarrass Root. He very well might have kept this up and directly attacked Roosevelt now that Root was gone. Due to a strange turn of events, this would not happen. Bierce had gone overboard with his attacks, even to the point of writing a story about a fictional Presidential assassination in which the victim was a thinly veiled clone of Elihu Root.

The story was published only a month before the real assassination. Bierce found himself under attack because of this, some even claiming that he was responsible for Indianapolis. It was not lost on anyone that Bierce was a mouthpiece for Hearst and the fallout hit where it hurt the newspaper magnate the most, in the sales of his papers. That was why Hearst wasted no time firing Bierce. The former army officer and prolific writer would eventually take to heavy drinking and working menial jobs before finally committing suicide some nine years later. Hearst would recover but he would not do so in time to take on the bear in the White House.

This all amounted to one thing. Roosevelt had a blank check like no other since George Washington. What is even more important was Roosevelt understood how to use it. In his years in the White House, his vigor and energy would seem boundless. He would also bring others with those same traits, not to the inner halls of

the capitol, but in places where things really
mattered more. Many of these men, later to be
saddled with the collective term Bull Moose,
would make silent but important changes.
Many would be forgotten while a few would
not, but what is important here is, all of these
changes were about to set the world on its ear.
Nothing would ever be the same again.

The Other Paris

Fort Bragg usually gets most of the fame
in Western Tennessee and it is the name we
associate with the entire theater, but the name
really only covered a network of prewar
fortifications and improved defensive points.
Many of these places were not even officially
under the administration of Fort Bragg which
was after all not exactly a traditional fortress to
begin with since it sprawled across a hundred-
mile sector of the Department of Western
Tennessee. There were actually three official
'forts' that administered the front that spanned
between the Mississippi and Tennessee Rivers.
Bragg was just the best known and the other
two Forts, Polk and Cheatham, were mostly
concerned with the defense of the two primary

waterways they were headquartered on and has since faded into obscurity.

Paris, Tennessee fell inside the zone of Fort Cheatham, which covered the Tennessee River Valley, even if this fact has long since been forgotten in pop culture. In this zone was a town that was named after an enemy capital, Paris, even if this fact did not spare it any wrath from the United States Army. In 1901 the actual town was still in Confederate hands, but this was a hollow victory since the civilian population was largely gone and the city had stopped functioning as such for over a year.

Confederate defenses sat just north of Paris, along what had been a creek bed. In 1901 it was barely recognizable as such since the ground had been fought over for nearly a year and a half. We have one picture of the area taken just after the war, and it shows us a shallow valley devoid of any plant life except for fallen trees that turned the creek bed into a pile of splintered logs. The damage shown in the area looks to largely be the result of conventional artillery, but this is not what Paris would be remembered for in the history books. That is understandable since the US Army had made no serious attempts to storm the city since 1899 and the CS Army was perfectly happy with that situation. That meant the fighting around Paris was static and had consisted largely of raids on the other side's trenches.

There are those who wonder why it was that General Shafter chose this particular area to try out his new weapon. It did not appear to be of any real importance to either side. and I propose that might very well be the reason he picked it. One has to remember that Shafter was not the most enthusiastic fan of the chemical artillery shells and never showed any sign that he had much confidence in their effectiveness. His detractors point out that he did take the time to travel to the frontlines to personally oversee the first operation using the weapon. They also point out that any failures were largely the responsibility of those who planned the missions, and this list also includes the commanding general of the entire US Army, since he approved those plans.

Looking back on the situation, the reverse seems to be the case in so much as it was the not the plans that Shafter approved, but the ones that he denied that were at the core of the matter. Shafter's staff, back at Fort Lincoln, shared their commander's sentiment about chemical weapons, and their recommendations seem to show this. They were in direct contradiction to Third Army's new commander, General MacArthur, who had a staff that saw the situation very differently. By this time, MacArthur's people were probably the most experienced command staff in the US Army. They had been the ones that directed the defense of Washington in the early days of the war. As a result, they had both the intimate knowledge of the problems at the front and a good reason to find practical solutions to those problems. Tragically, like so many other instances in this war, their superiors were not listening.

MacArthur supported the recommendations of his people who suggested that the new weapons be used in high concentrations on specific points that were to be exploited by specially trained infantry that went in almost immediately after the artillery. Fort Lincoln completely denied these plans and pointed out that MacArthur had no time to train any troops in new tactics. Shafter also personally noted that these plans were too radical and that the other units involved in the operation would be unable to support such an attack. This kind of attitude from above was not entirely unrealistic but, it also demonstrates another problem of general officers during the war.

There seemed to be two classes of Generals that developed as the war went on and hindsight affords us the opportunity to see that both schools of thought were just plain wrong. We met the first kind of General in the Balkan campaign. The Russian General Fok made the mistake of expecting his conscripted army to act as if they were prewar regulars. As the war went on Shafter very much became the mirror image of this in that he was seriously underestimating the abilities of his own troops. He understood that they were mostly civilians in uniform and as a result lacked any real confidence in their abilities. His plans at Paris, plans he forced on a theater commander that he had personally appointed to the position, show this basic lack of confidence. When combined with his pessimism about the new weapon, one can see that this 'test' was halfhearted at best.

The entire assault on Confederate lines was carried out as if it were any other attack. The chemical artillery shells were used as if they were just another high explosive round. They were given no specific targets for the new weapon, their rate of fire was one chemical round per every five salvos, and the preliminary barrage was no different than the countless others that came before. One has to wonder if Shafter, who was most definitely personally appalled by this weapon, wanted it to fail. If he did, he did not seem to have considered the ramifications of using chemical weapons in the first place.

The single biggest factor that Shafter's staff seemed to completely ignore, if indeed they even understood it at all, was the type of chemical being used. This is essential to any such operation of this type. They also did not make any allowances for the weather, most important of which was wind. These two crucial factors were not lost on MacArthur and his people. Their reports to Fort Lincoln stressed these variables multiple times and were not even addressed by Shafter's people. This goes a long way towards explaining what happened.

The artillery shells fired by the US Army on that day were a concentrated mixture of chloroacetone with a combination of herbicides, the latter of which was completely useless in this area since they were south of the major kudzu belts. In layman's terms the weapon was a primitive form of tear gas, and while it could be lethal in heavy doses, no such concentrations were fired on that day. Then the weather took its toll. It was springtime but the air did not feel like it and in the early morning when the barrage began, the temperature was still well below freezing. Most of the initial gas attacks did not vaporize once the shell exploded. It froze in chunks and much of it was buried in the mud as it fell back to earth.

Despite all of the problems and misdirection, US Artillery still managed to create a cloud that was more than just dust. Many Confederate soldiers fled their bomb shelters and shortly after that the front lines completely. Not all of them ran though. At some point, the Confederates figured out what was happening, and a swift solution appeared along the lines. Soldiers were dousing rags and bandanas with a combination of liquids. They even went so far as urinating on the cloth. These makeshift gas masks were far from perfect but given the haphazard manner in which the enemy was gassing them, it allowed more than a few pockets of resistance to make a stand along the trench lines.

When the US Infantry attack went in, they found the enemy resistance sporadic and varied all down the line. That might have been enough had the US soldiers not been told that there would be no resistance at all. The sudden return fire, much of it coming from locations that were thought secured, had as adverse effect on the US soldiers as did the gas on their CS counterparts. Even in locations where the US overran the enemy trenches, they faced yet another problem. Many of the chunks of frozen chemicals began warming up as the day progressed. As the US soldiers fought off counterattacks by Johnny Kudzu, their own gas began to form around them out of what appeared to be nowhere.

By the end of the day, the trenches were mostly back in Confederate hands. In three more days, the lines would be right back where they had started. Again, it is highly debatable if this was the conclusion that Shafter was looking for. There is also every possibility that it was a case of Shafter's staff simply not knowing what they were doing. Since Shafter never mentioned this in his own papers or the various writings on the subject, it is likely that we will never know for sure. What we do know for certain, is that Shafter had just unwittingly kicked over a hornet's nest. To the horror of his people at Fort Lincoln, the CS had not been completely unaware of what was coming.

Confederate Naval Intelligence had long since detected the activity going on in Delaware.

They were never able to discover exactly what it was that the enemy was up to, but they never really had to. Once the hard data was assembled many of the analysts realized that the sudden surge of outgoing railcars from Wilmington could only be so many things. They assumed it to be worst-case and that meant some sort of chemical weapon. As a result, the Confederacy was ready to retaliate.

They had not made any artillery shells, as the US had done, but what the Confederacy did have was a huge textile industry and that included factories that both made and used many kinds of dye. The biproduct of these processes was chlorine gas which had limited uses for other things but was largely discarded. The CSA also had a surplus of airtight containers that were now in use for their new Zeppelin industry. It was trivial for them to turn out a small trainyard full of bottled gas. None of it was as lethal as the next generation of gas, that was specifically made for the job of war, and earned the nickname 'Mustard Gas'. It was lethal enough for what the CS had in mind, even if when they were stockpiling it no one had ever seriously thought it would be used.

The biggest problem that the Confederates had with their gas weapons, which were brought to the frontline and released from hoses in a concentrated area, was the lack of good places to use it. Geography and wind patterns were mostly against them in this exercise, but on a front of nearly 1500 miles, it was inevitable that they would find one place. This spot was near Winchester, West Virginia, and had long since been scouted out as a possible location for this exercise. On the very day that the CS army was retaking the last of the trenches around Paris, their first gas cloud rolled over US lines in West Virginia.

On the surface it would seem as if the Confederate attack was far more successful than the one made by the US Army. We have no reliable figures on the casualties generated by the Paris attack, largely due to the haphazard manner in which it was done. The gassing at Winchester was an entirely different matter and even the conservative estimates put casualties at around four thousand men in a single day. Note that I said casualties and not fatalities since the largest portion of those men were wounded, many of whom would return to the front before that particular operation was even over with. Yet, still, that was not why these weapons were complete failures.

Contrary to popular opinion, war is not about killing the enemy. Casualties are a biproduct of war and not its goal, which is the imposition of will. In this conflict, that goal could only be realized by breaking the enemy frontline and here we see that chemical warfare was a total failure. Even the Confederate attack at Winchester failed to break the enemy front. They did manage to open a small hole in the line but infantry marching on feet were simply not capable of fully exploiting the breech. The US would plug the hole in their lines and eventually beat the Confederates right back to where they started from, even if it took longer than it did at Paris. Ultimately the end results were identical.

Of course, chemical weapons did have an effect, it was simply not what anyone had expected. It did not take long for everyone to figure out that they would not produce victory, but now that the genie was out of the bottle, to not use them could most certainly produce defeat. It did not take long before the Germans used them on the Russians, the French on the Germans, the Russians on the British, and so forth and so on. Within months everyone would be using them, and the types of chemical mixtures only kept getting more lethal, even if none of them were producing the desired result.

A lot of this failure could be explained by the inexperience of the armies, namely their leadership, in the prosecution of the kind of war they were truly fighting. Indeed, much of the leadership of the world still did not even realize what kind of war it was, let alone fight it in an effective manner. That was only a small problem compared to others and the most notable of these were the simple fact that chemical weapons are inefficient to begin with. They lack the one quality that is most desirable for any military weapon, that being the ability to be properly aimed. Chemical weapons simply can't be. This means, in order for them to be used at the right place and time on a battlefield to produce a decisive result is always a matter of chance. In a profession that does its utmost to reduce random luck, chemical weapons become almost useless.

Countermeasures to defeat the worst effects of chemical weapons were fairly trivial to devise by most industrialized nations. The gas mask was simple to produce and did not even make a noticeable dent in the rapidly shrinking rubber supplies. These masks varied widely in design, from one nation to the next, despite the fact that they all essentially worked the exact same way. When paired with gloves and hoods, they rendered most concentrations and types of gas essentially harmless. This was so much the case that the countermeasures themselves became the worst effects of the gas. Infantry commanders would do their best to get their men close to the enemy before he could unmask since fighting in the protective clothing was prohibitive and exhausting. Of course, this was usually balanced out by the fact that both sides were masked. It served only to reduce the offensive capabilities of all the armies and deepen the quagmire.

There was also one effect that no one saw coming or even thought possible and it was the fact that chemical weapons were actually aiding the very enemies that it was made to kill. A little fact that is almost never discussed about warfare, and certainly not unique to this war, is the little creatures that have followed every army since time began. Pestilence was an age-old problem for armies, and in this war with its miles of trench lines that were half flooded in water, polluted with feces, and a host of decaying bodies lying in close proximity, disease was a serious problem. For every soldier that was incapacitated by the direct result of enemy action, three were brought down by disease. A great deal of this was due to insects and this is not even counting the less lethal but annoying kind which had thoroughly infested the trenches, such as lice. These creatures were far more effective killing machines than any chemical weapon, and ironically, they were also completely vulnerable to the new weapons. Within months of the first widescale use of gas attacks on all fronts, the mortality rates from disease dropped by almost half.

The beneficial and surprising side effect of this particular aspect of chemical warfare would not even be realized until long after the war. In 1901, just after its first use at Paris, it suddenly became a major concern for world leaders. Even after Winchester, they were not so much afraid of its effects on their armies. If anything, the North American attacks seem to indicate that these weapons would not do much to change the battlefield equation. The national leaders had other concerns, however. By this time, they all had powered balloons flying high above cities and dropping bombs on each other's civilian populations. All of them gasped in horror and realized that if those high explosives changed to chemical weapons, the devastation could be more than they ever imagined. Here is where the chemical munitions had their most profound impact.

The Wright Choice

To say in those early days of spring, that Theodore Roosevelt was the busiest man alive was quite an understatement. This would almost seem obvious given the circumstances that thrust him into the White House. He was having to find his own footing, run all of the more mundane details of a government, a war, and even a personal home to some degree. Foreign dignitaries and diplomats were calling on him left and right. Most of them used the pretense of expressing their remorse and sympathy for the fallen Elihu Root, but in reality, most of them were trying to size up Roosevelt. This was very different from the days when John Adams moved into the house. At that time, nobody considered the Presidency very important. It was even different from the time when Abraham Lincoln took possession. Strangely enough, even Elihu Root's administration did not find that much different from either of the two President Lincolns. Now, not only was there a new man in the house, but the job had changed and ironically enough the house right along with it. Suddenly, it was all important.

This led to the very first problem of Roosevelt's administration. It was the reason for his first executive order, and it seems rather odd for an executive with the literal weight of the world on his shoulders. Roosevelt could not get any sleep and the primary reason was that his new home was more a military command center than anything else. Wires were crossed over each other on the floors and new holes were in the walls to accommodate the wires. Every room in the house was now occupied by its own private army and not only was there nowhere you could go where bells, clicking, and a hushed rumble of collective voices could not be heard, but also there was literally no room for Roosevelt's family that was still on the way.

Since no Vice President had yet to be confirmed, his old residence at the Naval Observatory was still vacant. That was why Roosevelt spent his first few months as president commuting to work. He also ordered renovations on the White House. Most of them would be finished before Roosevelt left office, and indeed the bulk of them before the end of his first term. It was the beginning of the modern building we know today and the establishment of one of its most visible traditions, the Oval Office. This was the centerpiece of what was ironically named 'The West Wing' which was also what Roosevelt's ad hoc cavalry command had been called in New Mexico.

For the time being, Roosevelt was stuck with what he had, and this is why his first Cabinet meetings were not even held at the White House. Root had the same problem, but he spent a good deal of time working out of his railroad car. Roosevelt did not have such a thing yet, so he chose a local hotel meeting room to sit down with Root's old cabinet. It was really the first big problem he would face in establishing his administration. None of these men really held any loyalty to him which is not that surprising since a good number had little loyalty for Root either. Roosevelt could not arbitrarily dispose of them since Cabinet level positions had to be approved by Congress. Apparently, according to his journals, Roosevelt had not even decided what to do about this situation until the gas attacks in Tennessee. The triggering mechanism being that not only was Roosevelt unaware that the attack was to take place, but he also had no idea that these gas weapons even existed.

John Hay, who had used the gas weapons to deflect one president, now found himself on the spot with another. He did make a reasonable argument that there had simply been no time to tell Roosevelt, which was mostly true. He also stated that as Vice President, Roosevelt did not have a need to know and the weapons were of a very secretive nature. This was also true, to a point, because while the President of the US had to find out about his secret weapon in the newspapers, Confederate Intelligence had known something was up right from the start.

Maybe that was why Roosevelt did not accept either excuse. He did not say that was the case but instead he then made a point that Hay had obviously not thought of. The cabinet was so horrified by what Roosevelt said that it was apparent that none of them had thought of it either. The new President told them in his usual energetic way, "The greatest threat we now face are these accursed flying trains. What happens when their ordinance stops exploding and begins to go woosh instead? I ask you that!"

One has to speculate here. Were these men afraid of Confederate gas shells falling on US cities, or were they terrified at the prospect of Roosevelt ordering such attacks on Confederate population centers? If such an attack ever occurred, no matter which side was responsible, there would be no peace in North America for centuries. Roosevelt had a reputation as a loose cannon, the US now had an infant air fleet that was growing weekly, and they certainly had a surplus of chemical artillery shells. It had to be rumbling in the back of every mind in the room when you consider that this was before people knew who the real Roosevelt was.

We do not know if Roosevelt meant to shock these men in such a way, but it certainly helped his cause. These men suddenly went silent and that was probably for the best considering that, right then and there, Theodore decided the best way to handle his cabinet was to simply ignore it. That is not to say that the President was going to try and do everything alone, he just now planned on doing things differently. The term that would later stick to this kind of circumstance is called a 'kitchen cabinet' and while that term would only be born years after Theodore's death, it was most certainly the kind of team he assembled.

For all of Roosevelt's life he had surrounded himself with people who were not only experts in their chosen fields, but many were quite gifted. Roosevelt's real talent was spotting people like this and fostering their support and loyalty. He had used this skill to assemble a Cavalry regiment and it worked out splendidly. Now he was going to turn it on the war as a whole. Roosevelt had just spent several years in the army and his list of personal acquaintances, that were both experts at war and owed him favors, was long and diverse. This list was from the very top of the command structure, like General Shafter, all the way down to privates in the field. He would call on many of these men in the months to come.

Some of these 'consultants' would be more notable than others, but right then in March of 1901 there was no other expert that seemed to be more important to Theodore than Samuel Langley. Roosevelt had spent his restless hours reading and trying to acclimate himself to his new job. He had turned both his office and bedroom into makeshift file rooms where, in between courting ambassadors, he was catching up on all of the information that Root had the luxury of years to digest. Somewhere in his reading he had determined that his old acquaintance, now out in Kansas, held the best chance in stopping the Zeppelins. The sudden appearance of chemical weapons now seemed to make this matter even more urgent.

Oddly enough, it was not Langley who would become most instrumental in this equation. It was a trio of siblings from Dayton, Ohio that Roosevelt had never heard of and of whom Langley had little use. Wilbur and Orville Wright were two brothers who had been for many years as divided as the former American nation. They were born into a family of deeply held Christian beliefs that were both passionate and as equally divided. They were a very typical example of their times and the issues that confronted the average American.

Wilbur had chosen a path of deeply held pacifism while Orville was very much a hawk when it came to the Confederate States of America. It must be noted that both of these beliefs stemmed from the exact same issues and, oddly enough, it was not because they viewed the Confederacy any differently, they just disagreed on how to approach it. Wilbur's attitude seemed to center around the idea that if you could only reach the hearts of their lost brethren then unification would certainly result. This attitude was most definitely the one fostered by his deeply religious father. Orville, on the other hand, held the more popular view that the only way to deal with the south was to stomp it flat. Of course, these two seemingly opposite views never appeared to interfere with the brothers working together. They even ran a small newspaper at one time and their opinion articles were quite often similar on at least one point, they both firmly opposed slavery.

Of course, the final abolition of slavery in the US in the late 1880s, may have been either a cause of celebration for the Wrights or it was the last thing the two brothers agreed on and only managed to start a family wide civil war. We're not really sure on this point. We are relatively certain that Orville and Wilbur's one and only sister, Kitty, played referee for many years. When their mother died, despite Kitty's young age, she took over the role of leading female of the Wright Family and some family friends noted that she kept her two older brothers from almost killing each other on many occasions.

Kitty was more than just a behind the scenes player. She had an advanced education, her own career as a teacher and she still managed to run the family even with her father's declining health. This is important to us because it now appears as if it were not for Kitty, the Wright's venture in the bicycle business would have fallen apart and probably right from the start. Wilbur was always the managerial sort, the natural leader, and Orville was more of the ideas man. Kitty kept them together because as she noted in her own journal, they needed each other. The only thing that Kitty could not seem to do was make them have ambition. Individually they both seemed to but once put together, their weaknesses began compounding on each other and as she noted, it was always "a terrible mess."

Bicycle shops of that time are not what we think of them today. Had it been more modern times then Orville and Wilbur would have had themselves a used car lot. In many ways they were what we would call shade tree mechanics. They were also running this business to fund a project that was completely unrelated to bicycles, even if many of the shop parts would wind up in their attempts to build a vehicle capable of independent, heavier than air flight. Just before the war began, their single biggest problem was the lack of resources and time. When the war started, this problem was trumped by almost constant bickering between the brothers. It was a situation, noted by their sister, that threatened everything they had done.

The heart of the matter was Wilbur's opposition to the war. This pacifism spilled over on their project because both brothers realized that what they were doing had military applications. In much of the popular literature, and something that historians even believed up until most recently, it was thought that letters from both the war department and Octave Chanute had set off a tinder box at the Wright home. This has now been shown to be false because we now know that neither brother ever saw the letters. As it turns out, Kitty had kept the correspondence from her brothers because a divide over the war was already brewing in their household. She did more than just hide the letters though. Kitty apparently realized the importance of them, and she actually answered both, signing them with Wilbur's name.

Kitty would also write another fateful letter, this one addressed to a family friend who lived in Kentucky. The man she sent it to was a published writer and someone that both of her brothers respected. He came to see the family in the hopes that his presence would help soothe the tensions. Paul Dunbar did exactly that, but not in the way that anyone had intended. As noted before, he died in Wilbur's arms on the J Roebling Bridge, hit by a bullet in a crossfire between Confederate raiders and Ohio guardsmen. This event would change Wilbur's life forever and when he returned from Kentucky, where he took the body of his friend, his attitudes on the war had changed dramatically.

Wilbur never told anybody as much, never said that he was wrong, and in fact, he never really spoke much at all about what had happened that morning on the bridge. All that is known, for certain, is that he stopped fighting with his brother and they both began serious work on their flying machine. At this point, their story could have very well ended if it had not been for Kitty. While the Wright Brothers were not well-known figures, even in the race to build the first airplane, they were not completely unknown. Both men had traveled to any number of fairs that were promoting this unproven technology, and in these travels, they had met many pioneers in the field, including Chanute and Langley.

While the Wrights might have appeared to the giants in the field as little more than what today we would call 'fan boys,' they did make an impression. Unfortunately for them, the impression on Langley was unfavorable and he particularly found Wilbur's personality quite abrasive, as he would later comment. Chanute was a different story. He actually found some of the Wright's ideas intriguing, but apparently not enough to ask them for any help until he found himself trapped in France and working on their aircraft project, where he had repeatedly hit one dead-end after another. The Boulanger Government had grown more desperate by the day and General Revenge was not the kind of man that Chanute wished to anger. He was looking for any help he could get.

Oddly enough, the letters that Chanute had sent to the Wrights were not really a serious plea for help. That correspondence was Chanute simply tapping every source of ideas that he knew about. His real call for help went to Langley since the Franco/American rail engineer was aware that his old acquaintance was working on a similar project for the US Government. Both men were hampered by security concerns, but they helped each other as much as possible. It was not until Theodore Roosevelt ascended to the White House that there was any talk at all of official cooperation between the projects.

Then the gas attacks in Tennessee and West Virginia got the entire project bumped up to a priority status and the new President of the

US declared, "time for talking (about airplanes) is over. We either do or we sink!" That was why Theodore, against the advice of his friends and advisors alike, took his first presidential trip. It would be the first of many and it concerned the building of an airplane. Oddly enough, he would not be heading to Wichita where the project was centered. In this case, Theodore went to Dayton, Ohio and the bicycle shop of the Wright Brothers.

How Theodore had heard of them was in his flurry of communications with both Chanute and Langley and is a long story all by itself. While neither of the engineers suggested that Roosevelt bring the Wrights into the project, what the President did notice was that their names kept appearing many times when almost no one else's did. Reading these telegrams, it seems as if Chanute first mentioned them in connection with something that Langley thought ludicrous. Roosevelt began to systematically pin down Langley on the matter, and finally, the head of the Smithsonian had to admit that this wind tunnel idea, might show promise. Langley was not used to anyone outside of the engineering field being so precise, or even interested, in the kinds of details that Roosevelt was demanding.

That was how the President of the United States paid an unannounced call on a pair of bicycle mechanics in Dayton, Ohio. The purposes of his trip were never reported to the public and for that matter there were no official government notes made either. The entire affair was so vague that even the film industry of later years never picked up on it. We have no idea what was said. All we do know is that when Theodore left Dayton, the Wright Brothers were no longer repairing bicycles and many local people began to note that an army major was staying around the shop and acting as if he owned the place. Eventually, Samuel Langley would be making calls there as well. The results would be dramatic.

A Wing, A Prayer, And A Transmission

The basic principles of powered flight have actually been known for several centuries. Figuring out the factors that allow something heavier than air to get off the ground, does not require an industrial complex to figure out. One merely needs to observe birds which are the ultimate proof that this is both possible, and even more important, not a miracle. Anyone who is familiar with Leonardo Da Vinci will know that the first useful plans for such a device were drawn up in the Renaissance and are not modern, relatively speaking. Yet, until 1901 no one had actually built such a machine that actually worked. The stumbling blocks were two-fold, one being the power plant required and the other being materials technology required to make that power plant both strong enough and light enough to be useful. The technology to build and hold together an airframe had been around for centuries at this point but was rendered useless by the lack of an engine.

Samuel Langley was very aware of these facts and that is why his project had mostly concentrated on producing a power plant that was adequate to the task. Steel technology, ironically pioneered by the British, had reached a point in 1901 where such an engine should be possible. The refinement of crude oil into a usable fuel had also aided in this task.

Strangely enough, Roosevelt had also aided in this quest when he was not even aware of the fact that he had. During the New Mexico campaign, his men had captured one of Astin Greene's trucks and the vehicle was quickly shown to many industrialists in the US, who were floored by many of its innovations. The compression ratios and the metallurgy (which was mostly a Mexican innovation) were far higher than any comparable engines in the US. The one innovation that was entirely Greene's was not really the engine, but the transmission of the energy it harnessed to the source of locomotion. You have to remember that this was at a time when most motorcars were still using bicycle chains to transfer energy from the engine to the wheels.

Chains, no matter how well made, can only be so strong due to the simple nature of what they are. If you put too much stress on one, then it will break. That is generally not a problem when the source of power are human legs, but gas engines were now at the point of being too strong for them. Greene's solution to the problem was to use a set of encased gears that could be shifted when required. This new transmission system both shocked and thrilled US engineers. Because of this, the blueprints for this system quickly made their way to Langley in Wichita. Ironically, despite these plans later being useful, it would be the reason Langley would make no progress for some time.

Langley's obsession with the power requirements would lead him down a dead-end path because he was ignoring several other fundamentals, all of which would prove to be far more important. No one dared point any of this out because so far, the only design that had any success at all was Langley's. His team had managed to get a glider fifteen feet off the ground for a forty-five second flight across his test field. That should have been good news only they were unable to repeat the test and no one ever figured out why it worked. Modern theories suggest that the most likely reason was that a natural updraft had occurred on that day, and that it gave the vehicle a little extra needed lift. Despite the failure to repeat the exercise, it only encouraged Langley to continue down the same path.

The Wright Brothers had different ideas that Langley did not agree with. They considered the most important element to be the wing and thought that more conventional power plants were adequate enough to do the job, at least that is if you had an effective wing design. You see, powered flight is all based on a simple physical principle. Air rushes over and under the wing, as it moves. The wing causes the upper air flow to take a 'detour' and because it wants to reach the back of the wing at the same time as the lower flow, it moves faster. This creates a low-pressure center above the aircraft and then the heavier air concentrations beneath it push the vehicle upwards. This was not disputed by anyone at the time, but how to achieve it was. The vehicle requires a certain amount of speed to do this, and this is why Langley thought the engine was important while the Wright's believed a more efficient wing design was the answer.

It was not that Langley ignored the wing but his methods for testing these designs were less than ideal. Langley was a model maker, and his wing tests were all based on any number of small gliders that he had built and were thrown into the air by a human hand. Langley obviously thought this was enough, but it did not give you adequate enough data on full sized wings because the larger you made one, the more drag you created and almost at an exponential rate. Drag rates are basically the non-aerodynamic characteristics of any aircraft that disrupt the airflow over the surface, hence reducing the efficiency of lift. Given the material that early aircraft were working with, the drag was significant and indeed most of the advances in the early aircraft industry were figuring out how to reduce it.

The Wrights had taken a different approach and long before their involvement with the US government. Their bicycle shop had aided them in the building of a genuine wind tunnel. Their main business meant that they had the parts, the space, and the machine tools required to build a descent apparatus where they could test full sized wings. Once they had access to government funding, resources, and access to Langley's notes, it did not take them long to find a wing design that they thought would work. The biggest problem was actually getting Langley to agree to test it. It would take their sister, Kitty, appealing to their army advisors, to appeal to the President, to get that test. When Roosevelt was updated on their progress, he wasted no time sending a telegram to Langley, ordering him to do so.

By the Fourth of July 1901, a prototype had been built. It was a double decked bi wing aircraft that was flown by Wilbur while lying on his belly. On that day he would fly it some four feet in the air, for over a minute, from one side of Langley's test field to the other. In the coming week it would make two more flights that both got higher and longer in duration. Its third flight was its last and oddly enough because of its success and not its failure. They had yet to develop a real means of control and the aircraft could not really turn. Wilbur, who enthusiastically wished to push the machine to the limits, flew it right into some trees on the far side of the field. He was only lightly injured but the prototype was completely wrecked and would never fly again.

This did not really matter since, after the second flight, they were already building a second and third prototype of different designs. They were also already working on the third and crucial factor in powered flight, that of controlling the X, Y, and Z axis of their aircraft. Here, the work of Chanute would be crucial. Since Chanute had almost no success with either wings or engines, he had been concentrating on a system of control surfaces. Langley had the plans for all of them by this point and now they only needed to incorporate them into the new designs. Langley would also get his own ideas involved. The first aircraft had used two very simple lightweight and less than powerful engines. Langley was sure that he could do better, and with the new captured Confederate engine, his people were certain that they could adapt the innovations to a truly dedicated power plant made exclusively for flight. If you will pardon the pun, the US aircraft industry was about to takeoff.

Battle of New Jersey

It was once noted that only those who remember war fondly are those who have had the least contact with it. This point has been debated for a very long time, but the evidence seems to indicate that it is very true. War has been often romanticized, and governments in particular always like to play up the heroic aspects. That is not to say that there are no heroes or villains, but one has to remember that tragedy makes them who they are. The exception, and not the rule, is what people pay attention to and the media business, without a doubt, makes its living off of this since the day-to-day norms are not really considered news.

This has been true since long before our era of faster than light communications whether it be the internet, the television, or even telegraphs and newspapers of the bygone era. Movies and websites have replaced books and periodicals which replaced poems and songs. The heart of the matter, for a species which is fond of storytelling, is glamorizing the day-to-day droll which is life. Our perceptions of war are no different in this respect, so it is not surprising that we elevate the horror that is war with the tales of those who have somehow overcome it. Still, there is yet another side of this equation.

What is not very well known is that every time the public has gotten a better look at war, usually thanks to a technological innovation, those who normally do not see it for what it is are horrified by the vision. The normal reaction is that something must be terribly wrong, and this war is not being fought correctly because the image they are seeing is not what they imagined it to be. Never does anyone seem to consider that this is what war has always been. The impact of these glimpses have had a very profound impact on the culture at large but almost never does anyone see it for what it is.

The first great example of this is a literary character that is still with us to this very day. Dracula, the famous blood-sucking monster, is now a staple and archetype for an entire literary genre, yet this character was based on a very real man named Vlad Tepist, sometimes called Vald the Dragon, and usually Vlad the Impaler by his enemies. In his time, he was universally hated and feared by both friend and foe alike. The reason why Vlad is still with us today is technology and war.

Vlad was one of a longline of minor dictators that controlled the border states between the constantly warring Ottoman and the Hapsburg dynasties. These buffer kingdoms were largely supported by either side in order to fend off invasion and larger wars. Vlad was a puppet dictator of the Hapsburgs and his job really only had one requirement, make the Turks fear and hate him by any means possible. The Hapsburgs were perfectly fine with anything that their proxies did so long as the border wars remained border wars. Such a situation was not uncommon in such regions throughout history. So, what went wrong for Vlad?

Technology changed the picture, and in this case, it was the printing press. Suddenly books were cheap, and as a result, more people could afford them. This led to people wanting to read and literacy rates jumped all throughout Europe. When you are printing books in a competitive market you need juicy stories to sell your books and the tales of the war in the border regions were just that. Being horrifying, charismatic, and feared as a monster was an advantage in Vlad's job until more people began to read solid tales of his exploits. Suddenly he became a liability to the Hapsburgs who eventually arrested him and then demonized him due to the political embarrassment he was causing in the rest of Europe. No one seemed to understand that the real monster was, and always had been, war.

The same was true a few hundred years later when England, France, and the Ottomans went to war with Russia in 1854. A new invention meant that people no longer had to read about the battlefields, they could now see them even if they were not there. The new invention was the photograph, and the Crimean War, as it would come to be known as, was the first widely photographed war in history. Since the technology of the time only allowed for pictures of the military camps to be taken, at least safely, that is what most people saw. They were appalled by the conditions and just assumed that the war was being prosecuted incorrectly. It never seemed to occur to anyone that camp life for armies at war had always been this way. The result of this public outcry was the International Red Cross.

The changes made after the Crimean War were far more profound than just the highly visible Red Cross. Armies began changing the ways that they did business for all of history. It was quite common for civilians to follow armies in the field. Many of these people were just families of the soldiers, most of whom lived with the army in war and peace. They were usually given mundane jobs that people always need to have done. An army is a small city on the move and their requirements for services are no different. This includes everything from washing clothes to preparing meals and for the more technical jobs, there were always merchants (known to the armies as sutlers) who provided everything from prostitutes to tailors. One of the services provided was also medical care, and by our standards today we would find it horrifying. The people in 1854 most certainly did and the Crimean War would put an end to the traditional camp followers. Most of these services would be put in uniform and under military control by 1898, all thanks to the photograph.

By the late 1890s, photographic technology had grown by leaps and bounds. There were two basic developments that would shape the war and for the first time ever this technology would be seen by governments as important, even if it was rarely discussed in any official manner. The two technologies would chart two very separate paths, but both would be influential in many ways. These two developments would also both be personified by the men who championed the technologies. They were both from the United States, they both would become extraordinarily wealthy because of the war, and they were both of a new breed that had been born in the late 19th century. They were literally the first class of 'rock stars' of science. One man was George Eastman and the other was Thomas Edison.

The Eastman company was primarily concerned with expanding the photograph industry and they largely succeeded by making it simple enough that anyone could afford to take a picture and did not require a trained technician to do so. His first 'Instamatic Camera' was released for general sale just before the war. It is likely that it would have been a success no matter what, but the sudden conflict made his cameras worth ten times their weight in gold. Everyone wanted to take pictures with their loved ones who were departing for the front and Eastman gave them a cheap and easy way to do it.

By 1901 the use of these cameras had expanded as people figured out they were good for more than just family portraits. These disposable cameras were small, lightweight and soldiers began using them right at the front. It was now possible to take pictures of actual fighting and many soldiers did so. Reporters also started using them and as a result this war became the most documented war in history up until that point. Now every aspect of the conflict was being seen as these pictures filtered back to the general populace via mail from the soldiers at the front.

The pictures were not so great, often blurry and of general poor quality. This did not matter to the people back home because it was not what they were seeing that mattered, but more to the point it was what they were not seeing. War was nothing like anyone imagined. There were no great lines of men in gorgeous uniforms who were heroically charging behind national banners towards the enemy. What they were seeing were men living in horrific trenches with dirty uniforms that barely deserved the name. They also saw explosions kicking up dirt in devastated and unimaginable landscapes. Last but not least, they saw mangled bodies that had obviously been lying exposed for days or maybe even weeks.

This was not something that many people talked about. The public record on the matter is silent unless you count the side effects. Maybe it was simply the over polite attitudes of the day, not wanting to shock a neighbor who had lost a loved one at the front, but it was still changing attitudes. The real effects were secondary in nature, and hence often overlooked. This can be easily proven by looking at events in areas where these cameras were most common. Anti-war sentiment was steadily growing in the United States where they were the most common. This sentiment became quite explosive in the market where these cameras were the second most common, in France.

There was yet one more piece of photographic technology that was counterbalancing these glimpses of the real war. It was the motion picture and in the mid-1890s both forms of it had become common in most industrialized nations. These two machines allowed people to see the most realistic form of photography that had been invented to date. They were called the Kinetoscope and the Vitascope. Both were produced and largely controlled by one man, Thomas Edison.

Our first glimpse of Edison's role in the war was in his submarine building competition with John Phillip Holland. Edison had not only managed to run Holland out of the bidding war but right out of the country and into the welcoming arms of the Confederate Navy. Not long after the Ionian Sea, the Confederate use of submersibles became widely known despite the best efforts of the CSN to keep them a secret. While the Confederate Navy was very good at keeping secrets, the Confederate Congress was not and as soon as the first legislature found out about their wonderful new weapon, the entire Congress knew about it soon after. That meant the entire world knew not long after that.

Needless to say, the news was not very good for Edison who had turned out one failed copy of Holland's designs after another. Fans of Edison point out that his submarines would have actually performed better than those built by the CSA, but we will never know. Their chief deficiency seemed to be Edison and his hardnosed approach in dealing with the US Navy who by 1901 had already fired him and awarded the contract to another competitor, George Westinghouse. Even so, Edison had many other military contracts, and the Holland Affair did not ingratiate him with some very key people. This is why he started looking for something to put him back in the good graces of the US Government.

The motion picture technology had been around for almost a decade at this point and exactly why it was that no one had produced any war films is anyone's guess. The most likely explanation was that simply no one had thought to do it. Edison did originate the idea however and it came to him as he looked through countless newspapers and saw pictures that were taken by Eastman's camera. Motion picture technology of the time was incapable of capturing the battlefield. The equipment was too bulky and sensitive. Edison hit upon an idea. His companies were already turning out short films for his machines so why not stage a battle? Since Edison controlled the only real film distribution system of the time, he could do pretty much anything he wanted.

Edison started with a single film that was staged in a public park in West Orange, New Jersey. We only have a few brief glimpses of the film since most of it has not survived. What little we can see looks quite ludicrous to the modern eye. In it there are two lines of opposing men rallied around flags wearing a mottled collection of uniforms that were thirty years out of date and shooting weapons that created huge puffs of white smoke. It has been written that the conclusion of this five-minute film showed the US troops (who could only be distinguished by their flag since they wore the same uniforms as the Confederates) running the enemy off in a valiant charge.

The movie was meant exclusively for the Kinetoscope market. These machines were basically one person peepshows that cost a nickel to watch. People would put their eyes next to a hole and turned a crank to advance the film. In 1901 you could still find these machines in hotel lobbies, restaurants, department stores, barber shops, and even one Broadway theater that had a bank of them installed in a hallway. Sales tripled wherever the film was shown, and oddly enough copies were being distributed through neutral Holland and Belgium, so this film became equally popular in allied nations as well. Edison quickly realized that he had something.

Stripes Over Bars became the pattern for an entire series of films that Edison quickly expanded to include his Vitascope, which was the first real motion picture projector. It was used for film screenings that could be seen by more than one person at a time. Contrary to popular belief, Edison never claimed that his war films were of real battles, however he never said that they were not either. Many people after first viewing these films, believed that what they saw was real. These films were also growing in length and patriotism with every new print. The detractors of Edison, and those who found the movies as ludicrous as they truly were, dubbed all of the films to be 'The Battle of New Jersey.' Over time this expression would come to be used anytime someone thought they were being sold a bad deal.

Edison was unconcerned with his detractors. He had many and was used to ignoring them. What he was concerned with was the fact that he had found his way back into the doors of government contracts once the effects of these films began to be realized in Washington. When President Roosevelt asked for a private screening of one particular film at the White House, Edison knew he had accomplished his goals. Despite this fanfare, ironically, it would not be the US who would first take full advantage of this new propaganda.

This is where the story takes another bizarre turn and while it is not a true case of life imitating art, it is a case of where the fictional world will drastically alter the real one. The two places where the propaganda war had already been going full force were in France and Germany. Both Boulanger and Wilhelm were intrigued by this film and both demanded to see it. Boulanger instantly saw the possibilities since he was a man who was growing more and more concerned with his public image. He ordered his own war films and even diverted French troops to help make them.

Wilhelm was impressed by the film, but still he only saw it as little more than a toy. It would be the suggestion of one of his staff members, a decorated soldier who was privy to his inner circle by the name of Helmuth Von Moltke, that a German film of this kind would be useful. Wilhelm eventually decided to order such a film and while Moltke had nothing more to do with it beyond that point, he would eventually get the credit for its success. This would lead to changes that would alter the entire war.

More Arts Than Martial

While the western world was weaponizing their artists, they were not going to outdo the

Chinese. The west certainly turned to a very hi tech approach but just because someone did not have a movie camera, telegraph, printing press, telephone, or other such modern conveyances, it did not mean that there was a lack of mass media. The Chinese did have all of the aforementioned technology, but it was not common enough to be an effective tool for use by the general populace. The reason for this seems to be that the Chinese take the old saying to heart, that if something is not broke, then don't fix it.

In the modern world we take the television, radios, the internet, and our phones for granted. We think of them as great wonders of communication and we scarcely give any thought to the days before any of this existed. We go so far as to just assume that nothing we do could have been done before our electronic toys were around. As far back as 1901 seems to us now, the truth is that it was not that long ago, and to look at China of the period gives us a very good glimpse in how mass media existed before fast as light communications. The Chinese were still doing things the old way and proved exactly how effective it was.

The video screen of the time was the local market. These were not just places where people went to buy things. They were full of everything that we associate with modern communications and that included commercials, news shows, and let us not forget the big thing, entertainment. For those of you that doubt these markets were any different from social media, a very common practice to get your opinion out was to write a handbill and stick it on a post in the market. There were almost no spaces in any market where you would see bald wood. It was a very common practice to write on the bottom of these handbills, "Copy and repost ten times or you will have as many years bad luck." Sound familiar?

By 1901, the Chinese government had never been more fragmented. The Dowager Empress, Cixi, had made her play to unify the country and had failed miserably. Her stand against the foreign invaders had been a ploy to bring the de facto independent governors back under her authority. It was a play that was aimed at the elites of China, and in the process, Cixi had managed to lose control of her army, the capital, and the throne with it. After that fiasco, the governors had naturally stopped listening to her at all and the country was growing ripe for yet another civil war. Even so,

Cixi was down but not out. She had one last card to play and she started no sooner than she stopped her headlong retreat from Peking and settled far up the Yangtze River in the interior.

One has to remember that Cixi was technically considered a Manchu and to the average guy on the street her dynasty might as well have been American, Russian, or British. She was every bit as foreign a ruler as any other invader and there had been a growing backlash against the Manchus that predated any serious incursions by the Europeans. One also has to remember that Cixi was not the legal head of state and maintained her power by manipulation. She was obviously very good at it and turning an anti-Manchu movement into an anti-European one was child's play for her.

The average Chinaman had seen the system that existed for their protection, either failing or being turned against them. This was never more visible when the Chinese populace went shopping for groceries. Flood and then drought had created a serious shortfall in food production, but the Chinese farms were still producing enough, only for the average person this food was not reaching them or was very overpriced when it did. The war had created a high demand for food and the English and

Americans paid with hard currency so most of the food China needed was getting sold off to the Europeans. Hong Kong actually had surplus food stocks during the war so what did the British do with it? They shipped it to Shang-hi where it was resold back to the Chinese at inflated prices. Naturally, this food was never the best.

So far, the various Chinese governments had showed themselves to be hopelessly corrupt and in general only interested in games of intrigue with each other. The Army had proven itself impotent and Europeans were taking China, one city at a time. The people of China became desperate and turned to the only thing they had left, that being their entertainers in the marketplace. Cixi was well aware of this and turned on her propaganda machine, backing these entertainers, and effectively weaponizing the peasants of China to do her bidding despite the fact that they were unaware that this is what was really happening.

One might ask what kind of entertainment would be useful in this situation, but China had something that almost seemed custom-made for such a crisis. In the latter half of the twentieth century, the west became all too aware of this once it was paired with the technology of motion pictures, but this was not the first glimpse the west would have. In 1901 no European really knew what to make of it and applied the name of the closest western analog, that being boxing. This was how the rebels of the uprising became known as 'Boxers.' It seemed appropriate since their stated weapon of choice was the human fist and their market shows, something that westerners were familiar with, showed an uncanny skill in using human limbs as almost magical weapons.

The term 'Martial Arts' would later be applied to this but the truth of it is that what the west has come to see as a form of fighting has far more in common with ballet dancing than with prize fighters in the ring. No one knows exactly where Martial Arts comes from, but one thing is obviously clear, given what we know of it, it is far more productive in entertaining the masses than in actual combat. This is why we have many records of entertainers performing elaborate choreographed scenes and almost none of these techniques winning battles. What few uses are stated as evidence of their worth in battle almost always fall into the category of 'unconfirmed myth' once they are examined by scholars.

I do realize that there are many defenders of this art form who have made many claims and would debate this; however, the historical record has shown conclusively that given a choice people always pick up weapons when marching off to war and that the blade trumps skin and bones while bullets trump blades. What has come to be known as the Boxer Rebellion proves this beyond a doubt. The one thing that the peasants of China lacked were weapons and in particular firearms. Entertainers being what they are solved this problem with a bit of fiction.

The fight dancers of the market would convince many that if you only believed in the cause, you would be immune to enemy bullets. This of course quickly proved to be false. Those who spread the propaganda would combat this reality by claiming that those killed by enemy fire were simply not true believers. It might also be worthy to note that when the fighting erupted even the masters of the marketplace fights never failed to arm themselves with weapons, even if it were only with sticks. There are no reports by anyone of magical super soldiers fighting with their bare hands, not even in Chinese records. All of this goes to prove a few very relevant points. The first is that the pen may not be ultimately mightier than the sword, but it is still mighty. The second is that it showed that what the Boxers were truly masters of was not fighting, but propaganda instead. No one can dispute that their circus acts were effective tools at recruiting a hungry and desperate populace.

It is of no great surprise that the uprising failed, of course one has to consider that the civil disturbances had no real aims to begin with. There seem to be have been none beyond venting frustration on the most obvious of targets and considering that, you could say it was successful since that is exactly what happened. Beyond that, it did not alter China's situation with the western world in any way that helped the average Chinese.

The 'rebellion' was largely an urban one and there were attacks by Boxers in most Chinese cities. It could not have been more poorly timed if it had actually been planned, which it does not seem to have been. The war had brought more foreign soldiers into China than had ever been before and due to the war, none of them were too worried about the diplomatic repercussions of shooting Chinese citizens en masse. The Europeans also had help from the Imperial Army in all three of her military districts. The governors were far more fearful of the rebels than were the Europeans and, as a consequence, they were far more brutal in putting down the rebellion.

Needless to say, Cixi did not need the rebellion to overthrow the Europeans. There is no evidence that she ever believed that it would. It did several things for her, not the least of which was to get rid of many of her own troublemakers while killing the invaders at the same time. She also managed to weaken her internal political opposition and it is reasonable to believe that this was her primary goal. Still, the aftermath of the rebellion did not exactly go her way. It might have strengthened the hold that Cixi had on her own exiled court, but it did not drive the regional Governors into her arms.

What the rebellion did do was alter the political situation on the ground and force the Western belligerents to act. Up until this point they had been content to let the Chinese theater of operations remain static since they had more pressing concerns elsewhere, but now they found China impossible to ignore. The weakened regimes inside of China, both military and political, had been sitting on the fence, but they no longer could. As they sought European alliances, they changed the balance of forces in the region and now active military operations would become required. There was no one who was happier about this than a certain American General by the name of George Armstrong Custer.

From Revenge to Restoration

Japan has been characterized in many ways. When people think of Japan, it often conjures up images of tie clad businessmen or pigtailed, sword wielding, Samurai, but the one thing that each of these images have in common is the trait that has survived in Japan through all of their historical periods. The Japanese do nothing in half measures and if there is anything to characterize them above all else, I believe that to be it. This was very true of Japan in 1901 but it was hard for the Europeans to see this because Japan was a land in the middle of a major transformation.

Europeans of the time understood that Japan was trying to make themselves into a European styled state, but they did not seem to ever grasp the significance of this and hence did not put it in its proper perspective. Indeed, this also seems to be the case of Europe's views of the rest of the world. By the first year of the twentieth century, Europe had come to so technologically dominate the rest of the planet that there was hardly anyone in Europe who believed that it could have ever been any other way. The truth was something else altogether and this was particularly the case with east Asia where the Chinese and Japanese had been far ahead of the rest of the planet in technology, economics and culture for many centuries.

There are those who claim that the Europeans, once they reached the far east, had stolen Asian ideas and made them their own. This is largely untrue because the Europeans did invent most of their own technology and proved to be far more effective at employing it. Even so, the Asians still remained more advanced for over a century after regular and speedy trade routes were established. In fact, this situation was ultimately the reason behind several wars between the Euros and China where Asian trade goods were so vastly superior that they were causing a trade imbalance that England and France could not tolerate, or they would watch their economies collapse. This is where China's overbearing attitudes of superiority did not serve her well.

From the 16th century onward, the world was rapidly changing, and these were changes that East Asia was not well-suited to deal with, mainly because people in this region valued stability over progress. These new changes would push the region for many centuries and would eventually cause the Chinese government to collapse. In Japan, they were faced with the exact same problems only the results were quite different. A civil war erupted, and while you can find many causes, again it was ultimately the result of the world globalization that was currently in progress. The Japanese isolationists would take the day. They would push Japan back to its romanticized medieval roots and this would hold sway over the country for two centuries. Then the Americans showed up.

The American fleet that demanded a treaty with Japan was met with shock by the Japanese. It was not the threat of force but the level of advancement that genuinely impressed the many factional leaders of this country. There had always been those who agitated for opening Japan's borders but until the US fleet was anchored in their harbors, this progressive faction had nothing to argue with. Now it was obvious that going feudal was futile and that

Japan was now not only no longer ahead, but way behind the rest of the world.

This started the movement that has come to be known as the Meiji Reform. While it outwardly appeared to be a complete makeover in the western style, the truth of it is that it remained largely Japanese in nature. The Shoguns (translation being a group of petty dictators who ruled their fiefdoms absolutely and the nation in a confederated style) were overthrown, and at least in theory, the power was restored to the Emperor. The reality of it was that the more progressive Shoguns ousted the isolationist faction and began changing Japan from the bottom up. The Emperor was largely a figurehead and the real power remained in the hands of a few key men, all former Shoguns, most of whom have names that have lived on to this very day in the names of the international companies that they founded at the start of the Meiji period.

These changes did not happen overnight, although in relative terms this reform/revolution did happen relatively quickly and was very thorough in changing Japanese society. It still took decades, and it had an important impact on the war. The Imperial Japanese Navy, that replaced the Shogunate

Fleet, was seriously lagging behind in its development in 1898 when the war broke out. The reason for this was that Japan was a nation with limited resources and due to the constant rebellions from many ousted Shoguns, they concentrated more on developing their new conscripted army and kept putting off the upgrades of their navy.

The changing point came in 1895 when Japan went to war with the Qing Dynasty over Korea. The Japanese army was more than successful in routing the Chinese and while their navy did well, they found themselves at the mercy of two Chinese battleships that were both built in Germany. The Japanese had no guns that could do any damage to them at all. Despite being ultimately victorious the weakness was seen by Europe and this is primarily what cost the Japanese their ultimate prize of Port Arthur. This would become their Casus Belli for joining in the war in 1898.

The only reservations that the Japanese had about going to war had not been any high-minded reasons about the immorality of war. In truth, it was all about the weakness of their navy. In 1898 the Japanese had abandoned the theory that they could make do with a coastal defense fleet, torpedo boats for offensive capabilities, and commerce raiding cruisers. As the war would prove, Japan's older and lightly armored cruisers (indeed considered corvettes by European standards) were not up to the job of slugging it out with the far more modern French and American ships of similar class.

Japan did have a battleship at the start of the war and, finally after great trouble with the British, got their second in early 1901. This was an empty accomplishment since the Mikasa was only half finished when it arrived in Japan. The ship was a rushed job. She was, however, completely seaworthy but she was also barely armed and actually had to be escorted by the Royal Navy from the shipyards in Britain where she was built. The truth of the matter was that Japan had not reached the point where she could build her own capital ships and this would not just be a liability for her naval operations, it would also cripple Japanese foreign policy as well.

Japan required Britain's help in everything that she did and despite the fact that this was for the common good, Britain did not do so freely. The British wanted something every single time the Royal Navy aided the Japanese. Considering the strategic situation, this was often and as the leaders of Japan realized, it was quickly turning them into a client state much in the same way that the CSA was. This would begin to slowly start driving a wedge between Japan and her allies, although oddly enough, it would be the beginning of a partnership between Japan and the Confederate States who were now players in the region since the CSA took possession of the Philippines from Spain.

What the small oligarchy of business interests in Japan realized by 1901 was that they were going to have to change the situation in order to come out of the war with their very independence intact. This was even in the best case scenario, which was an allied victory, and at the time there was no guarantee of that. In Korea, the Japanese Army had managed to hold their own, but it was now clear that they were never going to be able to dislodge the Russo-American Army who were occupying fortified positions along the Yalu river. Like in most theaters of war, Korea had become a stalemate but here it was becoming a liability.

The new commander of the British East Asian Fleet, Arthur Moore, upon relieving Admiral Seymour, had done a complete survey of the strategic situation upon taking command. Since he had been in theater all along commanding the Australian Squadron, he was already aware of this information, but he wanted it in writing so that he could present it to the Japanese government. It suggested the evacuation of the Korean peninsula and cited many reasons, all of which the Japanese already knew. Supplying the Japanese army in Korea was becoming expensive in terms of the ships that were lost due to enemy raiding.

Not only were the Japanese and British merchant fleets paying a heavy price for this, but Moore was having to use capital ships to protect the convoys due to the presence of the American Fleet at Port Arthur. The run from Japan to Korea was a short one but the routes were well known, and the restricted waters left few options of getting from point A to B. Enemy cruisers were having a field day. This also resulted in the supply operations being less than successful. The main thing that kept the Japanese Army, with their superior numbers, from overwhelming Entente forces in the region was the fact that they could never build up enough logistics to get a full offensive going. This is why the British considered Korea a write off.

The Japanese found a retreat completely unacceptable for any number of reasons. Just the loss of face was enough to keep this from ever happening but there were far more sound reasons. The biggest of these was that the loss of Korea would leave Japan open to an attack on her home islands. The other reason was that should the Japanese Army be effectively removed from the war then after its conclusion Japan would have far less say in the peace that came afterwards. During the conflict this would be a minor point but, after the war, it would become everything.

The Boxer Rebellion changed the entire picture. Not only did it change the situation in China, but it required a response from the Entente, and it was not the kind that Japan could easily ignore. Not only did it prompt Russia to send critical reinforcements from the west but now the Americans were also assembling troops to deploy to the region. As we will see, Theodore Roosevelt was looking far more outward than had Elihu Root and with Vancouver effectively neutralized, he had some soldiers to spare.

Up until this time, US troops in China had been a small expeditionary force consisting of mostly US Marines and some Cavalry. These were elite troops, and this made up for their lack of numbers in many ways but at the end of the day, there is no substitute for having the biggest battalions. The US was now preparing to send two entire divisions to join the rapidly growing Russian Army. The Japanese knew they would be hard pressed to hold that back, let alone achieve their war aims of taking their stolen prize of Port Arthur.

The Japanese leaders argued ferociously over what to do about this and ultimately, they settled on a very pragmatic solution. If they could not take Port Arthur, then another port in mainland China would be required for their future policy goals. The question was which one and the choices were limited at best. The majority of the Chinese ports were already under foreign control. Taking a French treaty port seemed the most attractive option but, if the Royal Navy could not take them then Japan realized it was beyond their ability. That left ports under friendly control and the Boxer Rebellion gave Japan its best option for establishing itself in China.

The Humanity of It All

In the spring of 1901, all of Europe was wound like a spring and fully prepared to release all of the energy on each other, once again. Both sides were fully aware of the economic damage that was being done on a truly epic scale and oddly enough this was not the usual physical damage that is associated with war, even if there was plenty of that. The truth is that despite being so widespread the war was largely a rural one. The armies had not fought over any major cities and with the exception of the Zeppelin bombardments, which were not as destructive as many have claimed, the physical infrastructure was largely intact. This seems at odds with many photographs that we have of the war, where more than one town was flattened, save maybe the ruins of a church steeple. The truth is that these were small towns that had the bad luck of being caught in no man's land since virtually the start of the conflict. They had been constantly fought over but, the fighting remained localized to these strips of land.

What was falling apart were not the buildings, roads, factories, or anything built by humans. That is not to say that things were not starting to collapse but the ultimate victim of the war was the human soul. War weariness had set in and all of the belligerents were feeling the pinch. The casualties that the spring and summer offensives generated certainly played their part in creating this situation but there was far more to it than that.

Here we have to turn to personal journals and letters to get a glimpse of what was going on in the minds of the average man. I would have liked to cite opinion letters written to newspapers but sadly even in nations that had a free press, such opinions in public forums were lacking. The reasons for this could have been either that the newspapers refused to print them, or the governments quietly forbid such dissension or people did not wish to be so public with their complaints. The most likely answer is that a combination of the above prevented such articles from appearing. The private thoughts are far more telling.

Over and over again the word 'normal' appears in private correspondence. This was true when it was obvious that the authors of such letters were not even directly criticizing the war. People not only wanted things back to the way they were but did not even seem to realize that it was too late for that. Their attitudes were definitely gloomy, and the results of such things are hard to quantify and measure. Still, we have some clue as to the effects of this. There are the obvious things such as labor troubles of which occurred across the board in the industrialized nations. There were also riots and demonstrations which happened even in nations such as Britain and the United States where we seldom hear about them like their counterparts in Russia and France. These things were only the tip of the iceberg because the real troubles lie in many small behaviors that alone seem inconsequential but as a whole can be devastating.

This is where we turn to the industrial output of each nation. By 1901 all of the belligerents (and even a few neutrals) had converted as much of their infrastructure over to war production as was physically possible. Those factories also peaked in their output. Every nation was setting production records for war related materials and none of them would break those records. The peak had been reached. On the surface this would seem to suggest that war weariness was not a factor however that is only on the surface.

Thanks to post war studies, we have discovered that it was not the quantity of what was leaving the factories that was at issue. The real weakness was how much in resources it was costing to not only maintain production levels but to expand it. This was in both direct labor and material costs and for reasons that are still unknown. When compared to pre- and post-war schedules, it was taking more of both. This was not uniformly across the board because the efficiency of some businesses increased yet at some factories, industrial consumption as much as tripled from their 1898 standards, and yet they were not producing anywhere near what they should have.

It is hard to explain such a thing and even harder to find an exact cause. That is why many a historian has dubiously ignored this. I can only venture an opinion here and that is of course that this was a definitive sign of war weariness at the most minute of levels. It was not just raising the cost of the war but of just plain living for your average man and woman who were nowhere near a front line. Of course, much ado is made of the high level of casualties that were being generated by active operations but again that is only scratching the surface. It is also horrifying to realize exactly how much higher those casualties could have been.

Despite what some say, I think it is more than adequately proven that the larger portion of humanity is willing to reasonably sacrifice for the greater good. People only become skeptical of such behaviors when these sacrifices no longer seem meaningful and I believe this is exactly what was happening in the middle of 1901. Every year people were hearing that this next push would break the enemy and every year this did not happen. Every nation had already paid a terrible price and so far, they had nothing to show for it. Most of the national leaders were becoming all too aware of this fact and those who ignored it did so at their own peril.

It was this fact that locked most governments into a war policy that gave them no leeway at all. It was becoming a commonly held view in the halls of government that the war had to be an all or nothing proposition. To talk peace and stop with nothing to show for it could be disastrous on the home front. For the minority of world leaders who were democratically elected it would mean that they would lose their job. For those who held power by heredity or force, they would lose their heads and neither of these wished to face these possibilities. This would not only dictate national policy but war strategy as well, and the 1901 offensives illustrate this perfectly.

While the military leaders of both sides tried to dress up their war plans as if they were new, the reality was that nothing had changed. This was not entirely the fault of the map studying generals because no matter how much they looked at their maps before or during the war the land was not going to change, and it was geography that dictated their goals. Their strategies were more or less sound, and this could explain a great deal why no one bothered to change them. The problem really lay in the fact that it was not strategy that needed to be examined. Both operational and tactical concerns had been largely ignored before the conflict and the firing of the first bullet had not changed this.

The European operations of 1901 are a good case in point. The allies had virtually an identical plan as they did in 1900. They focused their efforts on knocking Russia out of the war. Moltke even commented when he saw Waldersee's plan, "the only changes are a few pins on the board." What the plan boiled down to was that the allies were simply going to try and hammer the Russians into submission and the goal of taking Warsaw was at best a secondary objective that was almost irrelevant at this point.

Waldersee would not get his chance to put his repetitive master stroke into practice. Both Boulanger and Czar Nicholas had very good reasons for wanting to conclude the war as quickly as possible. As with the allies, the Entente did not really change any plans other than some vague promises to coordinate their efforts. This proved impractical since the allies were sitting in between them and neither French nor Russian military leaders seemed particularly enthused about the idea. The one thing the Entente did do better was with speed. They hurled their forces forward while Waldersee was being too meticulous about making sure that every last detail was finished before he moved.

The one thing that the Entente had changed was their focus and this gave them the early initiative in the Spring of 1901. Up until now, the main emphasis had been on somehow knocking Britain out of the war. They had now given up on the idea in the short term and both France and Russia decided to concentrate on Germany which was the more immediate threat to each. Boulanger was heavily relying on chemical weapons to allow his troops to do what they had not yet managed, capture the city of Strasbourg.

Russia had more room to move around but unfortunately for them, Nicholas had begun micromanaging the war and overruling his generals on a regular basis. As such he was ignoring basic military principles and practically negated the advantage of maneuverability in favor of using the space to mass more troops. Numbers look fine on paper, but the handicap became all too obvious to many Russian Generals, most of whom were being ignored.

Having a bad unit on the line might give you more numbers but given the fact that they are largely ineffective, and you still have to supply them, they become a liability instead of an asset. At this point Russia did not even have any reserve units left to deploy. All of the new corps that were being raised and deployed consisted of hastily drafted civilians who had at best a week of training before being sent to the front. This situation had hampered Russian efforts in the Balkans the year before. Now the problem of using largely untrained troops was far worse and becoming front wide. These new units were offensively useless, and when they were attacked, they would dissolve under very little pressure. They always took far more casualties than comparable prewar units and most important the larger percentage of their troops simply did not want to be there.

Despite these problems, and despite the fact that the French chemical weapons met with similar problems as did the American experiment, the Entente managed to make some gains in the opening rounds. French troops finally got to within artillery range of Strasbourg. The Russian offensive caused enough concern at the German General Staff that no one there wanted to be the man who had to brief the Kaiser every morning. The condition of both fronts would be enough to cause a shakeup in the German command structure but that is for later. The real question that needed to have been asked was why all of this firepower, more than had ever been amassed by the human race, seemed impotent and never did as expected.

Later wars, that used more advanced models of these exact same weapons, did not create such a stalemate. One has to remember that while the newer weapons were later generations, the fact is they were still the same weapons. With that in mind the real question becomes, how did this happen? There seem to be several reasons but, I think that two are more critical than the rest.

The obvious and first answer is that at the turn of the 20th century these weapons were so new that no one really knew how to use them properly. While the 20th century usually gets credit for all of the advancements in our lives, the truth is that it was the 19th that saw the lion's share of change. Put yourself in the shoes of a sailor like Jackie Fisher, who started his career on sailing ships that Christopher Columbus of the 15th century could have stepped on and figured out with ease. Fisher ended his career with ships that moved under their own power and had radios that someone like Columbus would have thought to be witchcraft. By comparison, a sailor from 1901 could look at a modern cruiser from a century later and still identify it as such.

The same could be said for the armies as well. While the sword usually gets most of the fanfare in war, the truth is that the most common weapon used by soldiers for most of human history has been the spear. The Great War of 98 was to end this forever. While it is true that firearms had been around for several centuries it was not until this war that they really came into their own. In all wars up until this one, infantry relied more on the bayonet than their accuracy with a firearm and that big, long blade transformed firearms into the more ancient weapon, the spear. In 1901, you still had general officers who had yet to realize that the spear had finally seen its day.

Artillery saw a similar transformation and I believe it was also at the heart of the second biggest reason for the stalemate. Firing a big gun had always been an exercise in mathematics, specifically an exercise in trigonometry. Besides breach loading, better metal and shock absorbers that allowed for greater rates of fire, the biggest advancement in giant guns was math. Further ranges meant more complex equations and more to the point, how to teach these to non-mathematicians who then had to do them rapidly enough to keep up with the rates of fire. This part was overcome but no one had anticipated the side effects or the fact that this technology had rapidly outpaced the communications required to effectively employ it.

For decades after the war, most armies would deal with the issue of the lag time between reporting moving targets and the fire missions meant to deal with those targets. It would not be until almost twenty years later that an accident at Fort Leavenworth, Kansas was to shed some light on an almost crippling weakness that up until then no one had even dreamed existed. The culprit of this weakness was ironically math and it involved the artillery shells that were virtually identical from one nation to the next.

This particular accident went ignored outside of the military profession for almost a century. Inside the profession it became critical. Several practicing guns fired a mistimed salvo, and they struck a group of civilian sub-contractors with what should have been a devastating direct hit. Everyone involved in the accident was shocked and relieved to discover that not a single contractor had been killed, yet they all realized these men should have all been dead.

This prompted the US Army to test their remaining stocks of artillery rounds left over from the war. After a few years they had discovered the problem and were confused as to how this could happen. The reality was that the most commonly used artillery ordinance was largely harmless beyond the initial explosion. Most artillery shells rely more on shrapnel to do the dirty work than on the actual explosion. The metal shavings from these shells were being propelled outwards at a less than lethal velocity. It took several years to figure out how this could happen given that all prewar testing had told them otherwise.

As stated before, the answer was the math done in those prewar tests. Mathematicians always like to point out the absolute certainty of their peculiar language. Their formulas and answers are resolute but what they often forget is that a formula can only be accurate if you have all of the variables and in life this is most often not the case. This issue was a most common mistake made by many 19th century scientists who were so eager to apply their method to everything before they stopped and looked at what they had. It was a case of did they search for the right question before seeking an answer?

The wooden targets used in the original artillery tests were constructed to be the exact resistance of human skin. In fact, the records kept by the company that made these test dummies bragged about their ability to make exact tolerances. Again, this was a good case of how they did not know everything. The tolerances might have been identical, but they were different kinds of tolerances. Human skin and wood strands are joined differently meaning that they split differently. Skin is also tougher than wood under certain types of impacts because it will give way to a certain degree, allowing it to take more of an impact and go unharmed. Wood will not budge meaning that the force of an impact is compressed into a much smaller space giving the source that impacted it more cutting power. The accident proved it; the prewar tests were invalid.

This means that all of the wartime guns were firing ammunition that was greatly reduced in its primary job. When you add the communications issues, this might go a long way towards explaining the failure of 'the king of battle' to win the war for any side. The final summary of the post war tests summed it up for a US Congressional committee when its author, Colonel George Marshall, added a personal comment, "the humanity of it all."

An Even Bigger Carrot

While Theodore Roosevelt would claim that his eventual policy was born in his days as Vice President, and there does seems to be at least some truth in these claims, it is most likely that he did not shape these incoherent thoughts into a more formalized strategy until his early days as commander-n-chief. We can use his own writings to prove this and even more important, we can point to one event in particular that must have put it all into focus for Theodore. That would be the rapidly escalating crisis in Northern China that occurred on the heels of the Boxer uprising. This was very early on in the administration and how Theodore would handle it set a pattern in the White House that told everyone what to expect from the new chief executive.

Unlike the laconic Root, Theodore would seem like a bloodhound on a trail when he would hear of new developments from almost anywhere in the world. If he judged them important, he would shove most other issues aside and personally push things along until he had the situation moving in a direction that he favored. Oddly enough, this first great crisis would be accidentally and unknowingly set in motion by Theodore himself. Roosevelt had never made any secret that he thought the only way America was going win any respect was that if they could play as equals in other people's backyards. It was what the Europeans had been doing for centuries and as far as Theodore was concerned, America would have to as well.

It was this attitude that prompted Roosevelt to override orders from the war department and change the destination of two divisions that were now being diverted from the Vancouver front. Originally these forces had been destined for Kansas where General Shafter had wanted to mount a large, but diversionary, attack against Sequoya in order to tie down Confederate reserves for yet another push against Fort Bragg. Roosevelt made no secret that he thought the entire operation was wasteful and even if successful would be useless in the larger scheme of the war. This was an important milestone for the United States.

Since 1861 the entire foreign policy of the United States had revolved around one central theme, that being the existence of the Confederate States of America. For the first time since before the administration of the first

President Lincoln, an American president was deliberately choosing to pursue a policy that in no way was connected to the CSA. Theodore believed that America needed larger, more noble goals. He argued this with his top soldier, General Shafter, who was making a case that the basic war strategy required taking the entire Mississippi river valley. That meant breaking Fort Bragg.

No one knows if Roosevelt actually realized the significance of sending those divisions to China or if it suddenly occurred to him as he ranted at Shafter. Either way, the idea did occur to Theodore and several journals recorded his exact words, "General, we have been fighting this war to achieve goals that have become entirely irrelevant. It is time that we own up to this fact and pursue the goals that are now required, that being a peace that we can live with." Quite often another statement is attributed to this speech but in reality, it was not until after the crisis in Shandong that Theodore said, "We've tried the stick, hell we've got the biggest stick on the block. What we need now is a bigger carrot." The reason we can be sure this statement did not come until later was because, as Roosevelt did record, it was in dealing with the Chinese that he realized

221

something else was lacking in the US War strategy.

This was not unique to the American Government. It is obvious when looking at all of the policies of the belligerents that they had forgotten any other options existed past the military card. It is likely that Roosevelt may never have thought of it had it not been for the unique problems presented in the Chinese theater of operations. In China, general global war was not enough to erase thousands of years of political intrigue and it continued right into the war. Once the Boxers had forced everyone's hand, the west suddenly found itself being drawn into this very complicated political situation that they had to play in order to get things from their Chinese allies. Oddly enough, it would also play a part in dealing with outright enemies.

As noted before, when Japan learned that the US was going to attempt to reinforce their troops in Northern China they became greatly concerned. They expressed this to their British allies but Admiral Moore, hampered by orders from back home, stated there was little he could do to stop them. To try might provoke another major sea battle that he had been expressly ordered to avoid. He was correct in his thinking because the new US commander in the region, Admiral George Dewey, had taken command with a new direction, under a new President.

While not exactly saying so, Roosevelt was encouraging his fleet commanders to be more aggressive despite the fact that it was not exactly welcomed news to those who were running the US Navy. They did their best to soften the orders, but Dewey still fully understood where his commander-n-chief was coming from. This situation left Dewey with far more options than did Moore and it made the arrival of US reinforcements all but guaranteed. In fact, the biggest thing standing in the way of this deployment was the battle between the President of the US and his own General Staff who opposed it.

The Japanese were not the only ones feeling threatened by this deployment that would alter the situation in China. Ironically, the man feeling most threatened was the American General, Custer. Up until now he had been the ranking US Army soldier in China, and suddenly he discovered that one Lieutenant General and two Major Generals were on the way. While technically speaking Custer had always been under the command of a Navy Admiral, the fact is that he always acted as if he were the entire show and both Mahan and Dewey allowed the man his perks just so long as he did not go too overboard. There was very little for Custer to do up until now anyway. By this time, he had only a little over three thousand men and without the Russian Army he could not do much of anything.

The Boxer Uprising was actually welcomed by Custer who found himself able to generate headlines again, however it ended too quickly for his tastes. Custer was mostly responsible for the occupation of Peking and while there were plenty of disturbances there, Custer's reputation amongst the Chinese, that of being dangerously insane, was enough to quell the majority of them with very little loss of life. The fighting was not enough to generate the headlines he needed. Now with reinforcements on the way, Custer realized he would not only be outranked by three others but suddenly he would only be one of nearly a dozen Brigadiers. It was a situation that he found unacceptable.

Fortunately for Custer, this situation created an ally from the least likely of sources. The Chinese General Jung-Lo, a cousin of Cixi and initially a supporter of hers, had come out in favor of the Guangxu Emperor not long after the Kansu Incident that had initially drawn

Custer to Peking. Despite his change of allegiances, Jung-Lo was nominally a conservative and not that favorable to the new Emperor or the Americans. He cooperated with them to get what he wanted, and quite possibly because his rival Prince Yuan was openly cooperating with the Germans in the Shandong Peninsula where he had recently declared himself Governor.

We now know that a great deal of Custer's moves were due to his own far-reaching strategy, that of one day becoming President. In this respect he was no different than Jung-Lo who was looking to his own position after the war. To this Chinese General, his rival Yuan must have seemed like a bad weed. Yuan had first created a power base in Korea until it was lost to the Japanese. Then he began playing power broker in Peking with direct access to the Forbidden City, until it was lost to the Americans.

Now with Peking lost, Yuan simply moved one province to the south and set himself up as a warlord of sorts. The Germans, who occupied Kaichou Harbor at the start of the war, were looking for a Hong Kong styled lease of the peninsula and Yuan was more than happy to grant it to them as long as they helped him rebuild his army. This was not just with weapons. The Germans were also promising to build him a railroad from their port to the provincial capital of Jinan. This went beyond military support in that all of it would give Yuan economic and political clout of the kind that Jung Lo could not hope to counter unless he built his own alliances.

Here is where the change of leadership in Washington would make its first impact on the world. The obvious choice for Jung Lo was to seek support from Russia. The problem with them was that Nicholas was not very interested in negotiating with Chinese Generals. Up until now the Americans had only been a little more giving on the matter but it was obvious to Jung-Lo that they only went so far as to meet their immediate needs concerning the occupation. It would be Custer's little problem and Roosevelt's new policies that would change the situation.

Root's administration had been content to deal with the Emperor only, and virtually ignored the fact that China was really ruled by her regional leaders. John Hay had also considered Jung-Lo to be less than trustworthy, but Roosevelt did not care. He was more than willing to deal with anyone who could make things happen. Jung-Lo got promises of small arms, ammunition and even artillery. He also got cash up front and this was the spark that set the entire theater ablaze. A Sino-American Army would be marching south, towards Jinan to scatter the forces of Prince Yuan who were building in the area.

Needless to say, neither Yuan nor his German allies were prepared for this move. If the American hand was weak, the German position was almost nonexistent. They had yet to even cement their control of Kaichou and the surrounding environs. The German 'Governor' of this new lease was a Danish born sailor by the name of Captain Carl Rosendahl. While he had always proved to be a competent sailor, he was not quite up to the challenge of administering a colony and this was particularly true of one that was only just now being organized. Rosendahl had only a handful of troops at his disposal and this meant his security was largely left in the hands of Yuan who was his buffer against the Entente.

Custer and Jung-Lo scattered Yuan's army at Jinan and took control of the vital transportation hub. This dangerous situation now escalated into an outright crisis for the allies that went beyond the peninsula. It was also the exact kind of situation that Japan had been waiting for and they wasted no time in rushing to the aid of their allies. It would only be a few days before the first Japanese troops began landing at Tsingtao. A week later, a major expedition would follow and a week after that the first serious fighting would occur along the Yellow River.

The Entente enjoyed the initial advantages in the fighting and the Sino-American Army was eventually able to compel the Japanese to pull back to their coastal enclaves where they were safe for the time being. The Entente simply did not have the kind of firepower to take the larger cities on the coast. A stalemate developed but it was not the military aspects of this operation that was really important, and this was true for both Shandong and the world in general.

Even as the fighting went on, an American couple that we have already met, Herbert and Lou Hoover, would become involved in the situation. This may never have happened had it not been for the fact that Roosevelt was now President. Hoover had written several letters to the Root administration concerning the plight of the average Chinaman. They had all gone unanswered and as the situation would prove, they had never even been opened until Theodore was confronted with this situation. The new President not only sympathized with Hoover, not only approved the plans of this young geologist but Roosevelt authorized the resources to make it happen.

Sending aid to China was old hat at this point but the new program that Hoover was placed in charge of would be different. In the past, when outsiders had sent aid to China it had always ultimately wound up in the hands of China's corrupt leadership. Very little aid ever reached the Chinese people. This time, with Hoover in charge, the relief effort would actually reach those it was intended for and the effects would be very long-lasting. It would slowly begin to transform the political landscape in northern China and make the military operations seem rather small in comparison.

This entire situation would also change a great deal in East Asia, not the least of which was Japan's eventual control of the coast of Shandong as they ousted the Germans in much the same way that they had been turned out of Port Arthur. This would drive a serious wedge between not only Japan and Germany but also between Japan and Britain. It would change the political alliances of the postwar world.

All of that was major but it could not compare to the immediate aftermath. It was in the handling of this situation that Theodore Roosevelt learned his job. The people who worked for him also saw that something new was happening even if they could not quite put their fingers on what that something was. The American people also got their first look at a dynamic new president and his actions were far more vigorous than any morale tour could ever be. Theodore personally would use this situation as a blueprint and quickly figure out how to merge his plans with reality. He had always known what he wanted to do, and China had taught him how. It was a good thing for Theodore that it happened when it did. The first real test of his new policy, 'The Big Carrot,' was almost on top of him.

Forty Mile

It can be said that on the Canadian Front, General Otter had outguessed his American enemy, General Shafter, in terms of strategy.

This might certainly be true to a point, but one might consider that Otter was forced to face several political realities that Shafter was afforded the luxury of never having to deal with. Shafter's basic plan shows his straightforward military thinking. His objectives were Quebec City, Montreal, and the Canadian capital of Ottawa. He simply chose the shortest distance and sent his troops in that direction. While it is true that these plans were drawn up well before Shafter became the top American soldier, you also have to remember that Shafter was not new to the General Staff and had helped draw up these pre-war plans. Once he relieved General Miles, Shafter never did anything to change them and, on many occasions, gave these plans his stamp of approval.

On the other side of the border, Otter was faced with any number of political problems that tempered his military plans. Even the British Governor General, Minto, knew these facts and this played greatly in deployments of military assets. It is one reason why the British Army, and not Canadian troops, were largely deployed in the region of Quebec. The Foreign Office in London was not too terribly concerned about a Francophone revolt, but they did not ignore the possibility either. It was judged that the British Army would be better suited to handle such a revolt should such an unlikely event occur. What puzzled both Minto and Otter the most was why the Americans never made any real attempts to alter the situation in Quebec.

The US government did try and foster assets in Quebec but here is where the bureaucratic weaknesses of the US come in to play. These attempts to force a political victory in Quebec were handled by the US State Department and the US Military had almost no knowledge of it. If Shafter knew anything of this it certainly did not impact his plans nor did he even show any sign of trying to play divide and conquer with his enemies. The one man who did finally become aware of the entire picture, and pay it due attention, was none other than President Roosevelt. He was furious with both Shafter and John Hay for not calling any of this to his attention right from the start.

Roosevelt may very well have never learned of the State Department's efforts in Quebec had it not been for a couple of other events that happened all the way on the other side of the continent. The first was the formal surrender of Vancouver which after much effort was no longer defendable by virtue of the fact that they had completely run out of food. Civilians in Vancouver had been boiling and eating their shoes for some time. The ammunition situation was almost as bad, and it had reached a point where the situation was simply no longer tenable.

The surrender of the city was not so much of a surprise to anyone. If anything, Roosevelt had thought that it took longer than it should have. As such, it changed very little inside the Roosevelt Administration. What the loss of Vancouver did do was kick over an ant hill in Alaska, something that only a few select people inside the Russian colony were aware of. No one outside the territory was even remotely aware of the chain of events that had just been set into motion. Up until that point one of the key destinations of gold smugglers had been Vancouver. It was in fact the largest gold market of all of the glitter coming out of the Czar's domain. One would think that the capture of this city by the US would have been welcomed by men such as Wyatt Earp, who was after all an American. The exact opposite was true.

In the shady business of smuggling, there is only one allegiance and that is to the guy who pays the best prices. Since almost the start of the war, that guy had usually been a British banker. Vancouver had become the center of that world where not only was a blind eye was turned towards doing business with the enemy, but had also been encouraged by the British Government. Buying Alaskan gold had become so important that Joseph Chamberlin got routine updates on its status. Then came the American army who laid siege to the city. That did not stop all of the gold transactions in Vancouver, but it did make the British look for alternate routes that were safer and less expensive since bribing US Army officers was now a part of doing business there. None of these alternate routes were ideal and all of them included any number of passes over the Rocky Mountains, all of which were dangerous, slow and only seasonably of value. Naturally, none of these qualities were much of a deterrent to smugglers such as Earp, Ulyanov, and Bullock. What was standing in the way of their literal pot of gold was each other.

What we do know of their dispute began over Earp's use of certain passes that Bullock demanded a toll for. Bullock claimed that he had fronted the bill for scouting and setting up these routes as well as maintaining them with provisions that Earp's men had used without permission. At first it seems that Earp was willing to pay even if there was quite a bit of haggling over the timing and price of these payments. For reasons unknown, Ulyanov got involved and the situation not only got hopelessly complicated but completely unworkable. Apparently, Earp lost any interest in the situation after that, tried to get back to business as usual and ignored Bullock completely.

This is where the situation is somewhat murky and exactly who did what is not clear, but what we do know is that it happened in a Ketchikan Brothel. Brothers, Bat and Ed Masterson, were very typical of many you were likely to find in Alaska. Their pasts are somewhat mysterious, and they have been claimed by others to be both Canadian and US citizens. It does seem clear that they lived in both countries before finding their way to Alaska, mostly thanks to Earp whom they were friends with. Bat Masterson in particular was one of Earp's right-hand men and he was well noted for keeping the peace between the various factions that at this point revolved around nationalities. It was helpful that Masterson could claim either country as his own and he switched his nationality as the situation warranted.

Not long after the dispute over the consumed supplies, several men, none of whom we have ever discovered the identities of, attacked the Masterson brothers at the Ketchikan brothel that had the very generic name of La Chez Amie. There are many who have claimed this to be very suspicious seeing as how it is known that Bat Masterson was not a patron of such places. The more conspiratorial minded always say this was some secret meeting place but what little evidence we do have suggests that Bartholomew was simply waiting on his brother. The aftermath of the attacks seems to suggest this since Ed Masterson was literally caught with his pants down and stabbed to death while his brother, Bat, managed to shoot two of the six assailants, none of which were carrying guns and wisely chose to flee at that point.

The fallout here was that Earp blamed Bullock for the attack on his friend and assumed it was over the recent dispute. At this point, Earp decided to take the supply cabins in the region that had come to be known as 'The Golden Hump.' This name could have been because of the high altitudes of this particular route or maybe it was a sexual euphemism. Any way you look at it, Ed Masterson's final hump was about to get one faction or another screwed if the situation was not resolved. This is where Vladimir Ulyanov looks very suspicious. Instead of playing peacemaker as was usually the case, he backed Earp.

A few days after the Masterson attack, when it was clear the Russian Army would do nothing about it, Earp personally led a small group of his men to a local saloon that was a favorite meeting hall for Bullock's men. They walked right in the door, caught the patrons completely off guard, and proceeded to shoot anyone that got in front of their sights. Three men were killed, seventeen wounded, and what seemed to enrage people even more was how many bottles of liquor were destroyed in the very one-sided fight. Because of this Earp did not win any friends in Ketchikan, but it was even worse for Bullock.

Seth Bullock got the message loud and clear. He was not in town when it happened and some point to this fact as Earp sending a peace feeler along with his forty-five caliber bullets. If that were true, and it is somewhat plausible, then Bullock rejected the message. He fled to the Canadian side of the border and eventually wound up in Dawson City, Canada. His final stop is important because this was at the time a heavily fortified military outpost. The town had only been laid down less than a year before the war and was meant to be a forward settlement for exploiting the gold finds. When the war broke out it quickly became an army town, mostly garrisoned with Canadian Militia and RCC troopers. These were who Bullock was seeking.

While later accounts of the Battle of Forty Mile portray an invading Russo-American Army being repelled by a valiant red jacketed detachment of outnumbered Canadian Cavalry, the real battle was nothing of the sort. Just like with Roosevelt in Mexico, there were no cavalry charges at this battle and even more important, no horses. There were also no red jackets or uniforms of any sort even if it is true that the RCC was a regular military formation. What is also equally true was that none of the men from the Canadian military who followed Bullock back up the Yukon River in small boats did so in any official capacity. Most of them had been paid in gold from Bullock's own personal supplies and had essentially become mercenaries. The fact that they discarded their uniforms is ample evidence of this. What also helped Bullock was that he had friends in Dawson City, many of whom had a stake in his control of the Forty Mile gold route. Because of this he had little trouble with the local political leadership or the military command structure when he borrowed their soldiers.

Unlike many actions in this particular theater, we actually know exactly where this battle happened thanks to the work of archeologists some four decades later. Earp and Ulyanov had heard about Bullock's flight to Dawson and deduced his intentions of seizing absolute control of the vital pass just a few miles up from the junction of the Yukon and Forty Mile Rivers. They quickly assembled their own little army and tried to beat Bullock to the prize. Bullock won the race and held the high ground when Earp and Ulyanov arrived as expected. Bullock had known they were coming all along. It seems as if that was the point.

It is true that the Canadians' (or Bullock's) soldiers were outnumbered, although not as much as we have been led to believe. The truth of it, as laid out by the archeology mainly by finding buried piles of spent shell casings, is that both sides were relatively evenly matched. What gave the Canadians the advantage seems to be two-fold. One was that they had a unity of command and all spoke the same language. Earp's forces did not and were being led by two commanders (Earp and Ulyanov) who disagreed with each other at nearly every instance. Their troops were also both Russian and American, and neither of these factions appeared to really want to talk to each other, let alone try. The second reason was that while the hard living smugglers and miners have a reputation as good fighters, this type of brawler rarely does very well against disciplined soldiers. Most of Bullock's force was just that.

From what we know of journal entries, the battle probably lasted a few hours on one single day. When the Alaskans were unable to dislodge the Canadians, they decided to give up and go home. We do not have a good count on casualties, but they seemed to have been rather light. The best estimate is that less than ten people were killed, on both sides combined.

The fallout from this battle for Earp and Bullock was nearly non-existent. Less than a month later, Earp paid Bullock his money and the gold smuggling went right back to business as usual. The same cannot be said of the relationship between Earp and Ulyanov. Many point to their disagreements in this 'campaign' as being the seeds of the eventual war that would erupt around these two larger than life personalities. While they both did eventually mend fences with Bullock the fight did place Bullock as the undisputed master of the gold trade. Apparently, Earp and Ulyanov blamed each other for this fact.

It was what happened far away from Forty Mile that is the most important. The further one got from the 'battle of Forty Mile' the larger the tales of the battle got. The facts that they were getting in Ottawa, London, Moscow, and Washington hardly resembled what really happened. Getting any concrete information was near impossible and I think that Czar Nicholas might have been somewhat angered if he had ever found out that his military intelligence was coming from drunks in saloons recounting their heroics in a battle they were not even really at. While some doubt this is the case it can easily be proven. Russian Officers collected over seven hundred interviews from participants in the battle. This is somewhat problematic when you consider that both sides combined had less than three hundred men.

At this point the reality made no difference at all because several critical factors were coming to a head elsewhere. Forty Mile alerted several belligerents about a front that while being important had not only been ignored but had largely been forgotten. It caused Czar Nicholas to realize he had to regain a firm control of his territory and this would lead to a course of near disaster for the Romanov Dynasty. It made Roosevelt suddenly realize that this front even existed, which led to his discovery of US State Department activities in Quebec. The most important result of all was inside Canada itself. For a war weary nation that was on the verge of collapse, a group of criminal thugs along a distant border, had been a shot of adrenalin. Seth Bullock, a man who barely considered himself Canadian, suddenly became a national hero. The timing of all this could not have been more critical and dare I say more opportune?

Conflicts Needs Conflicting

By that fateful summer of 1901 the lack of war material in Canada was starting to show itself in such a way that it was now impossible to hide. Governor General Minto had been aware that this situation was coming for some time. The quantity of munitions making it past the blockade of the St Lawrence Seaway had been steadily diminishing as the war went on. London's unwillingness to attempt to lift the blockade, coupled with the increasing demands of munitions for the BCEF in Serbia was taking its toll. The loss of Vancouver had only compounded the situation and to make matters worse, the only thing holding back what seemed to be an endless stream of US soldiers was an equally endless quantity of artillery shells. That is perhaps why Canada began running dry of this particular ammunition first.

The first thing that alerted the United States to their enemy's shortage was the rapidly diminishing number of counterattacks they were encountering along the front. It was almost standard practice at this point in the war, and considered automatic by company commanders everywhere, to expect a counterattack anytime you took a patch of ground. This was particularly true on the Canadian front where allied forces excelled in making the Entente pay for every inch they advanced. By early June, at the peak of the US offensive, the Canadian counterattacks were suddenly very rare.

Something else that was noticed by US Army troops was the clockwork regularity of harassment fire from enemy artillery. At the start of the war such fire was tossed about with almost no discretion at all, but in that summer some company commanders began counting the number of incoming artillery rounds and quickly discovered that the number everyday was always exactly the same. When you put these two observations together, it could mean only one thing. The enemy was rationing his artillery.

Minto was aware that his enemy was aware when US attacks aimed at Montreal and Quebec City began to grow bolder. Fortunately for him, a good section of this line was being held by British soldiers, a good number of whom were pre-war regulars. They got more of the artillery ration than anyone else and it was questionable if US troops could drive them all the way to the St Lawrence before winter set in once again. If that was the case, then it was likely that Canada could hold out until at least the following summer.

Even so, the desperation of the situation had become apparent beyond Canada. Chamberlin and Wolseley, back in London, had been of the opinion that the downfall of Canada was inevitable for at least a year. They never said so publicly, not even in cabinet meetings, but their actions speak louder than words. Collectively and very quietly, their staffs began drawing up plans that would keep the front active after largescale operations were no longer possible. They not only withheld this information from the Canadian Government but did not bother to tell their man, Governor Minto, either.

It is questionable if Balfour and by extension the ailing Lord Salisbury, were made aware of these plans but there is every reason to believe that they were at least partially briefed. It is not reasonable to believe that Wolseley and Chamberlin alone could have diverted the resources that they did without at least some measure of disclosure to the cabinet. I believe this was mostly a case of 'Ask me no questions and I will tell you no lies.' Still the men responsible for running Great Britain's war effort had to know what was coming and had to know that a man like Wolseley, who had always held a personal interest in North America, would not stand idly by and just let it happen.

One has to consider the greater ramifications that the war cabinet was facing, and this would go well beyond Canada. Great Britain's imperial power rested completely on the stability of her Commonwealth treaty.

Britain simply could not afford to govern such an empire without at least minimal consent and financial support from the very subjects they were ruling as imperial masters. The Commonwealth was their mechanism by which they did this, and the agreement rested completely on Britain's ability, namely that of the Royal Navy, to defend these lands. One could say that it was a very feudal arrangement. With this in mind it is understandable why the cabinet did not want to hear anything about the plan because it was essentially an admission that Britain could no longer fulfill their end of the treaty that held their empire together.

Still in defense of the cabinet, the US Army had left them with very few choices in the matter and there were also other strategic considerations that had to be taken into account. One can argue that the entire affair was handled poorly (most of the blame here rides on the shoulders of Chamberlin) but given the situation, the plan was sound enough. This is how a certain British Colonel, who also happened to be a prince, by the name of Arthur Gotha, commonly known as the Duke of Strathearn, was brought into the fold. As his name suggests, he was a son of Queen Victoria, he was a military man to the core and most importantly he had spent a great deal of time in Canada. Strathearn had worked closely with Minto during the years that the Canadian defense system was being built, so it was reasoned he was the perfect man for the very delicate task that Woseley and Chamberlin had in mind. This was the task of briefing Minto on the plans for the capitulation of Canada.

Strathearn's task was monumental to say the least. We do have official records of his meetings with Woseley and it is very clear that Strathearn's boss was expecting him to do more than just brief the Governor. Strathearn was not being given any official command since Bullers and Minto would be left officially at their posts, but what came after the collapse of the front would be Strathearn's responsibility alone. Apparently, it was Balfour's wish that their two top officials, namely Minto and Bullers, be recalled once it was clear that Canada was lost. From that point forward, Strathearn would command the resistance which was to be more than just partisan warfare.

For over a year, the Royal Navy had been establishing a chain of small bases at the lower end of the Hudson Bay. They had been stockpiling supplies at these bases and while they were limited in their usefulness, being only seasonably accessible and surrounded by wilderness, it was the perfect place to run a resistance movement. When the front could no longer be held, Strathearn was to lead the British troops that he could salvage from the front through the wilderness and establish himself at these bases. It would be very difficult for the US Army to reach him here and he would have a wide front in which to mount repeated raids against the enemy.

It was felt that this plan would accomplish the most critical need once the greater part of Canada was lost. There was no longer any hope of salvaging the agricultural importance of Canada. Most of the prime farmland was already being quickly overrun in the early summer of 1901. Canada's industrial usefulness was already negated by the fact that most of her prime industrial centers were now falling under enemy artillery fire and combined with the blockade there was nothing left for her to contribute here. That left only one thing that Canada could contribute to the war effort and that was the act of tying down as much of the US Army as possible. If this was not accomplished, then the US would be free to turn its entire might on the Confederate States and no one in London believed the Confederacy could hold that back.

This continued resistance was very important for more than just the obvious reasons. The effect that the loss of Canada would have on places like Australia and New Zealand would be devastating. There was already considerable opposition to the war beginning to bubble up but again this is also obvious. There would also be considerable problems with other nations that were not technically members of the Commonwealth but might as well be. The two chief notables here are the Confederate States and the fledgling Empire of Japan. Both nations relied heavily on London in the pre-war years and if they no longer saw Britain as a savior then their support was no longer guaranteed. The consequences to British interests in North America and East Asia would again be devastating.

One has to wonder if Strathearn realized the gravity of the situation as he boarded a destroyer bound for Canada. The man literally had the fate of the world in his hands. Success in this most sensitive mission would mean that Britain very well could pull something out of this huge mess. Failure could literally mean the end of his empire. While these two possible conclusions were on the extreme ends of the spectrum, the fact is that they were both reasonable possibilities that he had to consider. Unfortunately for history, and more so for Strathearn, we will never know what he thought. It is also the reason why we hear so little of the man today.

Duke Strathearn's fast destroyer was spotted by a US Zeppelin not long after it departed its final coaling station in Greenland. Since the BB-39, designated the USN Tweed, did not attack the HMS Druid, her commander felt that he was safe enough. The Druid was one of the newest and fastest destroyers in the flotilla, not even a year past her first sea trials. Everyone felt confident she could outrun anything the Americans had blockading the seaway ahead of them. They had good intelligence on the disposition of enemy ships and the run for Montreal seemed a straightforward proposition. What no one on Druid, nor anyone else in the Royal Navy, at this time knew about was what the US Navy Airships were really up to.

It is unlikely that anyone aboard Druid ever knew what hit them. The fact that the St. Lawrence Seaway had multiple belts of mines laid by both sides was nothing new to anyone. The Royal Navy had mapped out the American belts and naturally had maps of their own. What they did not know, nor realize at the time, was that the Americans were now dropping mines from their Zeppelins. It was something very new as the US Navy was now trying to turn the submersible mine into a more offensive weapon by randomly seeding cleared channels from the air. These weapons also had a very new feature in that they were magnetic and would detonate if the metal hull of a warship even got close. This is somewhat ironic in this case since the hull of the Druid was made of wood.

It was largely irrelevant in this case. How the HMS Druid struck the mine will never be known. What we do know is that almost nothing was left of the ship and there were no survivors. Strathearn, along with Woseley and Chamberlin's sensitive plans for the continued resistance of Canada, were gone in the blink of an eye. What is even more important is that the man who would have to deal with the fallout, Governor General Minto, had no idea that these plans even existed. When the critical breaking point was reached, Minto would already be completely disarmed, and he did not even know it.

Toronto

The new floating magnetic mine being deployed by the Americans was not being restricted to the St. Lawrence Seaway. Its success in the destruction of HMS Druid was discovered by the US Navy only a few days after it happened. Of course, no one in the US military, or even the civilian government, realized exactly what that meant for the entire Canadian Front. It was on another body of water where the US Navy was really cheering its latest technological terror. The target of this weapon is rather odd in that for some strange reason the American Navy and Army often consider each other the enemy more than they do their actual enemies. This is somewhat understandable in that while they only fight real wars every few decades, they are always fighting each other at the US congress in the dreaded battle for more money. As a result, their war of words can grow quite heated.

The victory at Toronto was not exactly the glamorous kind of stand-up fight that makes headlines that either branch of the US military likes to shout about, but it was a victory none the less and the Navy was more than happy to thump their chests over it. The simple fact was that the army had failed, and the navy had come to save them. Toronto had been under siege for over a year and repeated attempts to storm the city's defenses had failed rather miserably, only generating long casualty lists and little else. Despite the best efforts of the army, they had failed to starve the city out as well and naturally they blamed that situation on the navy. While the two branches of the US military were pointing fingers at each other, they failed to name the real culprits and those were the Canadians.

In this I say 'Canadians' and not the Canadian military because while the Canadian Army certainly gets its fair share of credit for holding Toronto, it was the efforts of the civil population that really held the effort together. Naturally, there are many stories of civilians contributing to the efforts along the trenches, of sacrificing, making heroic gestures, and while many of these stories tend to be true, they are also mostly anecdotal. The real battle for

Toronto was not waged on land but on the water and in this case specifically the Great Lake of Ontario.

As noted earlier, the brown water navies of the world had proven themselves largely irrelevant in the early stages of the war. The overpriced, oversized and awkward barges that were dubbed with names like 'Inland Battleships,' quickly became the butt of many jokes. On Lake Ontario specifically the United States found itself operating at even more of a disadvantage than the other great lakes to begin with. For these, and any number of other reasons, the US Navy had failed miserably at the attempts to cut off Toronto's watery lifeline.

This naturally led to the US Army's operations to seize the ports that supplied Toronto by land. The early stages of these operations were no more successful than any of their other operations in Canada. The attack across the river from Watertown, New York had been one such attempt and while the Americans did manage to cross the river, they came nowhere near their actual objective which was Kingston, Ontario. This operation did cut the Great Lakes off from the sea, but for the Canadians it was little more than a nuisance that had an easy work around. This was railing goods past the breach.

By 1901 the situation had changed for the exact same reason that the entire war in Canada had. The weight of the US was finally telling on the battlefield. For Toronto this meant that her plots were slowly drying up. The US Army gave up trying to storm the city and pushed further up the peninsula, specifically eastward towards Ottawa. A combination of factors began to take their toll. Not only was there a growing problem with rapidly shrinking stock of war materials but Canada was also running out of soldiers as well. By the summer of 1901 most Canadian units were at well below half strength and fewer and fewer replacements were reaching those units. It has been claimed that Canada spent an entire generation on this war, and in this particular case it seems to be less of an exaggeration and more of an understatement. The post war figures seem to suggest that the casualty rates in Canada was nothing less than apocalyptic.

Despite the severe losses, the fact was that those Canadian units still in the fight knew their business with deadly efficiency. They were taking a high toll from the fresh and inexperienced American formations moving into the line. This level of ferocity certainly made a difference in the attitudes of their enemies, but in the end the Canadian military could not overcome the single biggest disadvantage they now faced which was geography.

The US Army had now pushed them clear of the peninsula and had them on open ground. There were lakes that created some bottlenecks, but the simple fact was that the Canadian army now had to defend more ground with fewer men. The US Army took full advantage of the room to maneuver and by June of 1901 all of the ports that supplied Toronto save one were in American hands. This last lifeline to what had become the very symbol of Canadian resistance was the first port that the Americans had tried to take, Kingston.

The Americans threw one massive assault at Kingston after another from both the east and west. The attacks were repelled and losses on both sides were horrendous. General Otter was fearful that Kingston would become yet another siege and as far as the Americans were concerned, it was all they needed. Kingston did not have to be taken, it only had to be neutralized and, in this scenario, it would also pin down the bulk of the troops that Otter had left. Then the matter was settled from the most unexpected of directions. It did not come from the east or west but rather the final straw fell quite literally from the sky.

The real end came when the barge, Sara Pine, hauling munitions that were bound for Toronto, detonated a magnetic mine in the safe passage zone leading to the Kingston docks. The explosion rocked the entire city. At first the harbor master assumed that one of their own mines had broken loose from its mooring but when the waters were investigated one of the magnetic mines was found, safely disarmed and brought back to a warehouse in Kingston. It did not take long before the authorities figured out what was going on and reported it to the military. General Otter was notified of the new enemy activity in less than seventy-two hours and he knew exactly what it meant. He was also not the only one to find out about the problem.

The unions for both the dock workers and the merchant seamen probably knew about the new mines even before Otter did. Their leaders promptly notified Prime Minster Laurier that no barges or merchant vessels would be leaving the docks until the military could assure their reasonable safety. Laurier knew that he essentially had a mutiny on his hands now. His major problem in dealing with it was that, from his own pen, "these men have already sacrificed so much that I find it impossible to ask them for any more." His words were very accurate and probably even more than he realized. The effectiveness of the mines was not so much the issue here as it was the war weariness that they exploited. It was also not just the merchantmen who were demoralized, Laurier's own words bear out that he was as well.

Laurier might have been looking at the humanity of the situation, but he was also still a politician. He knew how to cover his ass, and in this particular instance he did so by the time-honored method called 'passing the buck.' Laurier notified the office of the Governor General and informed him of the work stoppage being threatened by the unions. What Laurier did not do was tell Minto the reason why. We have the official communications between the staffs of these two men and in them there is not a single mention of the magnetic mines or of Kingston. Maybe Laurier assumed that Minto was already aware of this? I think it more likely that the omission of these circumstances was probably for the same reason that Laurier did not call the Governor personally, he simply had no great desire to deal with Minto.

The inaction of Laurier in this matter created a power vacuum and like all such vacuums something will always rush in to fill it. While Laurier was considering his options, and Minto was completely clueless of the rapidly deteriorating situation, two men in Canada had all of the facts in front of them and were prepared to act decisively, even if they were not yet sure what that action was to be. One of the two men was General Otter and his communications with Laurier was met with little more than silence. His communications with Minto were met with deaf ears and then orders to follow, none of which were very realistic.

Minto ordered the Canadian General to send troops to either compel the dock workers and seamen to man their posts or arrest them and replace them with others who would do the work, even if it meant using army troops to replace them. It is easy to surmise that Otter was shocked by this order seeing as how when it first arrived he was completely unaware of the union situation. Still, Otter did not act rashly and found out what was going on before he considered his next move. It would have to be a very careful one because he realized that Minto's order was beyond their ability at this point. Even so, Otter would still have to do something because Toronto had to be re-supplied.

Strangely enough, it would be the US Army Zeppelin Corps that relieved Otter of his impossible quagmire. While much hype is made of the subsequent attacks on Nashville, the fact was that the first firebombing by the US Army was on Kingston, Ontario. Shafter had listened to Admiral Sampson boast of the success of their new weapon and Shafter was tired of hearing it. The Army had been working on their own strategic weapon, one aimed at increasing the effectiveness of aerial bombardment, so Shafter felt it was time for a test run. Everyone knew that Kingston was the most critical target on any front so all thirty-two airships in the US Army service were armed with the new incendiary munitions and began their journey from their bases in Ohio.

While these 'firebombs' are easily considered primitive by today's standards and are nothing like the combustible petroleum jelly that we call napalm, they were effective enough. They were not that different from the more conventional explosives of the time save their liberal use of phosphorus and magnesium. These weapons were a direct outgrowth of the anti-aircraft weapons being developed in France where gunners were looking for a method of seeing where their rounds went. While the French continued to develop their tracer rounds, once they shared this technology with their American allies, the US Army found another use for it. The firebombs were the end result.

An almost continuous train of zeppelins, with another two or three airships arriving no sooner than the last wave was leaving, bombarded Kingston for three days straight. At first it appeared as if the bombing would do insignificant damage but by nightfall of the second day when the US airships used the fires to guide them right to the target, it was clear that the docks around Kingston, as well as most of the downtown area, would be completely destroyed. It was not the kind of firestorm known in later wars but again it was enough. Now not only were the water channels out of Kingston blocked but the city itself had been rendered completely useless.

General Otter realized it was the end. When Toronto fell, Canadian morale would plummet, and Otter had little choice but order the garrison commander to seek terms for surrender. In a more practical sense, this would mean that a large portion of US Troops would now be free to join a push on the capital of Ottawa from the west. They would be able to roll right up the north bank of the St Lawrence Seaway, capturing Canada's remaining major industrial cities, trapping their best troops on the other side of the water, and conquer Canada. Otter no longer had any way of stopping this militarily.

Still, General Otter did not want to just give up. So many lives had been lost that he could not bring himself to do it. He had to find a way out of this situation and oddly enough it would drive him towards the only other man in Canada that seemed to know what was going on and had a will to do something about it. This man was someone that he had almost ordered arrested earlier in the war. The man was none other than the main leader in opposition to the war, a francophone, a political adversary and sometimes even suggested an outright traitor. The man was currently not even a government official and we have already met him, Henri Bourassa.

A Square Deal

General Otter's greatest dilemma was even more dire than the military situation on the ground. He suddenly found that his most basic loyalties were in conflict. If he followed the orders of the Governor General that represented the empire that he had served with complete devotion for his entire life, then he was dooming the home that he loved to complete destruction. Minto, absent any orders from the Home Office in London, had already decided on a course of action that could only end one way. He wanted to pull the troops back north of the St Lawrence, fortify Canada's major cities and make the Americans fight for each one, block by block. Otter knew the military realities and understood that this would only delay the inevitable and leave his nation in such ruins that in the end it would not matter who won the campaign. There would be no Canada left to rule.

At some point, as Otter agonized over this matter, he must have thought about the ammunition hoarding by the British Army. He must have considered the commitment of the troops, that were promised Canada, to the

Balkan campaign. It is hard to believe that these issues were not in the back of his mind when he contacted Henri Bourassa and began communications with the professional radical. These communications did not come out of nowhere. Bourassa had already been sending Otter any number of notes and hinting at his position and it is testimony to Otter's desperation that he now considered them a viable option.

Many have used Bourassa's influence in the antiwar movement, the anti-imperialist faction, and his communications with the US State Department as evidence that the man was a paid American asset and traitor. This is not true, and we know this because thanks to declassified US State Department records, we now know who the actual spies were. They were a rather mundane married couple, by the name of Lucien and Marie Chartres, who lived in Quebec City, had no known ties to any political factions, and apparently had conned the actual US spies into giving them money for services that they only pretended to render.

This became something of a lucky break, or at least it did for the President of the United States, Theodore Roosevelt. Once he had learned of this alleged independence movement in Quebec, one that was largely the figment of Marie Chartres' imagination, Theodore began formulating some plans of his own. When it was clear that victory on the Canadian front was within their grasp, and that there was little the Allies could do to reverse the situation, he sent a note to the Chartres' in Quebec. This was done over the very vocal protests of John Hay and even some of Theodore's political allies, such as General Bill Shafter.

Theodore would hear none of it, because apparently he had thought of the same thing that Chamberlin and Wolseley had. He lectured his veteran diplomat and soldier as if they were children and shook his finger at them while explaining in no uncertain terms, "gentlemen, we cannot have the bulk of our forces lying fallow in the great white north when we have real work to do elsewhere."

Those words recorded by Howard Taft, who was present at the meeting, seem to be as far as Roosevelt was willing to go in explaining his plans, or at least that was the impression of Taft who had not been privy to other meetings where apparently Theodore had no problem explaining at length what he wanted done. The basic lack of communications here did not seem to be with the President who above all else loved to talk. If there was a problem with the new US policy, it had to lay at the feet of others who simply could not see what Roosevelt was. One might call it a plan ahead of its time but for someone like Roosevelt, there was no such thing. If the history books needed to catch up with the man, then he was willing to turn the page.

Lucien Chartres was a bit shocked when he got a communication from his US handlers that was far beyond the scope of anything he had ever seen from them before. He was even more flabbergasted by the fact that they had delivered to him a letter that was hand signed by none other than Theodore Roosevelt. Lucien was not even sure he could do as requested since, despite his claims, he did not really know Henri Bourassa. Fortunately for the Chartres they did have some idea of how to get in contact with the man and the letter, signed by Roosevelt, was more than enough to quickly get them granted an audience.

When Bourassa was certain that the Chartres letter was authentic, he had all of the pieces he needed to act. While the US spy charges that were leveled against the man were false, there was also the case of those who accused him of using his influence with the unions. These turned out to not only be correct but an understatement. We now know that Bourassa had more than just influence, he was actually issuing orders to several unions, one of which represented the dock workers who were threatening to strike in the wake of Kingston. We have no actual documentation that he ordered this particular strike, but the timing certainly makes one wonder.

It did not take long before Otter and Bourassa met in person at Otter's field headquarters just west of Montreal. Bourassa presented him the letter and even before the francophone said as much, Otter realized that he might be looking at his last way out of the disaster they were facing. He certainly must have had his reservations and for a lot of reasons. He had to wonder if Theodore Roosevelt could deliver on his promises. He also had to wonder if his own government would go along with it. Otter had to know that no matter what Laurier said, Minto would never agree but at this point I think that the Governor General was the least of Otter's worries.

If General Otter had any reservations about Roosevelt they were soon laid to rest because to his shock the man who met with him under a flag of truce was none other than the

President of the United States. Roosevelt, and a small honor guard who were only armed with their colt revolvers, marched out between the lines under a white flag to meet with the commanding General of Canada's armed forces. General Otter wore his field khakis that did not look so different from those worn by the privates in his army. Roosevelt was dressed in his custom uniform made by Brooks Brothers, which had been worn during his time in New Mexico. The two men shook hands and Roosevelt requested that they put up a meeting tent and have lunch. Otter agreed.

The basics of Roosevelt's proposal was very simple. Canada could keep her independence and territory. The British Army of North America would have to surrender and would be interned but all Canadians would be allowed to stack arms and go home. In return, the United States wanted Canada to renounce all of her treaties with Great Britain. Furthermore, Canada would also be required to form a new government under a new constitution that officially stipulated the nation's status as an unarmed neutral.

Needless to say, Otter was not enthused with the deal, but he also knew the alternatives. Given the circumstances they were generous terms but there were many sticking points that would have to be worked out. He said as much to Roosevelt and quite possibly only then did he realize that Roosevelt was not the kind of man to be caught short. Roosevelt already had, in writing, a step-by-step timetable that began with a truce between the armed forces of Canada and the United States, starting twenty-four hours from the conclusion of their meeting. It is important to note that this truce was only with the Canadian military and the British Army of North America was not included. It also demonstrated exactly how shrewd and talented Roosevelt was.

While Roosevelt promised that Canada's borders would be respected that was not entirely true. He had built into his timetable, a formula for US withdrawal, that was dependent on the various conditions of the truce being met. Naturally, one of these conditions was the surrender of the British Army. If Otter could not make it happen then, as Roosevelt pointed out, the US Army would have to do it and that meant more territory would be occupied for what could possibly be a much longer period of time. He did not bother to mention the fact that it would also mean a great deal more physical destruction and in this case for a war that Canada was no longer fighting.

Six hours after the end of the meeting, both Otter and Bourassa were back in Ottawa and had a meeting with Laurier and his cabinet. After hearing the American terms, and discussing the matter at length, ultimately Laurier only had a question and not a command. He asked of his General, "Can we really make this happen?"

Otter only nodded and replied, "Do we really have a choice?"

Laurier never said yes. He simply nodded and said, "Then you know what to do."

At eleven hundred hours and eleven minutes on the following day, the guns of Canada fell silent. The same cannot be said for those that belonged to the US Army. An all-out attack fell on British lines just south of the St Lawrence Seaway. At the same time, US troops began marching right past their former enemies in other areas and were advancing on Ottawa and Montreal, virtually unopposed. Ironically, the city that started the entire process, Toronto, enjoyed its first day of peace in a very long time. US soldiers walked across the former no man's land and began distributing their rations with those they were trying to kill only the day before.

Soon, shipments of food and medicine would be coming in on the first trains to enter the city in over a year, only these trains had American flags prominently displayed on them. People had been expecting and dreading this day, but these trains were not filled with American soldiers, they only had relief workers who did nothing more than unload the vital supplies and then leave. The people of Toronto were stunned by this. Not only had their enemies showed an unimaginable kindness but as the day went on people suddenly began to realize, they had held out. There was no enemy parade coming down their streets. To the people of the formerly besieged city, it was to be marked as a day to celebrate for some time to come.

The same was not true in Ottawa, Montreal, or Quebec City. Here some Canadian soldiers had not laid down their arms. This was not in violation of the agreement with the US and in fact, Otter had notified his new American liaison, General John Pershing, of exactly what was to happen. Pershing actually accompanied Otter to the residence of the Governor General and when Minto saw the

271

American General Officer walking in side by side with Otter, he knew the day had come. As he would later record, he had just never expected it to happen like this.

Otter informed the man that he was now under house arrest but that he and his staff would be allowed to return to Great Britain just as soon as transportation could be arranged. He was then told that any soldiers of the Commonwealth now on Canadian soil were considered persona non grata and required to surrender their arms to the proper authorities of the new Provisional Government of the Republic of Canada. If Minto was at a loss for words, he did not show it. He simply thanked the men for the notification and asked if he could confer with his military counterpart, General Bullers.

With a nod from Otter, Minto retreated to his private study and called Bullers' headquarters. He was then informed that Bullers had received the same demand from this new 'provisional government.' Bullers went on to point out that while they might not take this new government seriously, they could not ignore the Canadian military which had now taken control of the river crossings and ports on the St Lawrence. The simple fact was that the

British Army was now without a real supply line and they could not hope to keep fighting for longer than a few more days.

Minto returned to his 'guests' and did not bother speaking with Otter. He directly addressed Pershing and told the young man, "So this is it. I recommend a truce as soon as practical and you will have our official surrender as soon as it can be arranged. Will this suit your President Roosevelt?"

The guns stopped firing in less than twelve hours. In under a week, Redvers Buller presented his sword to John Pershing at the home of the Governor General. After this ceremony, Minto had wished to have another that presented the nation of Canada to the United States, but under orders from Roosevelt, Pershing would not allow any such thing. It was contrary to the new US policy which was aimed at getting out the idea that the US was giving Canada back to the Canadians. No matter how much anyone believed this, it most definitely had an effect on the entire world which would be reeling from the events in Canada for some time to come.

Strangely enough, these events would give no small amount of grief to the man who came up with the strategy, Theodore Roosevelt. They would be affecting people in every nation and not just those at war with the United States. The two most prominent examples, probably impacted more than anyone else, were America's two biggest allies, Russia and France. If Frank Zolhus had aimed to start a revolution, this was it.

The Sneeze

It was once noted that when France sneezed, the rest of Europe caught a cold. Indeed, this statement was born of a century in which France spent most of its time in one kind of revolution or another. While much ado has been made about the social and economic revolution of Great Britain, what was going on in France has only generally been examined when bloodshed was the result. That could simply be the result of the fact that France was far less peaceful, at least compared to Great Britain, in its transition to a modern nation state, or maybe it was a result of the fact that Britain was better at selling itself. Either way, the fact is that outside of France few people dig that deeply into the collage of change that had been transforming France for the better part of a century.

It is true that most people know about key events that took place in France but seldom, in the English-speaking world at least, does anyone dig beneath its surface. The chain of events that took place in Paris of 1901 is yet another good example of this. Due to the events in Canada, where many Canadians claim credit for these events, most look on 'The Mutiny' as some grand gesture of peace when in fact it was nothing of the sort. While there are some who will be offended by this, the fact is that some stereotypes are born of at least a grain of truth. While this might drum up images of the laconic Frenchman, in reality the stereotype here is one of the private soldier who has little regard for much more than his own comfort. There was no better place to get that than in Paris.

One particular fact that is often overlooked is that Georges Boulanger already had a desertion problem of monumental proportions. This is not the kind of desertion that is most often portrayed by peace hobbyists, that being of a disenfranchised soldier who is questioning the ideological validity of war itself. In reality, this kind of soldier is at best extraordinarily rare and more often than not, when one sees examples of such, they are usually the result of a carefully manufactured image. No, in this case the problem was not with men running off never to return but it was more a case of soldiers taking their own self approved vacations and their most popular destination was Paris.

The destination speaks a great deal about the motives of the men who were now so commonly doing it. In the ranks of the French Army an unofficial system of official desertion had sprung up and was generally managed at the sergeant level. This system was usually very discriminately overlooked by officers who were smart enough to realize that they were powerless to stop it. Such was the life in an army of citizen soldiers, and this is really the key here. While it is true that some of these men went home the vast majority did not. That is saying quite a bit when you consider that some of these men were closer to their own homes than Paris, yet they chose the City of Lights instead.

This should tell you what these 'deserters' were usually interested in. The Parisian Bordello and Salon industry was quite literally booming due to the war. Most of these soldiers would spend a few days on their semi self-appointed leave doing what it is that soldiers are most famous for in such circumstances and then return to the front lines. There were of course some who either stayed longer or never went back at all. In the case of the latter, it was quite often due to the fact that these true deserters had found a niche in the night life of Paris where they were either making money or had a social standing much greater than in the army.

While much political hay has been made of this in the twentieth century, the fact is that what was going on in France was nothing unusual. It was in fact something that every army in the world was dealing with in one capacity or another and more important this problem had existed in every war in recorded history. The French General Staff, and this included Boulanger himself, were well aware of the desertion rates and completely unalarmed. There had been a suggestion of trying the time-honored custom of decimation where basically they shot ten percent of their army to restore order. Since the desertion rates themselves were at less than ten percent this idea was quickly dismissed since losing ten percent of their military in an attempt to recover five seemed rather ludicrous.

For that reason, the French policy actually swung dramatically in the other direction. Like much of what was going on in France at the time, Boulanger simply chose to ignore the situation to almost an extreme. It was so bad in fact that a deserter, on his Parisian getaway, could actually report to the war ministry and collect his paycheck while he was there. This might sound absurd but again one has to remember that at his core, General Revenge was more General than Revenge. He was a military man and understood the nature of armies and war. He knew this was so normal that many militaries had to invent another term for the behavior which was, most commonly called Absent Without Leave.

The real danger here went beyond the management of an army and this is truly what Boulanger had ignored to his own detriment. It is true that the numbers of deserters that were gone from the front at any given moment, were growing. It was equally true that the duration of time that these men took in Paris was also growing as well. It is also very true that the number of men who decided to take up a permanent residence was starting to drastically increase. These facts are well known but what usually does not get reported is why. The duration of the war certainly played its part, but the evidence seems to point towards the fact that the desertion industry was not only organizing but expanding and branching out into new financial opportunities for those who were in a position to exploit them. Most of the time these financial opportunists were enterprising deserters.

While some of these soldiers did open businesses, and as we shall see it was one such soldier that led to the mutiny, the real effect of this bizarre chapter of the war was that the desertion community of Paris was starting to take on a very permanent feel. In the beginning it was treated as nothing more than a diversion that seemed as temporary as the war did. By 1901 that had changed, and it was directly impacting the lives of the citizens of Paris in some very real ways. While Paris has quite the reputation for being a 'party city,' the truth of the matter is that most Parisians are no different from any other citizens of any other city. That is to say that they work, they sleep, and they wish to raise their children with as little complications to their lives as possible.

The desertion problem was impacting the average Parisian far more than the army, since while it is true that most soldiers of this period were solid citizens, a good number of them like in the population at large were just plain thugs. Now they were thugs with guns and trained to use violence, of which many had no problem doing so on their own fellow Frenchmen. The usual motive for these incidents was theft, and crime was skyrocketing in Paris as a result. The citizens of Paris were petitioning both their local officials and the national government to do something about it. What they got for their efforts was what Boulanger was becoming most famous for, silence.

Of course, this did not cause the mutiny which had its seeds on the other end of the spectrum. Since the start of the war, most of the soldiers who had slipped off for a few days of fun would return to their units. Once back they did what all soldiers do in such circumstances, they told tall tales and lied their asses off about the big one that got away. In this case, the 'big one' was usually a well-endowed prostitute with an even bigger bottle of wine. Some of these stories became legendary and the names of those involved, as well as the exaggerations, changed with each retelling. By 1901 these stories were no longer confined to the troops on the front lines. Some of them had managed to even make the newspapers even if they only received a byline on some back page. What these articles do prove, despite their seeming unimportance, is that these tales were everywhere.

What is absolutely true is that the men of the 401st Infantry Regiment, a unit that was largely conscripted in the Normandy area in the early fall of 1900, had heard a great many tales of these Parisian adventures. The irony of this is that they learned of this from the very men who trained them in a camp just outside of Orleans. Most of their officers and sergeants were men who had been serving for some time and almost all of them had partaken in the unofficial leave system that was now so common. The tales of women and wine certainly inspired the men more than guts and grit.

The problem that followed was largely due to the French rail service. Here the problem was twofold and the first one was the volume of traffic the system was being taxed with due to the war. Delays were common, even for troop trains, and the actual rails were greatly in need of servicing. This was not due to a lack of resources or trained professionals to fix the rails. The problem was more due to the fact that so much traffic was passing on them there was no time to do so. The schedules demanded by the Ministry of War were unrealistic to begin with and largely for this reason French Rail officials were unwilling to take any section of track out of service for something as mundane as routine maintenance.

The other reason for the railroad's involvement in this is simply that almost all the lines in Northern France converge on multiple points in the environs of the Parisian Metropolitan Area. For many provincial French soldiers, a trip to an army camp or the frontlines was the very first time they had actually seen this jewel of French culture known as Paris. Given the stories that were now circulating, for a great many of them it was simply too much. This certainly proved to be true for many in the 401st Infantry who found themselves stuck on a train platform for six hours.

In more normal times the men of this regiment could have traveled from Orleans to Nancy in half the time that they were just sitting on this platform doing nothing. They would also have been riding in cars with seats instead of the box cars they had been shoved into. It was summer so there was very little ventilation in the cars and despite the wishes of their regimental commander, there was no way to keep them in the cars while they were delayed in Paris. There was very little wonder that these men were restless, having just completed their basic training, and all the while they sat in a spot that gave them a view of the top of the Eiffel Tower. There was more than a little chatter about going to see the rest of it.

This chatter remained idle but by the sixth hour on the platform several men with vendors carts showed up on a nearby platform. These men were selling cigarettes and snacks. As it happened, they were also some long-time deserters who specialized in selling such items to other deserters who were fresh off the train from the front. The leader of this little band had been a sergeant, and this meant he knew how to talk to the troops. He seemed to hold much sway over the fresh conscripts that were drifting his way in dribs and drabs to purchase his smokes. What this former Sergeant was also selling was advertising for a collection of Bordellos and Salons that gave him a kickback for every patron that dropped his name.

Naturally, the green troops had been told they were restricted to the one platform but the fact that they were walking over to the next one to purchase cigarettes had been largely ignored. It turned out to be a mistake because once that invisible line had been crossed, combined with the monumental tales from the deserter/merchant, it was not too long before men were slipping away from the railyard and searching for entertainment. When their train was given the green light to leave, their officers were horrified to discover that nearly three quarters of a battalion of men had left. The regimental staff was even more horrified to learn that a good number of the men who had drifted off were also officers.

Had the regiment actually handled this in the normal manner, that of downplaying the problem, it is likely that this incident would have been swept under the rug. The problem here is that their colonel was looking at the end of his career and decided to handle the situation on his own. The result was an empty troop train leaving for the front that would not go unnoticed in Nancy. That alone would send chills up the spines of the General Staff once they learned of it. The other problem was in Paris itself. The colonel quickly rounded up some of his more dependable officers and sergeants as well as some of the local military and civilian police. He then began a hunting expedition for his missing men. It was an impossible task in a city filled with uniforms and given the fact that more than a few of those wearing them were not authorized to be there, it was a potentially dangerous task as well.

Now all of the factors were coming to a head. The sudden appearance of authority hellbent on their mission alarmed a great number of deserters and began yet another rumor mill that uttered a single word that tingled spines. That word was decimation. This convinced a good number of deserters to flee the city and many of them did not attempt to go back to the front. There were also any number of deserters who were both panicked and found they had no place to retreat to. These men were armed, and it was inevitable that some shooting would begin. Once that line was crossed the citizens of Paris had reached their limit. More than one mob was reported to be roaming the streets, looking for stray soldiers and hanging them from lamp posts.

By the time that the streetlamps should have been lit, it was too dangerous to do so. It did not help that another German bombing raid hit the city as tempers were already flared. The bombs also did nothing to quell the sudden violence as these riots began to grow. Political agitators, who had been waiting for just such an event, helped fan the flames and added fuel to the fire. Still despite the widespread violence, like in any riot, the majority of the citizens did not participate. Most of them were staying home and hoping not to become involved in a war that had suddenly appeared quite literally at their front door. For most of these people, there was only one question on their lips, "Where is General Revenge?

The Georgia Effect

While the plight of the average Frenchman left them with the perception that their national leadership had abandoned them to a degree, the exact opposite was true across the continent where Boulanger's main ally, Czar Nicholas II, was unwisely trying to give the impression that he was everywhere. From one end of the empire to the other there was hardly a street corner that did not have a poster of his face plastered on a building wall. If Nicholas had only known what people were saying about these posters, he might have had them all removed. Many of the posters had been up since the start of the war and nobody had thought to replace them. They were faded, worn and peeling at the edges and a good number of people thought them a perfect metaphor for the state of their empire.

Of course, much of the criticism that has been heaped on Nicholas is not so much unfair as it is missing the point. Nicholas was not an evil man that wished to make people suffer and if what the evidence suggests is true, he would not have known how to do so had that been his goal. Nicholas was very disconnected and not just from his empire. He seems to have had a very skewed picture of reality in general. The simple fact was that his army was winning, he knew it and assumed all was well as long as this remained the case. He only dealt with his internal problems when they blew up in his face and the very first incident of this was in Georgia.

While Nicholas was aware of the fact that he had bandit problems in much of his empire, up until now he had treated them as minor affairs best suited for local police. This is perhaps the reason why in a place like Georgia it got out of hand. The local population had no love for the police and found themselves far more sympathetic to the bandits. After all, as one man reasoned, "The bandits only rob me occasionally while the police do it on a daily basis." The validity of this observation is debatable but what is not is that people did deal with the police far more than the bandits who were now calling themselves rebels. The Tiflis Governorate had been hated before the war and their enforcement of domestic war policies was even more so.

None of the success of the rebels would have been possible had it not been for their leader, Joseph Jughashvili, who was now being called in the newspapers 'Tiflis Joe.' His nickname was a good example of exactly how effective Joe was. It also demonstrates exactly what kind of war he was fighting. All sources point to the fact that it was Joe who personally coined the nickname and that he put a great deal of thought into it. The name suggested and conjured up images of someone sitting on a throne in Tiflis when in fact Joe could not go anywhere near there without being arrested. The people inside of Georgia knew the truth but elsewhere in places where it really mattered, they did not.

There is also another aspect of the name that is even far more important. Jughashvili had to do more than invent his persona, he had to get it into the papers and the fact that he did is far more substantial. Russia's official press was state-run but that did not mean they could ignore things that began showing up in foreign newspapers or in unofficial handbills which were very common in Russia at the time. Once the name and story were out there, the state-run papers had to deal with it, and they botched the job horribly. Their articles seemed to be more aimed at appeasing their emperor than reporting information. They never seemed to catch on that the horrible things they said about 'Tiflis Joe' were only making him more popular with the population at large and more important not just in Georgia.

The real problem was that Nicholas was now believing the lies of his own propaganda machine that was at best incompetent to begin with. He felt he had to deal with this 'rebellion in Georgia' even if his own advisors tried to explain that this was a minor affair. His cabinet did have a point in that the collective actions of the bandits were militarily negligible. In fact, the single biggest action taken by Jughashvili was robbing a train in the Caucus mountains. Their haul had been the equivalent in today's value of a little over five hundred dollars, most of which came out of the pockets of passengers.

Still, Nicholas had a point and for once one can argue here that he was actually right. What is crucial to remember here is that the situation in Alaska had to be on his mind. The battle of Forty North appeared to be concrete proof that St Petersburg had lost control of Russia's North American colony. Now Georgia was up in arms and there were reports of incidents flooding in from all over the empire. Nicholas felt that it was time to deal with these traitors. The practical significance of the rebellions was not as relevant as the fact that everyone knew these things were happening. Given that logic, reasoned Nicholas, people had to see their emperor acting in the name of law and order.

One has to wonder why Nicholas felt comfortable enough to open up another front on his own nation and particularly when the military was already stretched too thin. The answer to this question was simple enough because at the time Russia was un-disputably winning the war. While things were not going as well as hoped in the Balkans, the situation was still under control. While there had been no decisive victories in the far east, it was clear the Japanese had been soundly halted. The most important of fronts, at least to Russia, was Poland and here there was no question about who currently had the upper hand.

Field Marshall Waldersee had been caught preparing to launch an offensive of his own and as a result his troops were not prepared to defend the ground they held. The Russians caught them by surprise and two months later it looked as if Prussia was about to fall. After that, the road to Berlin would be wide open and Nicholas could see that light at the end of the tunnel. When looking at it in his shoes, it's understandable why he thought this was a good time to begin putting the empire back together.

So it was, that the army was told in no uncertain terms they would maintain order in the empire. What Nicholas did not understand when he issued his decree was exactly what kind of operation he had just told his general staff to perform. Soldiers are generally not the most political of animals but in the case of the Russians this was not entirely true. They understood enough to realize that they could not do civil pacification missions with the kinds of conscripts their army was primarily composed of at this point. If a man is ordered to shoot at his neighbors, more times than not he will throw down his gun and flee or worse yet join his neighbors.

This meant using what was left of Russia's professional peacetime army. Currently those men were in Poland and driving on Konigsberg. This was the reason the generals argued against these orders, but Nicholas would hear nothing of it. That's why the Russian General Staff appointed a cavalry general, a man by the name of Alexander Samsonov, to command the pacification operation. They gave him some troops and then washed their hands of it. This would prove to be not just one mistake but many.

Lake Geneva

Even the war had not stopped all dialogue going on between the Allies and the Entente. There were always issues that needed to be discussed and could be worked out peacefully enough and for this reason there was a good bit of unofficial chatter between the belligerents. The majority of this conversation was happening in the most convenient place for most of the warring nations, Switzerland. The resort town of Lake Geneva had been a diplomatic favorite before the war and continued on after the onset of hostilities as if there were no war at all.

It was quite common to see prominent citizens of antagonist nations sharing dinner and social activities at Geneva, so very little attention was paid to one more. Many of the men who met here were actually personal friends no matter what their politics and nationalities were. This had been the sight of the negotiations for the sale of the island of Cuba which directly led to the war and some of the delegations were still around in 1901.

One of these men was an unofficial representative of the United States Government, who had decided to wait out the war in Europe. He was a business magnate and in adjusted dollars quite possibly the richest man that America had ever produced. He was responsible for the Standard Oil Monopoly that would in years to come put him squarely at odds with the sitting US President, but at this time Roosevelt was asking John Davidson Rockefeller for a favor. This was in late March.

At the time that Rockefeller had left for Europe, he had considered himself officially retired from business. He had been spending his time playing philanthropist and when his personal friend and a political benefactor, Elihu Root, had asked him to head up the Cuban delegation it seemed to Rockefeller as a patriotic duty. The problem now was that Root was dead and Rockefeller had about as much use for Roosevelt as did John Hay. Still, given the nature of the meeting, Rockefeller agreed.

The man he met with was the 4th Earl of Grey, Albert Henry George Grey, who had recently recovered from a shrapnel wound he received in Rhodesia the previous year. Grey was on his way back to South Africa where he would eventually take command of a reorganized army. He had been asked by the ailing Salisbury, personally, to take on this unofficial mission. The truth was that even if the real Prime Minister did the asking, the choice of Grey had been a compromise of the entire cabinet and the final straw in the matter was the simple fact that diverting Grey's travel through Switzerland would be very inconspicuous. The choice would prove to be a mistake.

Grey and Rockefeller did not hit it off very well. Grey was born into the aristocracy and his counterpart was the kind of man that he was taught to look down on. Grey made no effort to hide his disdain. Grey was also a radical liberal and he enjoyed both a good brandy and cigar. Rockefeller, on the other hand, was very religious, did not partake of alcohol or tobacco and found Grey equally offensive. Their one and only discussion over evening dinner went nowhere. One would think that these two men could have set aside their differences considering the general subject of their discussion, that of world peace. They did not have any more communications on the matter, and it was laid to rest until early summer.

The only reason any dialogue on this matter was revived at all was simply because Roosevelt would not give up on it. There were many in Roosevelt's cabinet that thought the idea treasonous. Again, even some of his own supporters were uncomfortable with the idea of talking this deeply with an enemy that was still not defeated. Theodore argued back that unless they knew what concerned the enemy, they had no real idea where to strike at him. This gave the President's plan some merit, but it took the capitulation of Canada before Roosevelt felt confident enough to make another move. He was already prepared to do so when the time came because Theodore had already dispatched his personal friend, William Howard Taft, to

Switzerland not long after the Rockefeller dinner fell through.

Roosevelt was confident that the British would come to him after the loss of Canada and he was not completely wrong although the first contact did not exactly come from London. There was another man in Geneva who had been sent there specifically to open a dialogue with the Entente and his name was Woodrow Wilson. He would be the first man who came calling on Taft and while Taft had no instructions to talk with the Confederate States on this matter, he did not see where there was any disadvantage in doing so. Taft had spent a good many years being the unofficial ambassador to the CSA, he understood how to talk with them, and he knew Wilson personally.

Even more important, and the ultimate reason why Wilson was in Switzerland, was that he knew both Taft and Roosevelt. Wilson had dealt with both men extensively during the Langley Mission just prior to the war. Taft had to recognize that if Wheeler had sent Wilson here then whatever the man had say must be serious. What Taft did not know was that Wilson's presence here was far less than it seemed. Wilson had not been Wheeler's choice to head up this unofficial mission. Wheeler had asked none other than the former President of the Confederate States, James Longstreet, to travel to Geneva and open a dialogue with the United States.

Since March, Wheeler had become aware of the Rockefeller dinner and while he had no idea what had been discussed there, just the fact that Britain and the United States were talking was disturbing enough. The fact that Balfour had not bothered to inform Richmond of this communications was even more so. That was why Joe Wheeler put so much importance on this mission and wanted to send the one man he saw capable of handling the situation and that man was not Woodrow Wilson.

At the time Longstreet was in ill health and living in an Atlanta hotel. His longtime family home, a hotel in the small mountain town of Gainesville, had recently burned down and a new structure had yet to be built. While living in Atlanta, Longstreet was often visited by the junior Confederate Congressman and former aide, Woodrow Wilson. The two men had long conversations about the future of their nation and Wilson expressed many concerns that he could not do so in public. As it turned out, these were some of the exact same concerns shared by Longstreet. While the former president was in a position to speak out on them, he was simply weary of politics at this point and had no desire to become embroiled in another controversy.

That is perhaps the reason why when Longstreet rejected Wheeler's request, he suggested Wilson should be the man. Of course, naturally Wheeler knew Wilson very well since Woodrow had also served him as an aide. Wilson also had extensive diplomatic experience, knew Roosevelt personally and had much experience as a litigator. This last reason is most likely why Wilson and Taft could talk to each other so well. They were both lawyers and understood each other's language. What neither man could get past at this point was that there was really not much to say. The war had reopened a good many wounds and made some new ones. It had yet to settle the real issues between the two American nations and at this point there seemed to be little that could be compromised.

The simple fact was that the concerns of the two warring nations were quite valid. Each nation was a threat to the other and both sides felt they still had the upper hand in the war. Despite a pleasant series of talks between the two unofficial representatives, and a very earnest desire for peace, they simply found that it could not happen as of yet. It was only after the British representative showed up that the Roosevelt Administration began to pay attention to the talks. The main reason for this was because no one in Washington knew who this man was, and it concerned them that Balfour would send such a fellow in the first place. This man's name was David Lloyd George.

If Canada had convinced the American administration of a need for some kind of dialogue, it had made such a move for the Salisbury Cabinet absolutely essential. The fallout from the loss of Canada was still being felt in London and there were even calls in the House of Commons to disband the current wartime cabinet. Balfour was able to hold off a vote, but he realized that the dove faction was gaining steam and he had to do something to head this off. He never really thought that the Geneva talks would go anywhere but what better way to disarm the opposition than to bring one of their emerging leaders into the fold, give him a seemingly important but do-nothing job, and get him out of the country. The Geneva mission seemed perfect. A recommendation from Chamberlin was all that was required at that point, and George was on his way to Switzerland.

George, also an attorney, found his talks with Taft to be somewhat frustrating. Both men tolerated each other even if they did not hit it off as did Wilson and Taft. Their conversations took on more the tone of what they were, that being litigators who were arguing a case. George also found that steering a ship was very different from advising the helmsmen. He was smart enough to understand that despite his desire to end the war tomorrow, this could not happen if Great Britain found itself with a peacefully sinking ship.

That was why not long after their talks began both men realized exactly what Taft and Wilson had, there could be no peace until something else happened on the battlefields of the world. Only when someone had a strong enough hand could they negotiate and currently despite the reverses and successes of both sides, nobody had this. What they did not know was that what they were looking for was coming and quicker than any of them thought possible.

Le 'Etat C'est Moi'

As the conversation between the US and the Allies had slowed down to the point that Taft thought he might actually do little more than enjoy the resort town he was staying in, events would quickly dictate otherwise. It is also an interesting testimony to the nature of speed of light communications that Taft was informed of the developing situation in France by Theodore Roosevelt who was still back in Washington. This is rather ironic given that Taft was much closer to the situation since he was sitting in Switzerland. It is relevant because such a circumstance could have never occurred in previous wars or even in the world of diplomacy.

It was such a development in technology, primarily the telegraph, that created the ability for world leaders to manage situations in real time when they did not even realize they were doing so, and thus helped contribute to the start of the war. It is easy to say that men, such as the Salisbury Cabinet, were only doing something that seemed commonsense, that of answering a telegram from subordinates on the other side of the planet, when what they were really doing was issuing orders outside the normal channels of diplomacy. Three years later, Theodore Roosevelt was doing the exact same thing with one important difference, he saw the relevance and understood exactly what kind of capabilities it gave him. He equally realized that others would not share these insights because up until now they had not really shown any signs of it.

Politicians, like everyone else, used the telegraph liberally but they also took it for granted. Most people of the time thought of it as little more than some kind of 'fast mail.' That is not to say that embassies and state houses did not have their own telegraph feeds, that diplomats did not use ciphered codes, or any of the other high technology of the time. Yes, they did their best to take advantage of the new technology which had been around for almost a half century at this point. What was not happening was more in the human mind. All the little gadgets in the world will not help your message if what the message says is trying to accomplish something that could be if the technology did not exist.

What is not certain is if Theodore realized this was exactly what he was doing, fully exploiting the technology. Given his lack of writing on the subject it is quite possible that he did not and was only reacting to another reality, that being his lack of faith in John Hay and the US State Department. That was most certainly part of the reason that one of the first people Roosevelt contacted upon the onset of the crisis was Taft. Ironically, as much as Roosevelt and Hay despised each other, in this circumstance Hay would eventually have to be brought into the fold. It would be this situation that prompted Theodore to send a host of new telegrams and would rapidly get a former President recalled to the White House.

The reason for former President Robert Todd Lincoln's arrival at the White House was mostly due to the conversations that Roosevelt and Hay were having in the upstairs office that is now named after Robert's father, the Lincoln bedroom. Lincoln was met at the door by one of Roosevelt's kitchen cabinet, his former regimental commander, Brevet Brigadier General Leonard Wood. Lincoln recorded that he was shocked and horrified by the state of what he referred to as 'my old house.' The White House was currently undergoing a serious renovation and there were easily more workmen there than staff and soldiers combined.

Lincoln was the last of the little group that Roosevelt was calling the 'pre-war conspirators' that he could find on short notice. The fact was that some of these men were dead, but the majority were simply too far away for the time being. Theodore now found himself needing these men since Hay had informed him of the behind the door diplomacy that the US had been involved in with France. The most important result of this cloak and dagger was of course the ascension of Georges Boulanger to the Presidency of the Third Republic. Up until now Roosevelt had been completely in the dark as to the depth of US involvement with General Revenge.

It was a great stroke of luck for Roosevelt, that Lincoln mostly lived in DC where he owned a modest townhouse on K Street which most people know rather well since it is now a highly visited museum and popular tourist trap. This meant that of all the men who had been involved in the Boulanger Affair, Roosevelt had the only two in the US who truly knew the entire story. John Hay was naturally one of them, but the problem Theodore was having was that his chief diplomat was being too diplomatic. Hay was picking and choosing his words very carefully.

The relationship between Lincoln and Roosevelt was entirely different as well as the fact that Lincoln was in a position, that of being retired from politics, to be open about his past dealings with Boulanger. Lincoln quickly spilled everything and now the key pieces of Roosevelt's plan were starting to come together.

The basic problem here of course was that Georges Boulanger had lost control of France. The 'mutiny' that had started on the Parisian rail platform had now grown into a general nationwide strike against the government. This is not to say that it was universal but things such as this never are, nor do they have to be. It is also not to say that the people of France were calling for an end of the war. There has been much hay made of this in the post war world and there is no disputing the fact that some did call for ending the war, but the evidence seems to indicate that most people participating in the various strikes, protests and outright riots were just frustrated. If anyone had ever controlled any of this, they certainly did not now. People were just venting and the one thing they wanted above all else, was just something else. It is not clear that anyone in France really had an idea of what they wanted, just what they did not.

Of course, at the time what they most definitely did not want was General Revenge. When it became clear in the Sedan that the local authorities could not control the situation in Paris, Boulanger decided it was time to actually leave his military headquarters. He had been running both the war and the government from the Sedan since the very outbreak of hostilities. Many have pointed to this fact as the real key to his downfall. Being outside of Paris separated Boulanger from the very heart of his government and he was never fully informed of situations and attitudes in the heart of France.

Sure, Boulanger got detailed reports but there is always much that is lacking in such bureaucratic dribble which is often boring, too detailed and written with an eye towards finishing the job instead of being thorough. It also cannot convey attitudes and Boulanger's next move certainly demonstrated his lack of understanding for that particular facet of the situation. That is not to say he was entirely ignorant of such things. We do know that Boulanger was a routine reader of Clemenceau's opposition newspapers. It is even reported that he was a fan of his former patron's writings and that he often read Clemenceau's opinion articles with a grin and occasional chuckle. It is quite possible that Boulanger was so used to reading nasty things about himself that he took most of it with a grain of salt. This can be detrimental if you are so used to it that you suddenly do not realize that such articles go beyond the author and are no longer just bitter personal ramblings.

This must have been why Boulanger thought he could personally turn all of this around. He quickly boarded his personal military train for Paris. He was urged by his General Staff to send troops into the city to restore order but promptly told his Generals that it would be "of most hazard and completely non-essential." In other words, Boulanger had become completely isolated from even his staff at The Sedan and was no longer listening to anyone. This had probably been the case for some time.

Once in Paris he was met with a troop of lancers, ceremonial cavalry who were wearing their best dress uniforms and riding large white horses. They saved the biggest one for Boulanger and he rode at the head of the column as they ceremoniously and slowly clopped their way towards the Arch De Triumph. It would be there that Boulanger planned on mounting a platform and giving a speech. We have no idea what that speech was going to be because even though he wrote it down on his train ride to Paris, he never gave it to anyone else and the paper has since been lost.

Needless to say, this bombastic parade was the last thing anyone in Paris wanted to see. Many of those who were partaking in the disturbances were either soldiers or veterans who had already been to the front. This display of military splendor would not work on them and even had the opposite effect. While Boulanger's column was never shot at, it was attacked before ever reaching the platform that was being erected for his speech. Most of the assailants hurled food at the dictator and in the end this actually seems more fitting given the state of supplies in France at the time. Boulanger was forced to retreat, and as it became clear to the crowds and spectators, the mob only grew in size and ferocity.

Before Boulanger even reached his train car, the Council of Deputies were calling for new elections to appoint another President. This particular act makes it clear that there were those in Paris, and Clemenceau was most definitely one of them, who were just standing by and waiting for Boulanger to make a mistake. The riot he caused most definitely fell in that category. Of course, he may have still salvaged the situation, but Boulanger made yet another mistake. Once out of Paris he stopped at the first military depot that allowed him to hook up the telegraph in his train car to the network. He promptly began issuing orders to marshal troops required for the "restoration of order in the capital." These orders fell on deaf ears, and in fact, tipped the balance against him.

While Boulanger might have misread the Paris riots, his Generals had not. As Boulanger fled the city, they were already receiving telegrams from men like Clemenceau, all of them giving detailed information about the emergency meeting of France's elected body of legislatures. Still, the Generals were not entirely sure where they fell on the situation, but it was the one telegram from Boulanger that decided the matter for them. Even if they had first suggested using troops to quell the riots, they now understood the nature of these riots and realized that ironically Boulanger had been right not to try. Now they chose not to do it and the fact that Boulanger had reversed himself was the final straw.

If French troops marched in too French cities, the Generals reasoned, then it was likely that the entire army would fall apart in short order. The war would be lost, and the Germans would once again occupy the nation and the consequences of that would be devastating. That is quite possibly why the Generals chose to not only quit listening to Boulanger but did not even bother to reply to the man who had led them for almost twenty years. When Boulanger finally realized that no one was listening to him and that his military support was rapidly evaporating, he did the one thing left that he could do, he fled to neutral Belgium.

Naturally, it goes without saying that this was a disaster for the Entente. In Washington, Roosevelt was faced with the realization that all of the military gains that had been made in the past three years were about to come unglued in a matter of hours. Roosevelt handled it by doing what he was best at, studying the situation in detail and digesting the facts in such a way that he could devise a workable solution to the problem. This was mostly in the form of grilling the men that he had discovered were largely responsible for putting Boulanger in power in the first place.

Roosevelt might have been angry that he was now stuck with a mess that had been created by other men long before he was even in politics. Now that there was anarchy in Paris, it was most definitely possible that the details of US involvement in the Boulanger Coup could come to light. If that were to happen then France might very well feel as if they had been betrayed and manipulated by their wartime friend, as indeed they had been, and seek a separate peace with the Allies. This might even happen if the information remained buried. Such a situation would leave the US at the mercy of the Royal Navy and suddenly both the US and Russia might have to sue for peace on Allied terms. This situation was unacceptable to Roosevelt.

Oddly enough it would be the most junior man in the meeting, General Wood, who gave a very practical solution to the crisis. This suggestion would become US policy and it was, "If we put one man in power it seems to me that the solution here is, we do it again." Hay and Lincoln were at a loss as to how they possibly could. After all, they had spent decades working on the Boulanger conspiracy and now they had only days at best. It would be a man not in the meeting, William Howard Taft, who offered a solution. More specifically, that solution was living two doors up from his rented Geneva lake cottage.

The Road to Smolensk

German war plans had always condensed the entire Russian front, one of the largest of the war, down to a few critical points. The German general staff reasoned that if these points could all be captured then Russian capitulation was all but assured. While this might sound like the perpetuation of some kind of comical German stereotype, the truth is that it was the methodical and detailed madness of the German General Staff of this period, that treated their war plans like they were some kind of elaborate clock, that were largely responsible for most of the facets of the stereotype that we know today. In fact, the German staff officers of that time were the very source of making the comparison of wars and clocks. They were not entirely wrong.

There is an old joke about a man getting on a German train and not hearing the stations being called at each stop. When he questioned the conductor on the matter he was answered with a question about the schedule. The German conductor was told by the man that the schedule reported the train's arrival at his departure station at eight-oh-five. The Conductor then told the man, "So, at eight-oh-five just get off the train." The man did and he was where he should be. It was the late nineteenth century that developed this mentality and it went back to a lesson that the German's had learned in 1870. It was that war runs on rails, and rails run on clocks.

The fact is that the Germans invented what today we generically refer to as a General Staff. Each nation has invented and reinvented names for these collections of organizations but prior to just before the Franco-Prussian War of 1870 it simply did not exist anywhere. After that war, and by the time of the Great War, every nation had one. The Germans had proven quite spectacularly that they were indispensable. A lot of the reason for this development in warfare is the emergence of the railroad.

While most people are familiar with cartoons of buffoonish generals pushing pins on a map safely in the rear and know the glorified names that these organizations call themselves, what has never truly come to light is exactly what the General Staff is. To put it simply, the General Staff was the point at which someone applied Scientific Method to warfare, with a liberal helping of bureaucracy. In other words, the Germans had not just married the idea of critical thinking skills to warfare but, they had inadvertently done the same with middle management. While this has been the butt of many jokes, it has also proven itself crucial to the implementation of large-scale warfare. It would be entirely impossible to do so without it.

The early versions of these systems had some serious flaws and this war brought almost all of them to light. This war would also be the seed of how these flaws got fixed. While I have already mentioned the lack of attention paid to tactical details, such as those used by Jesse James and his "Confederate Foreign Legion" at Roswell, there was still another aspect of warfare that was also being equally ignored. That was at the Operational level.

For the uninitiated student of the military who may have heard these terms but are not quite sure what they mean, it's really quite simple. Unfortunately, the military like any other profession tries to hide its inner workings by inventing a vocabulary that makes the job look more challenging than it really is. That's why most people hear these terms, apply their own meaning, and then water down the term until it sounds stupid, at which point the military makes up another word that sounds better until the cycle repeats itself. The truth is that while the terms might change, the job itself has remained largely the same for all of human history, the basics of which are the three levels: strategic, operational, and tactical.

Your strategic concerns are quite literally the big picture. This is the level where you consider resources, your entire military force, and how to channel these resources to get the most out of them. On the opposite end of the scale is the tactical. You could almost say that strategy is why you do things and tactical is how. In the middle of this is the art of operations and it is a curious blend of both. The operational commander has to blend the why and the how into a cohesive plan on the battlefield proper.

While there had been some thought put into tactical planning, mostly revolving around the new technology that was available, primarily long ranged rifles that were easy to reload, as we have seen it was nowhere near what it needed to be. At the same time, the operational level of warfare had not only been completely ignored but, this ignorance was defended vigorously by most professional soldiers. The time honored 'rules of war' had worked, and no one had seen where they should change. The actual terminology for these rules differs from one nation to the next but they can all be summed up to the most common which is most often called 'economy of force.'

While the professional soldiers were not completely wrong in their stubborn insistence that the economy of force was still quite valid, they held to it so rigidly that it can be easily argued that the problem was in the very definition of the term that they had all come to universally accept. It was such religious conviction that they had completely forgotten why they were doing it in the first place. They kept doing it even after there was plenty of evidence that something about it had gone horribly wrong. They were also at a loss to fix this.

Traditionally, a commander on a battlefield has only a few basic considerations and this is where the economy part comes in. His troops have to have beans and bullets and they all have to be at the same place and time when they meet the enemy. The commander, Robert E Lee, was an exceptional operational commander even if his strategic thinking has subsequently shown a great deal to be desired. Lee was successful because he was good at scattering his forces when they needed to be and pulling them together when it was at the most critical of moments. Why scatter your men in the first place? It's the beans and bullets part. An army is more than just the guys pulling the trigger, it needs all of those people in the rear to keep them in good enough shape to pull that trigger.

As anyone knows, a packrat is a horrible person to take a vacation with. They tend to load down your car with everything imaginable. That makes the trip uncomfortable, increases your time on the road, only to find out that most of the junk that they packed is useless when you reach your destination. Military supply people are habitual packrats, and they have a very similar effect on armies. The way around this is to scatter your forces into smaller groups that makes living off the land practical because the more land you cover, the more supplies you will find.

This tactic also solves the problem of insufficient roads. Anyone who has driven in rush hour traffic knows that the more people trying to use one road, no matter how well regulated, always results in a traffic jam. It is something that city planners have become intimately familiar with in more recent times.

They had thought that the answer to rush hour traffic jams was to simply add more lanes. What they discovered was that no matter how much you widen a road the traffic always fills it to beyond capacity. Governments spent large sums on figuring this out when all they really should have done was ask the army for they have been intimately familiar with this problem since ancient times.

Of course, Robert E Lee did not invent this operational tactic. He was a student of Napoleon who did not invent it either. Napoleon was a student of Julius Caesar and while we do not know if Caesar invented it, his campaigns in Gaul were the first recorded uses. We also know that by 1901, with the widespread use of railroads, a lot of these commonsense practices had fallen into disuse because many commanders on the field were overly relying on the technology that they saw as the ultimate answer to victory, even if so far it had failed to deliver.

What they were concentrating on at the front was just that, concentration of force. This is the flip side of economy and was best described by Napoleon when he said, "God is on the side with the biggest battalions." It also comes down to what Nathan Forrest said, "Get there first with the most." Unfortunately, this was not working in 1901 and again everyone was at a loss to explain why. With the advantage of hindsight, we can easily see what the problem was. The simple fact was that they were not achieving concentration. Nobody was gaining numerical superiority because, again, they were so tied to those rail lines that it narrowed their front of advance.

Physical reality dictates that one piece of solid matter can only occupy one point in space at one point in time. Soldiers are solid matter and in order to get the kinds of numbers that are required, a minimum of three attackers to one defender, to make a successful attack one needs a broad front to accomplish this. You would think that with all of the space on the Russian Front, one of the two sides might have used this advantage, but up until 1901 nobody had thought to try. They had spent too much time working on their rail schedules.

That situation was changing though. There had been divisional commanders who were clamoring for the authority to do just that, using the space to maneuver more effectively. Most notable of these men were two by the names of Erich Ludendorff and Paul Von Hindenburg. While Hindenburg was already a divisional commander at the start of the war, Ludendorff had risen rapidly to that position after its start. He had also spent some time working as Chief of Staff for another key figure, that man being Helmuth Von Moltke. This connection would serve to be crucial in the months to come.

The Moltke name was already well known in the German military when the war began. That is why our Moltke had picked up the moniker 'The Younger.' His uncle, with an almost identical name, had been largely credited with the defeat of France in 1870 and gained something of a hero status in Germany for the last part of the 19th century. Even so, The Younger had yet to really prove himself in battle. His personality did not help matters and strangely enough this is not because he was stereotypical of what we tend to think of as German Field Marshalls today. Those men somewhat earned the stereotype of being loud and bombastic while Moltke was most often described by those who knew him as a quiet and unassuming introvert who liked to read.

By 1901, his lack of volume was no longer a handicap and more of an asset. The simple fact that Waldersee had failed was enough. The term 'the road to Smolensk' had become something of a joke amongst German enlisted men. They had been hearing that jargon since the start of the war and three years later they had not gone much further than their own border. Smolensk was the last fortified point before Moscow. It was reasoned that once Smolensk had fallen then the primary Russian manufacturing center was no longer defendable. So far, Waldersee had not even managed to capture his month one objectives like Warsaw.

Now that a surge of Russian conscripts was threatening to break the entire front, Waldersee was recalled. He and the Kaiser were reported to have had a furious argument, although we have no idea what the two men said since no one else was in the room. It was recorded by others, however, that the volume of this argument, which echoed past doors and down the corridors, was more than enough to give us the gist of the conversation. In the end, the fact that Waldersee left that room and retired from service is all we really need to know. The only question after that was who would replace him?

Today, the ascension of Moltke seems to be set in stone. It looks like one of those decisions that was so automatic that we rarely even question it. The truth of the matter is there were any number of men vying for Waldersee's job. The two most prominent of these were not Moltke. The first was, of course, Schlieffen who wanted a posting that would allow him to prove some of his theories. Unfortunately for him, the ferocity of the French offensive had required that he do the one thing that the General Staff had told him to avoid, and that was ask for more troops. Wilhelm was tired of listening to Schlieffen, at this point, anyway. He often called the general an 'old nanny,' and the Kaiser probably did not see himself dealing with Schlieffen on a daily basis anyway.

The other man vying for the job probably had the best chance of getting it. He was Waldersee's deputy commander and had personally overseen the fighting around Warsaw. His name was Hans Beesler and he has been largely forgotten in history. His record has been commented on as mostly unremarkable and at the time it must have seemed that way to the Kaiser as well. Still, there are those that say Beesler had proven himself a competent commander. They also like to point out that he was senior to Moltke and that it was Moltke's political ties to the Kaiser that ultimately got him the job.

How much of this is really true is open to speculation. What we do know is that when the Kaiser stomped out of that office, where he had just dismissed Waldersee, it is likely that he was tired of dealing with bombastic generals with giant plumes of feathers on their helmets. There was Moltke, who had been sitting quietly behind a crowd of military men and had just sat down the book he was reading as he waited for his Emperor. The Kaiser obviously took notice and probably remembered that this quiet man had been at the heart of any number of key suggestions, one of which was a movie they were supposed to be screening later that evening.

The Kaiser looked at the faces of those around him, then stomped right up to Moltke and told him, "You are in charge. Bring me victory." Wilhelm said nothing else to anyone. He left, obviously still enraged and nobody wanted to bother the man because of it. Moltke later recorded that he was as surprised as anyone and was at a loss for words when all eyes shifted to him. This indecision would not last long. In this matter Moltke was very much like Roosevelt in that he had been at the heart of the German war effort long enough that he already knew the facts. He also had the presence of mind to quickly summon others who might have some idea about what to do with the situation.

That was why two days later Moltke had a meeting with most of his front-line commanders. He listened to them instead of making speeches, then he retired to his private quarters where he read and thought. A few days later, some serious reorganizations were implemented and key among them was that both Ludendorff and Hindenburg were raised to corps level commanders and given a virtual freehand in what they did. In less than a week, this would prove decisive.

Disjointed Empire

If the war at large was reaching a crescendo, it was nothing compared to the political campaign that was being waged in Richmond amongst the halls of the Confederate Capital. It had been no secret that the Confederate States had been looking to expand its borders since before the war. Most thought, and this included elected officials as well, that this expansion was limited to the island of Cuba. It was a non-controversial issue since any idiot could look at a map and see that the island colony was a security problem unless the Stars and Bars flew over Havana. The deal with Spain, largely brought about by the coming war, had included a good deal more than just the one possession. When added to the territories seized by the Confederate Navy since the commencement of hostilities, the Confederacy suddenly found itself with a small empire on its hands. This did not sit well with some.

One might think that there might be moral objections to controlling an empire and this was particularly true of a nation that had itself once been a colonial possession (to Great Britain) and then followed by being a virtual colony in all but name (to the United States). If any such objections were raised, then no one bothered to write it down. Most of the anti-imperialist sentiment was centered in the more conservative Home Party and their basic objections seemed to have been rooted in paranoia over the power that it gave the national government in Richmond.

Most of the elected officials of the time were old enough to remember having been citizens of the United States. They remembered the problems that came with territorial expansion and the unequal power that it gave the Federal Government in Washington. This had been one of the leading causes of the American 61 and now some of these hard-core states' rights politicians believed they were seeing the cycle repeat itself. There was no small amount of dissension in the Confederate Congress and much of that was directed right at President Wheeler. There were even some congressmen who accused Wheeler of using the war to become a dictator.

While the more radical claims grabbed headlines, they were largely ineffectual in budging Wheeler. If that was all there was then he may not have had a problem, but the fact was that not all of the points raised by the HP were without merit. Many claimed that the Confederacy simply could not afford to administer such far flung territories, let alone defend them. As the war dragged on, the last part of that was even worrying Wheeler as he watched the Royal Navy sit passively in their ports and do little to nothing. It was no secret in Richmond that British support was critical to such a venture and by this time that was no longer a foregone conclusion.

This basic problem led to some serious changes in Confederate Foreign policy. Prior to the war, the Office of State had been one of the most non-controversial agencies of the CSA. Foreign policy was very simple for the Confederacy and it all revolved around keeping the British happy in return for support. By the summer of 1901 it was very clear that no matter what the outcome of the war the world was about to be a very different place. The Royal Navy was no longer going to be the undisputed master of the ocean and the Confederate Navy was going to have to pick up a great deal of the slack.

At the time it was not very well known but it was in the shadows of these realizations that the Confederate States began looking for new allies. This would eventually lead to cementing relationships with nations that were already friendly to the CSA such as Brazil. It would also bring about new overtures between the CSA and Mexico. Despite Mexico's dismal performance in the war, anyone who knew anything about economics of the time were well aware that the Mexican Empire was a rising star. With a little help, Mexico could become a serious power to deal with in North America. Richmond was more than willing to offer them assistance.

These moves were logical and with only minor grumbling about various treaties and overtures to Mexico, there was little in the way of opposition. Of course, none of them did a great deal in cementing Confederate policy in the Pacific Rim and it was here that several diplomatic moves drew fire, and not just from Home Party politicians, but even from London. A great deal of this had to do with the fall of Canada which had caused a political fire storm in places like Australia and New Zealand. The anti-war factions in these commonwealth nations were slowly leaning towards becoming anti-imperial and Richmond began courting these factions with an eye to the future.

All of these would become future issues in many nations, but none would become more crucial than when the Confederate State Department began seriously talking with Japanese officials. The Meiji Government itself seemed largely closed off. They were polite, seemed receptive but at the end of the day not much came of the talks. The same was not true of the Japanese military and in particular their navy. While the civilian government of Japan was playing a wait and see game, their military leaders had almost reached a unanimous conclusion about the postwar world. If Japan were to stand on her own two feet, she would no longer be able to rely on Great Britain or anyone else for that matter.

Despite this realization, it was still obvious that Japan could not proceed completely alone. Western nations still had too much that Japan required. That was why the view amongst many Japanese Generals and Admirals was that if Britain wanted to treat them as children then just maybe what they needed was a friend who wanted a partner instead. When it became obvious to the Japanese military that the Confederacy was making some very friendly overtures, they became instantly interested.

Back in Richmond, while this seemed a logical move, there were many who were not so happy with the idea. They saw Japan as being too far away to be of any use and while nobody said as much, there were hints at racial problems as well. To our modern eyes this might seem almost a childish opinion and yes, it is very out of step with our modern world, but the concerns of many Confederate citizens had practical implications that could not be ignored at the time. One has to remember that racial beliefs of this time were not just confined to Europeans, everyone held such attitudes.

While it is unfair to constantly pigeonhole the Confederacy into one giant racial issue, because that was far from being the case, the simple fact remains that this problem that they inherited from the United States made governing the CSA very complicated to say the least. The racial issue almost always surfaced and even in issues that seemed to be completely unrelated. As long as times were relatively calm, the issue that involved nearly a third the population of the Confederacy proper, was largely manageable. By 1901 times were anything but calm, and the situation was growing worse.

The white population of military age was being wiped out and even in 1901 this had become obvious to the power elites of the CSA. They said nothing about it and indeed it was a tightly held secret that required no enforcement because those in charge were afraid to even mention it. It was also a problem for down the road and not the only one that was being faced in 1901.

The Bureau of Colored Affairs, the national agency that managed the CSA's free black residents and slaves, had been going through a quiet transformation as the war went on. At one time this agency was the model of efficiency, and despite what some modern authors have claimed, it was also largely fair. The reason for this is easy to understand when you consider that Richmond had no desire to give a third of their population a reason to revolt. This did not mean that the CSA was prepared to grant equality to blacks because there was no mention of that at all. What the BCA did do, while maintaining the laws that made blacks second class, was curtail excess that can occur when one human owns another.

Prewar records demonstrate that they were quite effective at this job. The BCA even had its own court system, which was largely confined to free residents, where it was possible for a black man to sue a white man. There was also a criminal division that enforced such laws as those against rape, and by 1901 this did extend to slaves. While modern human rights advocates tend to ignore such things, these laws were enforced without exception but of course you have to remember why. The white leaders of the CSA were not stupid, and they realized the implications of a revolt. They certainly had no intentions of granting citizenship to anyone with dark skin. This is why the foreign policy and the new territories suddenly became a problem, because for the most part there were almost no white people living in any of them.

It would have been impossible for Richmond to enforce the pre-war employment laws in places like Cuba, or anywhere else in the Caribbean for that matter. Blacks living in most Confederate States were restricted on how much they could earn per year. The national government set standard rates for everything from factory workers to barbers and while these were not absolute, they were more or less the standard. There were a few exceptions because there were some black residents who became rich in the CSA, but these were all extreme exceptions. These laws also restricted the jobs that could be held by blacks, both slave and free resident.

In the island nations of the Caribbean such laws were completely impractical. At the time no one even knew exactly what percentage of the population of Cuba was black, but no one doubted it was substantial. On the islands that were former French possessions the black populations were easily more than ninety percent. The people who lived under Spanish and French rule might have been subjects, may have been largely impoverished but they had also lived under laws that were very different from those of the Confederacy. Neither Spain nor France actually had any racial laws, and the peoples of these new Confederate possessions were not so receptive to the idea. These people also contributed to many technical professions and to suddenly fire them all would cause the economies of these islands to collapse.

Naturally, this would cause a problem back home for the CSA. Many realized it would only be a matter of time before certain black residents would question why it was that they could not work certain jobs for certain pay when in Confederate Territories it was perfectly normal. This was far from the only problem that the sudden Confederate Empire would cause. The question of what a race was would ultimately have to be questioned as well. At the start of the American 61 this question seemed as simple as black and white. In a nation as insular as the Confederacy, there were no shades of gray. The sudden inclusion of people who were neither white nor black, would shake up the very notion of race, and once this kind of thing happens it is a small step to wonder about your justifications of suppressing others of different skin colors.

On this subject it has to be noted that this was far from the first instance that the CSA had to deal with this issue. They had been dealing with native tribes and Hispanics since before they were even a nation. While these people were not considered white, they were also not suppressed by racial laws as were the slaves and former slaves. Since natives were only a majority in Sequoia and the Hispanic populations were largely confined to Texas, these exceptions to the entire black and white view were swept under the rug and ignored by the national government. Unofficial social customs took care of the rest in the individual states. With the acquisition of former French and Spanish territory, this could no longer work.

The real sticking point was also one of the furthest away. The population of the Philippines was very cosmopolitan and had been so for a very long time. Not only was there a Hispanic segment, mostly descendants of Spanish colonists, but you had the various Polynesian populations that were far from homogenous. If that was not enough, there was also a substantial Chinese population that lived in the archipelago, mostly in the environs of Manila. None of these people even took the new Confederate officials seriously when the race laws were brought up. At the same time, CSA authorities were having their own problems because none of the racial laws seemed to fit the situation that was Manila, let alone the countryside of Luzon or the thousands of other little islands they now ruled.

There were many in Richmond who were not happy with that situation but there was little they could do about it. Initially, they were also able to divert attention away from the race issues because in nearly all of the new Confederate territories they had a more immediate problem. Most of them had been in various stages of revolt against the Spanish and now that the flags had changed, these rebels showed no signs of quitting. All that had happened was that Confederate marines and sailors were now replacing the Spanish garrisons who were more than happy to leave.

Many of these rebels knew that the Confederacy had a much larger war on its hands. They also knew that it would take time for the CSA to militarily establish themselves. There was also quite a bit of unrest that stirred people who had otherwise avoided the rebellions. It has been noted, by the leaders of two of the biggest rebel factions in Cuba, that black recruits rallied to their causes in large numbers after the first Confederate warships showed up in Cuban harbors. They would not be the last in the new territories. These rebellions, no matter how downplayed they were by Richmond, sent quiet shivers up the spines of white Confederates in every state.

At the time that was a future concern for President Wheeler. His big shock came when the Philippines were formally handed over to the CSA because not only had he inherited a war of rebellion from Spain, he had in fact inherited two. It was well known in Richmond that there was a rebellion of Spanish speaking Christian Filipinos on Luzon and they were also aware that several other islands were in various stages of revolt. Wheeler's people had already contacted many of the rebel bands and were confident they could work out a deal that would eliminate much of the trouble. What they did not know was that the people of the largest of the southernmost islands, Mindanao, had no interest in peace. They were further horrified to learn that the Islamic Morro had been fighting everyone, neighbors and colonials, for longer than anyone could even remember. To date the Morro war still stands as the longest running known conflict in the history of mankind. Now the CSA had no choice but to pick up where the Spanish had left off.

Needless to say, none of this was particularly popular in the CSA. The young nation was now in charge of administering large populations of people who did not share the same skin color as the dominant ethnic group of the CSA. These people had their own histories, prejudices, and most were only vaguely aware of those held by their new masters. A lot of these people were already in armed rebellion and on the streets of Richmond, Atlanta, and New Orleans white citizens of the CSA read about these far-off places and wondered, how long until it spread right to their own front door?

The situation would only get worse and before the summer of 1901 was out. The reason why the citizens of the CSA could worry about their new empire was because up until now they thought the big war had largely gone their way. They had mostly stopped the invasion of their nation by the US. They had taken territory away from their enemies and their navy had performed spectacularly. Even the most pessimistic never thought they could lose. These naysayers had been mostly talking of not winning and that is not quite the same thing as losing. When the United States began to turn its full attention to its lost southern states, that would begin to change. Then came the disasters of the kind that no one could have ever predicted. The literal winds of war were about to change.

The Sixty-Ninth

Historians have never really paid the due attention required to a certain and nearly anonymous US Army captain by the name of Woodbury Cane. This is despite the fact that we have ample evidence of his contributions in the presidential library of his personal friend, Theodore Roosevelt. Cane was not some military genius nor was he some extraordinarily brave hero that rushed enemy guns and sacrificed himself for his men. I could go so far as to suggest that this is why no one has paid him very much attention, but I think it most likely that his true contribution to world history is just so obvious that it looked perfectly normal and hence was forgotten for just that reason. It was simply taken for granted.

Cane's primary contribution to the war was the very unheroic act of being at the right place and time while he happened to know someone worth knowing. If you will recall, Cane rejoined the US Army for reasons known only to himself, was not very well received, served on the Canadian Front and along with a good number of other soldiers who were considered a problem by their commanders, was sent to New Mexico in what was little more than a political dodge by General Shafter and the War Department. This move was to have unforeseeable consequences that would prove to be a game changer. While it is true that Cane was only one of many involved in the subsequent developments in Albuquerque and not even a primary player at that, there is still the issue that without his pen, nothing would have ever come of it.

The men that had been moved to New Mexico from Canada had not arrived in time to be integrated into the command structure of the department when the serious fighting took place between the US, Mexico, and the CSA. It was largely over and done with before any of them were even assigned barracks. Just before General Pershing was reassigned by the new President Roosevelt, he had only just gotten around to figuring out what to do with these men. The war had kept him busy and they had been overlooked by the General's staff. Since

Pershing left before he could do anything, these men were forgotten about once again, despite the fact that there were a substantial number of them, all doing nothing or you might say doing nothing official.

The reality was that none of these men had taken a vacation, but this was all of their own initiative. While most of these men had been thought of as problems while serving in Canada, the truth was that a large majority of them were just like Cane. The majority of them were not derelicts even if it is clear that there were a few. Most of them seemed to have been men who fell into the category of being too bright for their bosses and as a result were generally feared as potential replacements by those very same commanders who were more than happy to get rid of them.

Of course, that was only the ring leaders. Men like that tend to gather a group of core supporters and fortunately those supporters were all transferred as well. Once they were in New Mexico, and virtually ignored, they suddenly had a chance to compare notes, form their own improvised command structure and begin doing things that they wanted to do. Most of this activity revolved around 'fixing' what was wrong with the prosecution of the war, and not on the level that Generals are used to dealing with. All of these men were seasoned veterans and they all had ideas. They all knew that sooner or later someone would remember them, and more fighting would follow. Collectively they vowed to do it right this time.

Cane and his conspirators had some unexpected help from the most unlikely of sources, that being Confederate General Jesse James. Many of the survivors of the ill-fated Roswell Garrison, that was crushed by James, found themselves in Albuquerque, and before all was said and done Cane and his fellow officers had interviewed every single one of them. While no one in the Confederacy had thought to even question how James had done the impossible, and very few in the US as well, Cane and his conspiracy took an active interest. They actually drew up a timeline on a school chalkboard and pieced together the events of the battle. They figured out what James had taken nearly three decades to develop and incorporated many of these ideas into their own plans.

All of this would have come to nothing had it not been for Cane and his correspondence with Theodore Roosevelt. By the time that Theodore became president he was already aware of what was going on out in Albuquerque and he hardily approved. One of his first orders directly concerning the war was to have these men turned into an official command. The war department did not even protest and seems to have ignored the order as much as they could. They did not see the utility in doing this, but they did not see the harm either. General Shafter personally shrugged the order off and passed the buck until a minor functionary on his staff had them dust off the regimental standards of a deactivated unit from the Canadian Front. The excess soldiers in New Mexico would become the 69th New York Infantry, even if most of them were not even from New York. That was the last time that anyone at the War Department would pay them any attention until late summer of 1901. They were considered so unimportant that no one even thought to assign them a regimental commander.

That was just fine by the men on the ground who had already formed their own chain of command largely by the force of personalities. These men began to train and develop new tactics that today have become almost standard in small unit drills even if in truth many of these techniques were not invented in Albuquerque nor were they even modern. A good number of these tactics had simply fallen into disuse over the past century as technology had changed. The collective army heads of the world had thought that such things were now antiquated given the new weapon systems. What the 69th did was incorporate the new with the old, and just like James, developed tactics that were both effective and quite lethal.

This was not all that happened in New Mexico and the repercussions would spill out and begin to impact other things like ripples in a pond. Again, this was largely thanks to Woodbury Cane and his letter writing campaign with a man who had the power to literally grant wishes. One of these requests by Cane resulted in an unexpected visit from a man by the name of John Browning. He was a firearms inventor and had been one of the main driving forces behind the revolutionary US Army battle rifles. By the time of the war, Browning had fallen on hard times. Ironically, and fortunately for Cane, Browning's problems were similar to that of the men he visited in New Mexico.

The main problem that Browning had was that he was just too ahead of his time. It also did not help matters any that he also happened to be a Mormon, most of whom were looked on with a great deal of suspicion after the American 61. Even so, Browning was just too good at his job to be ignored and that was how he wound up working for Winchester until barely a year before the war he had a falling out with the company over some of his designs. Winchester had too much invested in their lever action technology and Browning had an idea for a system that would not only render it obsolete but the bolt action rifle as well. Today we refer to this system as the gas blow back which channels the excess gasses from the barrel to push back the bolt of the weapon. This eliminates the need to cock after firing and is the method by which truly rapid fire can be achieved. It was not entirely new in 1901 as the system had already been successfully employed in machineguns but Browning was ready to take his innovation to the next logical step. He was quite alone in this desire.

Things had gotten so bad for Browning that just before the war he was shopping for companies that might wish to manufacture his patented shotgun design. The only taker he could find was a company in Belgium, but the war had put an end to that deal. Cane and Roosevelt offered Browning an opportunity that he jumped at with both feet. The 69th was looking for a rapid-fire weapon that could be used to clear trenches. Browning had a design that just might fit the bill and he simply called it the Browning Automatic Rifle.

The BAR was not exactly a machinegun, but it was not a battle rifle either. It had a high rate of fire but a limited magazine capacity which could not really be increased because to do so would mean eventually melting down the barrel. Indeed, the barrel problem had been the main obstacle in developing a truly man portable light machine gun, something that would eventually be solved by the Germans with the simple and practical solution of just changing barrels when one got too hot. The BAR was never intended to be this so that was not exactly a problem that Browning had put much thought into. What the BAR did become was the forerunner to a class of small arms known collectively as the 'assault rifle.'

Cane and his fellow junior officers were impressed with the prototype that they eagerly test fired. It seemed to be the perfect weapon to fit their needs. Cane wasted no time reporting this to Roosevelt who was equally eager to pursue the manufacture of this weapon. Unfortunately, not a single BAR would ever reach the 69th, nor any other army unit. The mass production of the weapon called for an entirely new industrial process that no factory in the world was set up for. This did not stop Browning who would go on with support from the White House to produce a small quantity of his revolutionary weapon and almost all by hand. It would prove crucial elsewhere but that is for later.

The 69th had its finger in a few pies that went beyond small arms. Another technological development they inadvertently ushered in was a weapon system that was so simple, logical and straightforward that it is a wonder no one had thought of it before then. In many ways it was easily comparable to the tactics they would put into use because the weapon itself was anything but new. The hand grenade had been around for centuries but again due to technological developments it had fallen into disuse. Grenades, or any hand thrown bombs, prior to this war had been largely homemade devises and improvised. The only truly mass-produced bombs used hand lit fuses to detonate the explosive. These weapons were not practical on the modern battlefield nor was the modern industrial complex set up to manufacture them.

When the 69th examined the tactics of the Confederate Foreign Legion, one of their primary observations was the use of dynamite to neutralize strong points. As it was discovered, James and his Missouri rebels had hand thrown bundles of dynamite into machinegun nests. They did not use standard fuses though. A burning fuse was simply not reliable enough to do the job. James and his men had wired the explosives to electric detonators. The drawback to this tactic is obvious since the dynamite has to be rigged with a wire which in turn degrades the range and accuracy of the man who has to throw it. It also requires time to set up and the carrying of bulky equipment.

Fortunately for Cane, one of the many things that Roosevelt became introduced to, once becoming president, was a horde of inventors who were clamoring to get money for their ideas. Several of these inventions proved to have working plans for a practical hand grenade. Roosevelt sent many of them to New Mexico and it was found that the most practical of these was a design based on yet another tried and true technology that had fallen by the wayside, the percussion cap.

The idea was both simple and eloquent. A spring driven hammer was held in place by a spoon. Once the spoon was released, the hammer would strike the ignition cap which would set off a short fuse. This in turn would detonate the explosive which was encased in a metal shell. It was not a perfect solution, but it was a workable one. It also had the advantage of being easy to produce. The US had more explosive compounds than it knew what to do with. Stamp machines could easily be tooled to make the spoons. Springs were a common part of many consumer goods and last but not least the metal shell was little more than a round metal ball, easily manufactured. The primer cap was even easier since there were still gun manufacturers who were making them for civilian weapons. The first crates of these new weapons reached New Mexico by March of 1901.

The President would travel to Albuquerque that same month and personally view a demonstration of the grenades in use as well as the new tactics being employed. Roosevelt was so impressed that when he returned to Washington his first order of business was to command Shafter to expand the program that Cane had been working on.

Shafter was rather reluctant to devote any
resources or manpower to something that he
had almost completely forgotten about.
Roosevelt would hear none of the protests from
his military and he got his way. By August, the
US would have 12 specially trained 'Bull
Moose' battalions organized into three
regiments and ready for deployment. As events
would prove, this would not come at a more
critical juncture.

Angels and Germans

When Theodore Roosevelt was fully
prepared to unleash his war machine on the
Confederate States, it was with some sense of
irony that it was a move that was calculated to
impact his friends more than his enemies. It was
also because of this factor that his top Generals,
Pecos Bill Shafter being chief amongst them,
were not so happy about the timing. The
American General Staff was becoming very
cautious at this point and they had good reason.
The last three years of war had been taxing and
the fact that nothing had gone as planned bred
a certain sense of apprehension in the war
rooms of the world.

Even the victory in Canada did little to offset this pessimism. The US had finally achieved a solid win, but the cost had been higher than anyone had ever dreamed possible and it took three years when the original prewar plans had predicted only six months to a year. There was also the peace factor that had to be considered. Sure, the US had won the campaign but given the peace that Roosevelt had negotiated, many were starting to ask what had really been gained? There were some in the US who were quietly fearing that a Boulanger styled coup might take place in Washington as well. The first signs of a revolution were already rearing its head in Russia so these apprehensions seemed well founded. In the summer of 1901, it appeared to many as if the Entente was becoming unglued.

Naturally, the only man who did not seem to think this was Theodore Roosevelt. At the time there were many who saw his unbridled optimism as the delusions of a wannabe savior who was rapidly sinking with his ship. There were many, John Hay chief amongst them, who thought that he was just insane. The old members of the administration, those who were primarily loyal to the late Elihu Root, were even beginning to openly talk of a conditional surrender to the allies. France was on the verge of capitulation. There were riots and demonstrations in the Russian capital of St Petersburg where troops were being used to suppress their own civil population. If the stronger allies of the US fell how long could they hope to hold out against the combined weight of the Allies?

Where many were seeing disaster on the horizon, it was quite clear that Roosevelt was seeing these events as an opportunity. Once again, Theodore was calculating more than just the all-out military card that had so far proven useless. When his closest friends would even express their own doubts, Roosevelt pointed out that despite being decapitated France was still in the war. He also understood that this was the key because Roosevelt understood that France's motivation was plain and simple fear. No matter what any Frenchman thought of his own internal politics, the one thing they could all agree on was that they did not want to be occupied by Germany once again. Roosevelt had been playing on that fear since Boulanger had fled to Belgium.

Of course, the problem faced by Roosevelt was that this fear would be useless as a tool if no one thought that the Entente could win the war. By the late summer of 1901 it was certainly starting to look that way, even if the reality was something else entirely. The fact was that the French Army was still holding its own against the Germans. While France had failed to make any substantial gains, the reality was that Germany had not either nor was it likely that they could. Without invading the low countries, something that politics now rendered impossible, the front was simply too narrow for either army to advance. Unfortunately, most people are not military experts and the situation looked grimmer to the average man on the streets of Paris.

What civilians do in times of war is largely the same thing they do in times of peace and that is they pay attention to the news. In 1901 this was largely the domain of the newspaper and just like with the modern media, their primary objective is to make money and not report the actual news. Exceptions sell papers and with the war an everyday constant the headlines were not about that. In France, more people were reading about the endless conflict going on in their own government and those who were vying to be its new ruler. The fact that their own leaders could not reach a decision about who should be the head of state was just one more indicator to the French population that the war was all but lost. It reminded too many of the dark days of 1871, just after the collapse of the French army at the Sedan.

This situation was only aggravated by the aerial bombardment of French population centers. Despite the best efforts of the French military, the bombings were becoming almost constant. The German aim was also getting better as time went along and some secondary effects were beginning to show. The fact that French Zeppelins were doing the same to Germany was unimportant. The average Frenchman only seemed to care about what was happening to him and to hell with Germany. It was summed up by one newspaper column who said that "The skies are no longer safe for angels because now only the Germans are brave enough to tread."

This appraisal of the situation was not exactly accurate. The truth was that no one really controlled the sky even if both sides were using it. The zeppelins were unstoppable, but this was true of everyone's zeppelins. Again, this was not a great concern to the people who had to cower in their basements every night. They wanted something done about the bombing and if that meant surrender many were talking openly of this. With no coordinated government effort to combat these rampant attitudes, France was slowly slipping out of the war.

It was with this in mind that the Roosevelt administration placed a top priority on urging the Ministry of Deputies to appoint a provisional leader. The problem was that the French were literally getting in their own way. The factions, which were divided between Communists, Republicans, Monarchists, Bonapartists, and even a few Anarchists, all had their own ideas, all saw this as a golden opportunity, and worst of all were relatively equal in numbers. Some of them were also as afraid of each other as they were the Germans.

The situation seemed to be a hopeless mess and one that was rapidly spiraling out of control as France began to descend into revolution. This is what Roosevelt waded into and he did so in the guise of a three-hundred-and-fifty-pound man by the name of William Howard Taft. The American diplomat did not show up in Paris unarmed. He came with the influence of his president, as much cash as was required, and a certain twenty-three-year-old

French exile by the name of Victor Jerome Fredrick Bonaparte.

Known as Napoleon the 5th by his supporters, Victor was something of an uninspiring little man with only one true attribute, that being his name. His supporters, who were not even unified in the Bonapartist camp, had been trying to crown Victor ever since the abdication of Louis Napoleon. Very little had come of it and Victor had been living in self-imposed exile, as well as relative obscurity, ever since the rise of Boulanger. In the spring of 1901, he also happened to be living two doors up from the cottage occupied by William Howard Taft, at Lake Geneva. Victor had moved there just before the war from his more permanent home in Belgium for fear that one side or both might invade his host country.

Victor was an odd choice for Roosevelt to back. Everyone who knew him, and this included Taft, had reported the boy to be dull, unimaginative and less than charismatic. Taft even advised against it in at least three separate telegrams. John Hay, who had met the boy on several occasions, was absolutely livid over Roosevelt's decision and refused to talk to the president for weeks. That was not a situation that Theodore was upset over even if once again people thought him insane, irrational and reckless.

The fact was Roosevelt was playing a bigger game and not one that was readily apparent to everyone, including his own secretary of state. Roosevelt had long since proven he was no fool, only everyone kept forgetting this fact. Theodore had consumed every scrap of information, about the situation in Paris, that he could find. He had come to one inescapable conclusion and realized that the man he needed to reach was not named Victor Bonaparte. The real guy with the power was named Georges Clemenceau.

The problem with directly approaching Clemenceau was not that the man might be unreceptive and in fact he showed every sign that he was willing to have a dialogue with Roosevelt. The problem was that Clemenceau's hands were tied due to the constant wrangling of multiple factions inside the Ministry of Deputies. For Clemenceau direct communications with Washington could possibly label him as Revanche, particularly given Clemenceau's past dealings with Boulanger. If this were to happen then Clemenceau's support could evaporate in an instant and France would likely descend into anarchy, because as far as Theodore could see Clemenceau was the only stabilizing factor there.

Napoleon V was Roosevelt's offering to Clemenceau for a possible solution to the problems of both France and the United States. France was in dire need of a name like Bonaparte, but no one was willing to put up with the usual pains that went with it. With this in mind suddenly Victor's liabilities became something of an asset. Because he was so young, seemingly dull, and less than leadership material, this also made him very unthreatening. Of course, none of this would have helped Victor ascend to the throne of a new empire had it not been for the real asset he was bringing to the table and that was American dollars. It was the combination of the two that made him a serious contender.

There was also another factor that was sitting in the way. Most of those sitting on the left side of the Ministry did not want to do away with the Third Republic. Georges Clemenceau was first and foremost amongst them. This is where Taft became worth his weight in gold. Many thought him, due to his size, quite buffoonish but this was very much an illusion. Having served as the representative to the

Confederate States, Taft was now a seasoned diplomat who was quite used to dealing with issues of a very sensitive nature. He was also an expert litigator and he put both of these skills to use in Paris. No one knows if the idea originated with him or Roosevelt but as Taft would later express the problem came down to one side wanting a new empire and the other wanting the republic. What Taft would offer them was a compromise as he asked the logical question, "Why not have both?"

The idea was one that Clemenceau could live with or at least until the crisis had passed. As he would tell many in his camp, "this plan has worked in Britain for decades, why can't we do it here?" The basic idea was that Victor would be installed as a figurehead emperor while the real power would rest with a President and the Ministry. Of course, both Victor and Georges had very different ideas about how that would work but for the time being it only had to appear to work and the rest could be figured out later. It was a workable solution to many but unfortunately it was not the main sticking point with a radicalized few.

There was a sizable faction on the left that realized the implications of such a compromise. Not only did it offend their political sensibilities, but they also knew that this new compromise government was nothing less than a referendum on the war itself. Most of these men were openly calling for an end to the war, suing for peace on any terms short of a German occupation. If that meant crossing the Americans and Russians, then so be it. At the time this seemed like a realistic option to many because the Germans were losing in Poland. It was thought that the Kaiser would gladly offer an acceptable peace to France if it meant freeing up troops to hold back an almost unstoppable Russian onslaught that had even gone so far as to threaten Berlin. Then came the news from Prussia.

The new German front commander, Field Marshall Von Molkte, had pulled off what seemed like nothing short of a miracle. His forces were on the verge of absolute defeat when two if his key corps commanders, Hindenburg and Ludendorff, accomplished something thought impossible. Not only had they stopped the Russians cold in an obscure forest just south of Konigsberg, but they had counterattacked, surrounded an entire Russian Army group and completely destroyed it. The Russian army now found itself with considerable gaps in its line, entire divisions deserting en masse, and a sudden reversal was quickly developing that might spell the end of Czar Nicholas and the Russian war effort.

In Washington most saw this grim news as the beginning of the end. In the White House, for those around the President, it looked to be yet another example of Roosevelt's growing insanity. When Roosevelt was informed of the collapse of the Russian Front, Theodore stood up, pounded his fists on his desk, gave his famous toothy grin and proclaimed, "God bless that Molkte! By Jingo, if he was here, I would pin a medal on him! Bully!"

Leonard Wood recorded this incident and even he admitted to being at a complete loss as to why his longtime friend would be so happy about the news. Roosevelt did not waste any time explaining himself, but instead he went right to the telegraphs in the next room and began firing off a storm of paper to Paris. His most important wires were his first direct communications with Clemenceau. He asked the man bluntly, "What do you think your chances with the Germans are now?"

Clemenceau was equally direct in his response, "I am afraid desperation grows by the hour."

Roosevelt replied quickly, "We can still win this war."

Clemenceau was not so optimistic in his response, but he did manage to ask, "And how do you propose to do this?"

Again, the American President kept it short and blunt, "I do not propose anything but to show you." In a flash of the dramatic he did add, "You can either choose to dare mighty things or be amongst the poor timid souls who know neither the sweet flavor of victory or the vile taste of defeat. The choice is yours."

At that point, Theodore went from telegraph to telephone. He called across the river to Fort Lincoln and talked directly with General Shafter. His words were recorded in both Shafter's writings and several journals of those who were present at the White House. Roosevelt eagerly told his top soldier, "General, it is time. Let all hell fly and God be merciful on those poor souls who stand in our way because I don't expect you to be."

The day that every Confederate citizen had lived in fear of for four decades was about to happen. It would be felt well beyond the borders of the CSA.

Gone With the Wind

Writer and journalist, Margaret Mitchell, was not quite a year old when her mother wrapped her in blankets and fled their home during the early hours of a warm August morning. Mitchell's father was an attorney, and her family was prominent in the social circles of Georgia. Her cousin was none other than Crawford Long, the man who took away pain during surgery. She had other relatives that were of more local prominence, including the Hollidays who founded the first dental school in Georgia. Despite her high standing family, Margaret would go on to outshine them and all for an event that it is doubtful she even remembered.

It is often suggested that what she did remember, and what inspired her tale that became a bestselling novel, was the fact that she grew up without a father. Eugene Mitchell was a local civic leader and for that reason after sending his family away, stayed behind to help organize a citizen firefighting brigade when it was clear that Atlanta's professional firemen would not be enough. No one is exactly sure when or how Eugene died. All that is known is that both he and most of the men with him never came out of the blazes they rushed into.

The firestorm that engulfed the city of Atlanta, a vital Confederate rail hub, was neither accidental nor unique. The series of bombing raids that were carried out by the US Air Corps in early August have remained controversial on both sides of the border. Strangely enough, they were firing up heated debates in the upper echelons of the US government before they were even carried out. They are also the reason that the name Roosevelt is a much hated one in Georgia and other parts of the CSA. Before the war, Roosevelt was viewed as a somewhat sympathetic figure given that he had relatives who lived in close proximity to Atlanta. By late summer of 1901 this image would be changed irrevocably, and it would also cement a split in the Roosevelt/Bulloch family, forever.

What the raids truly were once you get past the emotional scars were the first strategically effective bombings of a large-scale nature. Ever since the Kingston raid, which was tiny in comparison, the US Air Corps had grown from less than twenty Zeppelins to nearly a hundred. This had all happened in a few months' time and it was largely thanks to one man, a car engineer by the name of Henry Ford. Ford had heard of Astin Green's production innovations that were being tried out in Mexico. He saw merit in them and where Astin had to fight to make every little improvement, Ford had a near freehand when he found himself employed by the war department.

At first Ford got into some serious hot water over his assembly line ideas. Months went by and he had not produced the first Zeppelin. The reality was that Ford had spent his time gathering materials and then organizing both them and his labor force. When they went into full production the calls for his resignation abruptly ceased. Of course, Ford was not running the only production facility. There were three others and before all was said and done all of the US Zeppelin factories were using his organization charts. Word of this filtered up to Roosevelt who then promptly sent Ford out to Kansas where he was tasked with doing the same thing to the new US airplane shop.

The US raids were aimed more toward short term operational goals than in the past. Prior to the use of incendiary bombs, the zeppelins had shown a distinct weakness in their ability to effect combat operations on a tactical level. Most of their targets were factories and most of their bombs were seldom hitting the target. The solution to this problem was fire and once testing proved that the munitions could adequately combust, several key factors were realized. The single biggest of these was that the zeppelins no longer had to hit their targets. This led to a theory that would be put to the test in Atlanta, Nashville, and Chattanooga.

The real targets that the US Air Corps were salivating to wreck were the Confederate rail lines. These targets proved to be beyond their ability. To hit an actual track was once compared to trying to hit a cotton thread with a penny from fifty feet in the air. There were attempts at bombing railyards, but they met with only limited success. Even the bombs that hit the actual yards did not cause enough damage and most of it was easily repairable. The military effects were negligible but now the US aviators realized that they did not have to directly hit their targets to render them neutralized.

The first bombings that occurred in Atlanta were some of the quietest that the citizens could remember. They were so quiet in fact that few paid them any attention at all. What they did not know was that these initial strikes were only meant to light the targets for the real payloads that were still on the way. Some fires were started but they were minor, and the fire brigades were dispatched to handle them. Some of them had already been put out when the next wave of Zeppelins came in. They had no problem finding their targets because they were no longer trying to spot buildings from high above. These fully loaded bombers were targeting the initial fires set by the advanced wave. Every wave that came after that had a much larger target to hit.

The attacks were not universally successful. Nashville was actually the primary target in the first round of attacks. Much of the city burned to the ground but as near as US military intelligence could determine, the rail system and the military stores there were only partially affected. There were also later attacks on the steel center at Birmingham, as well as one attack against the nearby Confederate Zeppelin base. Those attacks would utterly fail but at that point it no longer mattered.

The destruction of Atlanta and Chattanooga, despite being secondary targets, did more than make up for the failures at

Nashville and Birmingham. It has been theorized since the war that weather and terrain were largely responsible for the successful US Strikes. Chattanooga sits in a valley that is quite literally bowl shaped. Atlanta sits on the threshold between the cooler continental weather and the more tropical Gulf of Mexico climate. This ensures that Atlanta is usually breezy and for what the US Air Corps was trying to do those were perfect conditions.

The heat of the firestorms fed on themselves. In Atlanta it was aided by the breeze while in Chattanooga the unusual terrain reflected the heat right back on its source. In both cases the rising hot air formed a low-pressure center that began sucking the surrounding oxygen right into the rising column. This not only made the fire hotter, as it began to reach points where it melted metal, anyone who may have found some degree of safety from the heat found that they could no longer breath. It is all too likely that this is what happened to Eugene Mitchell.

It took three days of continuous bombing to create the firestorms but once they were going the zeppelins could no longer even approach the cities due to turbulence. That was just fine at Fort Lincoln because they no longer needed to, the mission was accomplished and after seeing the first pictures of the effects Shafter was eager to begin a full bombing campaign. The only thing stopping the complete destruction of the Confederacy was the fact that the US had used up its entire supply of incendiaries. They could be replaced but that was going to take some time. That's why Shafter had never put all of his money on the air campaign. It was only the beginning of an all-out attack.

The effects of the raids were also long-lived. Rail traffic from the eastern part of the CSA to its western states came to a complete halt for several weeks. The rail lines were thought to have survived the firestorm, but this proved to be an illusion. The heat had warped rails and not only had it turned the ties into useless charcoal but the beds themselves proved to have been weakened. Service was only resumed by diverting traffic to alternate tracks that took them a long way out of their way.

As for the damage in the cities, no one even knew where to start rebuilding. The rails were an obvious priority but in order to fix them you had to have workers. After the attacks, there were precious few. Nobody knows exactly how many people lost their lives but in the immediate aftermath it might as well have been everyone. Workers tend to skip work when their homes have been burned to the ground and this obviously happened.

Strangely enough, the most important side effect of the bombing was not the direct damage that it caused. It was yet another one of those unforeseeable circumstances that was an indirect result and also one in which mother nature would come back to prove that she would not be outdone by man. One of the very first reactions to the attacks, even while they were going on, was the immediate sortie of the entire Confederate Fleet at Mobile. The CSN had no desire to see their ships caught at anchor with a firestorm raging around them. As a result, most of the fleet retreated to their secondary base at Galveston, Texas. It was reasoned that the further they were from enemy bombers the better. Some were sent to the Caribbean but even a light examination of the records show that these were on scheduled patrols.

There have been many who have criticized this decision since it happened but the reason that the CSN had for keeping their fleet together seems logical enough given the circumstances. The US Navy no longer had the chore of imposing a full blockade of Canada. There was still a blockade of sorts but given that the British were no longer trying to run it, the number of ships required by the US Atlantic fleet had now been greatly reduced. The only thing that was now holding the USN in check was the threat of an attack by the CSN. Of course, the Confederate Navy was nowhere near as strong as the US fleet, but it did not have to be. It only had to exist to do its job.

The move to Galveston would wreck all of that. Less than a month after the move had been completed, the city would suffer a literal shot from the dark that came on them as much by surprise as the US firebombing did in Atlanta. This should have never happened because the CSN's primary operating theater was the Gulf of Mexico and they were no strangers to hurricanes. The CSN actually spent a lot of money studying the storms and had some of the foremost authorities in their employ. Their fatal weakness was that they knew this fact and had failed to heed warnings from similar experts in the new Confederate territory of Cuba. Apparently, the only reason for this was that the men warning them had a darker shade of skin.

This storm occurred before the habit developed of naming them after girlfriends and wives, so we have nothing more to call it than 'the hurricane.' What we do know about this particular storm is that it passed over Cuba and that Confederate Naval Authorities had been alerted to its presence. They also received all the relevant data concerning the storm's path and intensity.

While over Cuba, it is believed that the storm was what we call today a category 3. It was also believed to be turning out towards the Atlantic and weakening. Due to the multiple reports from any number of merchantmen who put in at New Orleans over the following week, we know this did not happen. The storm had actually turned west, over the warm waters of the Gulf, and was gaining strength as it zeroed in on the southern coast of Texas. When the first bands of intense winds and rain struck Galveston, given the reports we now have it is believed that the storm had increased in strength to a category 4 or quite possibly even a category 5.

The city proper sits on what is a coastal barrier island even if the casual visitor might not notice due to the roads and bridges that have been built up in the region. These barrier islands are really nothing more than glorified sand dunes that have piled up over centuries to the point that their tops form narrow strips of usable dry land. While meteorologists had spent a great deal of time studying the winds and rain, none of them had ever considered calling in a geologist so that they could factor in the land equation. The fact was that Galveston sat only inches above sea level and the storm surge raised that by feet. The city was flooded, the CSN shipyards destroyed and a good deal of the fleet right along with it.

Navies generally have one strategy in dealing with such storms. That is always the act of pulling up anchor and getting out of its way. The Confederate Fleet got absolutely no warning at all and by the time they realized this was truly a significant storm and that Galveston Bay would not be any protection at all, it was too late. Some ships did attempt to raise anchor and head for the high sea but by the time they did as soon as the anchors came up the winds would push them towards the land. Some of these vessels would collide; several smaller destroyers would partially capsize. A few more would take on too much water and bottom out in the shallows.

The larger vessels, such as the battleships, would fare the storm well enough. The CSS Alabama clung to her anchor, put her bow in the wind, and managed to escape with only minor damage. The CSS Texas, the revolutionary new battleship, was not so lucky. The destroyer CSS Hawkins had been one ship that pulled anchor when it became obvious that wind and water might capsize her should she remain in place. She collided with the Texas, which might not have been such a big a thing had it not been for the fact that she smashed two of the ship's anchor chains in the process. The only one left that was still holding was aft and the Texas drifted into a position where her superstructure caught the full brunt of the wind. That in turn pushed the Texas harder. The last anchor lost its grip, and the ship was literally blown towards the shore.

It became one of the most sensationalized photographs from the war. The CSS Texas was no longer the terror of the sea and not because she was wrecked. It was because the Texas was no longer on the sea. When the storm surge retreated, the Confederate battleship was sitting in the middle of downtown Texas City, almost a half mile from the water. It dwarfed the wreckage of the buildings around her.

It was an odd sort of disaster for the CSS Texas and also quite ironic because her crew actually fared much better than the ships who managed to remain in harbor. Not a single crewman had been killed in the entire incident. Still, it did not matter. The CSN would eventually get the battleship Texas back into the water. A crew of military and civil engineers would eventually cut a channel from the water, through Texas City and right up under her. This operation would be an engineering masterpiece and it would also be too late. While the damage to both the battleship, and the fleet that she belonged to, was far from totally encompassing, the fact remained that the Confederate trump card had been neutralized. It would take years to repair the damage and the Confederacy's pride would not play a significant role in the war from then on.

Retreat

By the late summer of 1901, for the first time since the very start of the war, it was clear to everyone that something was really happening that was of monumental importance. The problem was that no one, from the man on the street to the highest echelons of government, actually knew what this something was. Breakthroughs had been made but once again, as had been the case for the entire war, the gains by one side were being negated by the gains of the other.

In Poland, the German High Command's long sought-after prize of Warsaw was finally taken. The way it came about was not in the manner that anyone had thought, much to the relief of the city's residents. It had always been assumed that there would be a be a battle or siege and that the Russians would defend every last building of the city. There was good reason to believe this since the Russians had spent the entire war fortifying and stocking the city for just that eventuality. When German Cavalry came riding into the central city, not a single shot was fired. The Russians, with much larger problems on their hands, had simply fled east as fast as they could. They would also leave behind, unmolested, almost the entire stockpile of supplies that had been accumulating for the better part of three years. Ironically, the only supplies to be destroyed were by German Zeppelins.

The heart of the Russian problem had been created by their own monarch, Czar

Nicholas, when he ordered his army to suppress the strikers and demonstrators that were becoming common throughout the empire. Most of the troops that were sent were the core of Russia's prewar regular army and they would be sorely missed on the front. When it came time for one last push against Konigsberg the troops that moved into the line had only been at the front for less than a month and had not even received that much training before they arrived. It was these scraped together conscripts that would run headlong into Ludendorff and Hindenburg's seasoned veteran troops. The Russian conscripts would melt like the spring snow in wave after wave of fruitless attacks.

To make matters worse, the staffs of both corps commanders had reliable intelligence on the composition of the Russian units. Quickly, Hindenburg chose to concentrate his counterattacks on the newer units, blowing huge holes in the Russian line, and leaving the more veteran units sitting next to the newer ones with no other option but retreat. The Russian position disintegrated so quickly that events were happening faster than they could be reported to their higher headquarters and hence the situation became confused and the retreat turned into a rout with no one knowing what units were where.

The Russians did have one saving grace and it was by no efforts of their own. It was the traditional Russian defense that had saved them from Napoleon. In this case it was not winter, but it was rain. That is not to say that some sudden and major deluge fell on the German advance because it did not. It was just the usual amount of precipitation that fell on western Russia every year. It was enough to turn roads not made to handle heavy volumes of traffic into muddy rivers and leave fields as unstable as quicksand.

The weather factor did little to stop the reinvigorated German Infantry who now smelled victory. They marched as fast and with as much spirit as any army ever has in what was a maneuver campaign that would be studied for years to come. Unfortunately, their logistics system could not keep up. Once Ludendorff and Hindenburg began moving away from their rail lines, which became far less dense the further east they went, the more they had to rely on horse and mule for their essential consumables. It was the supply lines that could not keep up and, hence denied the

Germans what could have been a total encompassing victory of the first order.

There was also another factor and it was simply that the Russians were running faster than the Germans could advance. It gave them the commodity they most needed and this was time. The Russian Generals gave up on giving orders and simply began setting up collection points where they could ferret out their troops, reorganize their units, and prepare new lines of defense. They did so with amazing speed but still had plenty of their own problems including supplies. It was even more critical for the Russians because their officers discovered to their horror that many of their retreating soldiers had ditched all of their gear, including weapons and ammunition, as they ran. Now being closer to their own bases of supply, the Russians should have been able to replenish their troops much easier than the Germans, but this was not the case. They had stockpiled too many supplies to close to the front lines and lost most of it when those depots were overrun.

It was turning into a slow disintegration of the front line but in the end, it was not a complete collapse. The Russians still had the advantage of distance and weather and for the time being it was enough or at least it was for

Theodore Roosevelt. Oddly enough for the American President the problem with the Russian situation was not a military crisis but a political one. Theodore stated that, "If Russia could survive Napoleon in Moscow then it could weather Moltke in Smolensk." The real problem was keeping Nicholas on the throne which day by day was starting to look more and more impossible. Again, just like with France, the real problem with that was Nicholas himself.

While Nicholas might be getting in his own way, much like the Council of Deputies in Paris, that was the end of the similarities. Where the French populace had understandable reasons for wishing to continue the war, no matter who was in charge, the same was not true in Russia. The vast stretches of the largest empire on Earth meant that, for most of her population, war and peace meant almost nothing at all. In the cities where the war had impacted lives the greatest, the strongest sentiments definitely did not favor a continuation of the conflict. Unlike in France, there was almost no one who believed that the Germans would one day show up on their doorstep to stay. Germany was simply too far away for most people to contemplate such an event.

This all came down to one thing, Nicholas had to stay on the throne. Unfortunately for Theodore, and it gnawed at him greatly, there was little he could do about it besides send some telegrams of advice, most of which fell on deaf ears. As we now know the Czar considered Theodore to be something of an upstart, a peasant, and decidedly inferior, despite Roosevelt's pedigree. For that reason, Nicholas chose to confine his communications with the American President to official memos between the diplomats of both nations. This was why the telegrams from Roosevelt never even made it to the Czar.

Roosevelt was determined to help the Czar even if the emperor of Russia did not want it. This left Roosevelt with only one real option. His new military offensive against the CSA was already getting underway and it had largely been for purposes of making an impression on France. Roosevelt was under no illusions about it making an impression on Nicholas, however it did not have to. The only viable options, as Roosevelt saw, was that if he could not keep Russia in the war then he would have to end the war before Russia capitulated.

This seemed an impossible task. Theodore walked across the street to the War Department and spent many days visiting the office of General Shafter where they discussed the southern offensive in great detail. In the end Shafter convinced the President that even if the offensive succeeded spectacularly, it could not knock the Confederacy out of the war. In order to do that, as was seen by the war department, they would have to conquer most of the southern states and even with the full weight of the US Army that might take years. One only had to look at Canada as a blueprint.

Roosevelt did not concede defeat, even if he conceded Shafter's points. Once again, Roosevelt realized that the problems they were facing were ones that were largely the trappings of a lack of imagination that was running rampant through the halls of the world's war rooms. Theodore had come to the conclusion that if he could not conquer the Confederacy in time then he needed to wrestle what he could out of them, just like he had with Canada. He had to figure out where their true weaknesses were and use those to bring them to the mat. As he would later tell Leonard Wood, "If we cannot bring them under our thumb then the situation dictates that we must make them yell uncle!"

Fortunately for Roosevelt, the pattern for what needed to be done was already developing in Tennessee. This was largely in thanks to his personal friend, Woodbury Cane, and the much scoffed at Bull Moose Battalions that were largely thanks to his pen. These special operations units were seeing the last skepticism from the US Army. They defied much of the conventional wisdom that was associated with offensive operations. While the Air Corps had begun this offensive with a flash and a bang, the new infantry assault went in with absolute silence. There was no preparatory bombardment and for that matter, there was absolutely no warning at all.

The first waves of infantry crawled out of their trenches under the cover of darkness. They were very small teams that moved along pre scouted lines of advance and once they reached their objectives they waited patiently until just before dawn. Their opening salvo came as a hail of grenades against enemy strong points. The following waves did not advance along a wide front or even spread out, but they moved along narrow paths now cleared of enemy direct fire and were in the Confederate trenches before there was any time to even react.

Even the second wave was not as large as was usual for a standard assault. The conventional wisdom up until that point had been that the more men you tossed at the enemy the better. These groups slipped into Confederate trenches, almost unmolested, and began worming their way along the trench line. This reduced the size of the fight, normally between thousands of men, down to just a handful at any given time. Suddenly the extensive maze of trenches was no longer protection for their owners, they had suddenly become death traps.

The assault teams used flags to mark their advances for covering teams that were located in no man's land. These sharpshooters had occupied shell holes, clumps of kudzu, and any concealment they could find, and their fire kept Johnny Kudzu pinned down beneath the trench line preventing counterattacks on the assault team's exposed flanks. As these multiple assault teams worked their way towards each other, the Confederates found themselves growing more and more compressed and vulnerable to the new hand grenades. Once enough strong points were knocked out, the general assault from the standard US infantry went over the top and advanced against sporadic and weak enemy fire.

The results were several big gaps that formed in the defenses of Fort Bragg and this time the US Army was ready to take full advantage of it. They shoved as many units into the breeches as they could. Again, this was limited by how far a man could walk in a day and compared to breakouts in later wars it was at a snail's pace but a breakout it was none the less. It was aided by the fact that the Confederate logistics system had been hampered by the fire raids. While the front-line units had plenty of supplies, the reserve forces, those meant to plug holes in the lines, were running short. In the end this made the holes larger, but the Confederates were still able to plug them even if it was not as well as they liked. This is where Roosevelt once again stepped in and went toe to toe with his top Generals.

As the situation on the battlefield developed, Roosevelt saw the basic problem and once again he walked across the street to the War Department and began his usual rants. "You are trying to take ground, General," Roosevelt bellowed. "As you have pointed out that is something the enemy has in almost endless supply. Your own figures show that what they are short of is manpower. This needs to be your target!" Once again, Roosevelt's force of personality allowed him to get his way. Suddenly the target of the offensive was no longer the Confederate States, but it was their army instead. Operations were no longer being planned along the lines of seizing land but to actively grind the army of the CSA into nothing. It would not take long before this began to be felt.

The More Things Change

By the time that Taft returned to Lake Geneva, several significant events had unfolded across the globe and he was certain that one or two other unofficial diplomats might come calling on his door. He was a bit surprised that his dinner invitations remained somewhat scarce. What Taft was unaware of was that due to those events David Lloyd George was not even in Switzerland at the time. He had been recalled to London where he was 'consulting' with the cabinet. That was the official story for the unofficial diplomatic mission. There is no hard evidence concerning Lloyd's recall but given that he never actually met with the cabinet, it's more likely that they simply did not want him talking with Taft at that time. Balfour and Chamberlain had more than enough motivation to do this.

Despite the fact that the armies were moving for the first time since the beginning of the war, each side had made breakthroughs at roughly the same time. It was yet another case of balance that left the issue still in the undecided column. It was a fact that all of the national leaders of the time were firmly aware of and for men like Balfour and Roosevelt, it left them calculating the possible outcomes of some very separate theaters of war and guessing as to where it would leave everyone in the spring of 1902. While the Russians were in a headlong retreat it was fairly certain they could rally and hold the Germans once more, even after surrendering a good deal of territory in the process. The Russians had land to spare and for that matter so did the Confederate States.

The CSA was not in quite as desperate a situation as Imperial Russia, but no one doubted that they were quickly headed in that direction. This may have been why Wilson did not seek an audience with Taft in the early fall of 1901. To do so would have appeared to be desperation and the Confederacy still had her allies, although at the time it was unclear how much help they could be. One has to wonder how nervous this was making Wilson and not to mention Joe Wheeler who was back in Richmond. The fact was that Britain was being unusually silent and we do know that Wheeler was reading this as a message from Balfour that basically said, "Don't get any ideas. We are the big kids on the block."

Wheeler had more than enough experience when it came to dealing with his British allies and understood the inner workings of their government, particularly when it came to dealing with his nation. The average Confederate may have had a great deal of animosity when it came to their cousins in the US, but this is not to say that they lacked any for their British cousins as well. Any suggestion that the CSA even appeared to be a British Commonwealth was outright insulting to most southerners and this included Wheeler. That was why the silence and diplomatic doublespeak he was getting was so troubling at a time like this. Wheeler understood it was due to British concerns over the state of their Commonwealth and he wanted them to know that his nation was not a part of it.

Wheeler's assumptions were fundamentally correct. The cabinet was not just concerned about the state of the Commonwealth, they had become quite paranoid over the matter. Oddly enough this was not so much from the noise being made in places like Australia and New Zealand but the silence that was coming from inside of India. The cabinet had completely misread the signs. They were well aware that the Indians now had a position of strength to negotiate from and could not imagine why nothing had been made of this. It made men like Chamberlin see ghosts in every shadow and some serious plans were made for how to deal with a rebellion in Britain's crown jewel.

One might think that this would lead Britain's wartime cabinet to a desire to end the conflict as early as possible, but it had the exact opposite effect. They felt that they now had to pull a clear victory out of the entire mess or India would go over the cliff that they supposed it was teetering on. Anything else as they saw it would leave Britain having to fight another war, if not several smaller ones, after the big conflict ended. At this point, Britain simply was not strong enough to do this and that was particularly true when they considered having to do so without the aid of their German allies. As time would prove the cabinet was completely wrong about a great many things.

That would be in the future and men like Balfour and Chamberlin were not in a position to see that. We have to remember what it was they were calculating at that time. It was simple math and aptly provided by Wolseley and his statisticians at Pall Mall. When the numbers were crunched the situation that they got was this, the Allies could survive the loss of the Confederate States and the Entente would be severely handicapped by the loss of Russia. This put time on the side of the Allies, and if this plan had been followed through, the war would have definitely continued into 1902 and possibly even 1903. Given the poor shape of the world in the Fall of 1901, there is no telling how much devastation this would have caused. Fortunately for the world the cabinet was wrong about three very key facts.

Most of it had to do with the seasons and weather. Wolseley's people were well aware that most operations inside of Russia were highly dependent on the weather. The rains had already slowed Moltke down to a snail's pace and once the snows set in, he would come to a complete halt. They never considered the more moderate winters in the Confederate States where cooler weather was a blessing and not an obstacle. This meant that the United States, no longer hampered by Canadian Winters, could keep their operations at a maximum tempo while German troops remained huddled around fires in an attempt to keep from freezing to death. This would more than offset the fact that the CSA was in better shape than Russia.

There was also another situation boiling and one that was not completely overlooked in London but was definitely on the backburner. The situation in South Africa had stabilized but the area had almost completely descended into anarchy. No one had done much to alleviate the troubles of the various territories and nations there, but no one felt really compelled to do so. They were calculating the area's effects on the war and as long as the situation remained stagnate everyone outside of South Africa was more than happy to let it remain in anarchy. The second basic assumption that the war rooms missed was that there were forces inside of South Africa who were not as content to starve to death as those in government halls were prepared to let them. This was followed by the third and final big overlook here. It was not Autumn in South Africa, but rather, Springtime instead.

While there were those educated enough at Pall Mall to note the differences between the northern and southern hemispheres, what they completely failed to grasp was the effects it had on the situation in South Africa. Traditionally, wars usually begin in the early autumn, not long after harvest when food stocks are at their highest. There were no excess food stocks in South Africa and there was virtually no one there who believed that the situation would change. What they did have to factor in was the condition of the grass lands since combatants like the Boers were largely dependent on cavalry. The best time to go on the offensive with such a force is in the spring when you can maximize your resources. This is exactly what happened in late 1901.

The Boers would not go into battle alone and this would be a direct result of the last, and possibly the largest, factor that was misread at Pall Mall. They completely ignored the Teddy Bear in the room. Roosevelt was obsessed with ending the war now, and while many have raised Theodore up to be some sort of saint on this point, the truth was that he was as aware of the numbers as Wolseley. The longer the war dragged on the worse the situation would become for the United States and France. That was why when the South African situation presented itself, Theodore jumped on it with both feet.

Natal was an odd sort of place for a worldwide offensive to begin, yet that is exactly what happened. It was also a great irony that a world war began by men who had white skin would end because of the actions of those who did not. It was almost a prophetic statement of the century to come and there were none better suited to bring this about than the Zulu microstates of northern Natal. While Dinuzulu did not control most of Zululand he had the ability to do so if he could bring something to the table. While it was true that most of the leaders of the microstates supported the British, the reality was that most of their subjects did not. Even the support of the Zulu leadership was now wavering since aid from the British was dwindling by the month. The area was ripe for the picking and Roosevelt was more than prepared to give Dinuzulu a ladder.

Again, the single biggest problem that Roosevelt had was not with his enemies but with those who called him friend. While the Zulu might have been famous for using the stabbing spear, the truth was that this weapon was even on its way out in Shaka's time. The throwing spear, that had been forbidden by Shaka, made a comeback no sooner than he had died and even more important, more than a few Zulu had firearms by the time of the war in 1879.

It is just a legend that the Zulu picked up and used the firearms of the fallen British at Isandlwana. This was not the case. The Zulu kingdom had many Impis that were equipped with firearms by 1879, and most of those weapons were purchased privately by the individual Zulus. The point being that while the Assegai might have been a point of ceremonial pride with the Zulu, they were not married to the weapon when it came time to fight. In 1901 they wanted guns, they wanted a lot of them and in particular they wanted the same kind that were being used by the Boers. These were the Colt and Winchester battle rifles that had been provided by the United States.

Kruger outright forbid such a transaction and communicated to Roosevelt that he would never allow such a thing. Roosevelt treated Kruger exactly like he did his own cabinet and ignored the man. The fact was that Zululand had its own coastline and Roosevelt did not need Kruger to make such a thing happen. Roosevelt could not act alone though, and he knew it. He did have one ally that he required complete cooperation in this endeavor and as it so happened France's dark cloud turned out to have a very interesting silver lining.

The South Rises Again

This was not the first time that the Zulu issue had come up, and in fact it had been going on since practically the start of the war. Botha and Dinazulu's calls for aide largely fell on deaf ears. Boulanger had no interest at all, and Root was typically laconic about the situation, often paying lip service but not prepared to act. This was most likely due to the resistance coming from Kruger of whom both Presidents considered to be the final say in all matters concerning South Africa. Now there were some new players in the game, and they were not prepared to settle for the old rules.

Botha had friends in Washington and oddly enough Dinazulu had some of the most unlikely of allies in France. This odd situation was also due to a death and that in and of itself was ironic. A member of the house of Bonaparte actually participated in the Zulu campaign of 1879. His name was Eugene Louis Jean Joseph, and he was the son of Louis Napoleon. Eugene was considered the heir apparent to the empire but due to the abdication of his father found himself living in London at the time of the Zulu War. He went to South Africa carrying the sword worn by Napoleon I at the battle of Austerlitz. Eugene was killed with the sword on his person and it would be taken by a Zulu warrior named Zabanga.

This might sound like the odd sort of way to start a relationship, but Eugene's mother traveled to Zululand after the war. She actually met with Zabanga and was much taken with both him and the Zulus in general. This rubbed off on many of the Bonaparte family, and now suddenly with Napoleon V being announced as the heir apparent to a new French Constitutional Monarchy many of Napoleon's descendants were returning to Paris. They had no real power, but they did have influence. The combination of this and Clemenceau, who was holding the real power, was enough to get the Zulus what they were asking for.

French and American Cruisers began showing up along the Zulu coast as early as April of 1901. By the Springtime, not only did Dinazulu have a usable military force but he had managed to either sway or force most of his internal opposition to capitulate. Naturally, the British were alarmed by this sudden uprising in Natal but found that there was very little they could do about it. The new commander in South Africa, the 4th Earl of Grey, was not surprisingly alarmed by the new forces on the board and he did wire Pall Mall asking for more reinforcements from India, but very little aide reached Durban.

The fact was that Chamberlin expressly forbid it. He also had much support in his adamant demands on Pall Mall. It was felt that altering the situation in India either by sending British regulars, or even native Indian troops, might help the situation in South Africa but it would kick over an ant hill in India. If India descended into revolution, then South Africa would be meaningless. Grey would simply have to use the resources on hand in dealing with the uprising. That word 'uprising' was also the exact word being tossed around in London and it goes a long way toward explaining their lack of concern over the matter. What Grey had failed to impress upon the cabinet was that this was no uprising, this was an all-out invasion and his troops were being hard pressed to hold it back.

Of course, Grey's failure to communicate was not entirely his fault. The situation in South Africa had been complicated since the very first days of the war and more importantly the nature of the fighting had taken on a very distinctive flavor that was quite contrary to other fronts in the conflict. The 1901 offensive was no exception and while Grey might come to see it as an all-out attack, to those in London it looked to be nothing more than the raids that had been going on in that theater since day one.

Given the official wires from Durban, it is understandable how this might have looked to Wolseley and the cabinet. Contrary to many pop culture tales that followed the war, the Zulu had not joined together in a grand army as in the days of Shaka. This was not some clever tactic on the part of Dinazulu, but rather the result of the fact that he simply lacked the political clout to unify his people in such a grand scheme. Either way, it worked in the Zulu's favor, and given their past reputation along with their current desperation, the impression they made far outweighed anything that they did on the actual battlefield. This also led to the first big mistake made by Grey.

The Zulu resurgence had an even larger effect on the black population of South Africa than it did on the white Europeans. If one is not that familiar with the complicated politics of this very large melting pot of ethnicity, things might seem as they did to Grey in 1901. The fact is that South Africa is not very black and white, which is why it is with some sense of irony that the man who took over command in the region was named Grey. The simple fact is most blacks in south Africa are not Zulu, nor are they even Bantu which is the group that the Zulu split off from. Most of the local ethnicities consider the Zulus as great enemies and fear them. While the whites had armies to defend them, the blacks did not quite see those armies as their own. What they felt like in this new wave of Zulu attack was in a word, defenseless.

Grey found himself deluged with more than just requests for troops from white settlements. Those coming in from black settlements were even greater and there were many young men of color who were rushing to the British Standard, volunteering their services or asking for guns. Grey took in a few of the volunteers most of whom would be used for manual labor until they realized this did nothing to help their situation and deserted. The calls for protection did not go entirely unheeded but given that Allied forces were already hard pressed, not much came of this effort. The request for guns was rejected without even a second thought. This might sound rather ridiculous to the modern observer but at the time Grey's decisions on these matters were not questioned nor were they even considered controversial in either South Africa or back home. They were considered nothing more than plain and simple commonsense.

Since the war, much has been made about the ferocity of the Zulu raids. Much of this has been attributed to the warlike nature of the Zulu but a much closer look shows an entirely different picture. This was not the time of Shaka nor was it even 1879. While the Zulu had not given up their ceremonial traditions, they had also been living peacefully enough for the past two decades. In 1901 very few Zulu had actually ever seen battle and there are many instances that show this to be the case. They made mistakes like anyone else, but they also had a drive that their enemies had failed to consider. I believe this had a lot to do with their overeager campaign against British outposts and supply lines. The fact was the men waging this war were hungry, not for power or violence, but for nothing more than food. The Boer cavalry who was assisting in these large raids were not far behind them either.

At first these attacks did not even alarm Grey. Raids were extremely common and one more group of them was nothing exceptional. It wasn't until the attack on Kimberly, located not that far from the old battlefield of Rourke's Drift, that Grey became alarmed. The longer these raids continued, the more alarmed Grey became. He was smart enough to see a pattern developing and realized something. He was not wrong. What the Zulu were doing was using these raids to gain experience. Subsequently, Dinazulu was also using these cheap and easy victories as a means of consolidating his power. There might not be a combined Boer-Zulu army just yet but the threat of one was becoming very real.

This is what led Grey to make his second biggest mistake. In order to defend against such an eventuality, he would have to have a force large enough to meet that army on the field. At the time his forces were spread out all over South Africa defending heavily fortified camps or patrolling and raiding, which was not that different from what his enemy was doing. He would use his advantage in this situation, along with his control of the railroads, to slowly begin concentrating a force that he hoped would be large enough to contend with this new threat. This concentration would naturally be in the area where the threat was most viable and that would be from the central to eastern part of the theater. What Grey's enemies knew, and he was completely unaware of, that this was exactly what they were hoping he would do. The real threat to the Allies in South Africa had yet to show up but it was coming.

A True World War

One of the biggest problems that Roosevelt constantly clamored about once he was in the White House was the fact that while everyone knew they were fighting a world war, nobody acted as if it were the case. Once Roosevelt was introduced to the details about how the various operations were planned, he was horrified to discover that almost no cooperation was going on between the far-flung members of the Entente. In a lot of cases even their armies in the field failed to communicate with each other. As Theodore would go on to write, "They were all planning for this picture that they were not even looking at!" With Canada out of the way, the Confederate fleet wrecked, and a more sympathetic ear in Paris, Theodore suddenly found himself with enough breathing room to do something about that. He did so with typical Roosevelt energy.

What Roosevelt brought to the picture was a central purpose and scheme that had been lacking before his arrival. He had established some clear goals that went just beyond the obvious, that of winning the war, and he was slowly charting a path out of the conflict with something that he could sell as a victory. What Roosevelt equally realized was that in order to get any kind of dialogue going he would also have to leave the Allied leaders with a similar situation. If anyone tried to rub the other side's nose in a defeat, Theodore reasoned, then not only would this war go on, but it would most likely lead to many others down the road.

As much as Roosevelt would have loved to order an invasion of England, if it were even possible (and it really wasn't), there would be nothing to be gained by such an act. Still the British were cooperating in one aspect with

Roosevelt's personal desires. It had been the United Kingdom with which he had first sent out peace feelers, and while nothing had come of it, the act did tell Roosevelt one thing about his enemy. The British were the primary block to a peace settlement, and for that reason, it would be the British who got a kick between the legs. The Zulu had come along and given him the best opportunity for that.

It would not be in Natal where this new and ambitious operation began. It would start in the far reaches of the Pacific Ocean at Port Arthur and in Manchuria in general. US and Russian forces would launch an all-out attack on the Korean Peninsula. Entente forces were now reinforced by two US Infantry divisions that consisted of troops who were largely seasoned on the Canadian Front. The ferocity of the initial attacks was unexpected by the Japanese but not the attack itself. Entente forces made some initial gains and did manage to force the Japanese to fall back on Pyongyang. Even so the attack quickly bogged down after that. The terrain in Korea is extremely difficult and if faced with an opponent who is ready and determined, and the Japanese were, such an eventuality is the most likely result.

This would have been just another quagmire except it was only really a diversion for a diversion. It was quite a bit of resources to spend on something that is seemingly so trivial. It appeared to many, particularly the US General Staff, that the wasted resources in this offensive would cripple the Entente in the following year's operations. What they did not seem to get was that their President was not planning on there being any operations in the following year. It was also nothing compared to the resistance that Roosevelt was getting from his own Navy.

The real operation that the fighting in Korea was designed to effect was something that had not happened since the start of the war. Generals Wood and Pershing had been largely responsible for this plan, and because it was two upstart Army Generals, the Navy was not on board with the concept. Fortunately for Roosevelt he was in a position to ignore his Admirals as much as he was his cabinet. He communicated directly with his man on the scene, Admiral Dewey, and issued the orders directly from the White House communications center, completely bypassing the War Department.

This act would set up the first possible full-scale naval battle since the Yellow Sea. It was not something the leaders of the US Navy were all that thrilled over. One miscalculation could cost them the largest portion of the Pacific Fleet and as a result the entire theater would have to be handed over to the Allies. This battle did not occur for several reasons and the most prominent of these reasons was the sudden demand for supplies that were placed on the Japanese army in Korea.

Admiral Moore found himself having to divert even more resources to supplying the Korean Peninsula as well as protecting the merchants who were doing that job. His resources were being stretched thin and suddenly he was alerted that a large task force of American ships had departed from Port Arthur, destination unknown. Naturally, just like Grey in South Africa, Moore found himself at the center of a bombardment of telegrams screaming for protection. Everyone, from the new Confederate authorities in the Philippines, to the City fathers of Tokyo, were convinced that they were the target of this America attack. The only way Moore could deal with this threat was to assemble his own task force and give battle. That stood in direct contradiction to his orders but under the circumstances he felt he must disobey.

Dewey had quite a jump on Moore and despite this there almost was a battle. Dewey steamed his force south in order to confuse the enemy about his true intentions. Moore assembled as many ships as he could in the time allotted and departed from Hong Kong which was where he personally thought the enemy would strike. Then nature took over once again and a storm of the type that had wrecked Galveston, called typhoons in this area of the world, intervened. Unlike the Confederate Fleet, Moore managed to avoid the storm and even tried to use it. He followed along its southern edge and placed himself where he supposed Dewey would have to pass if he were heading for Hong Kong. The Americans did not show up.

The real target of the American taskforce was far to the east. It was a little known and unremarkable island known as Guam. It had been sold to the Confederate States in the deal they made for Cuba but as of yet no one from the CSA had shown up to take possession. There were exactly two Confederate Officials, both of whom were from the CSA's State Department, that were on the island. They were operating out of Japan and had come to Guam so that they could coordinate the official handoff.

As of September of 1901, with the CSN being completely tied down in the Philippines, the exchange had yet to happen. When Dewey showed up off the coast of Guam the Spanish flag was still flying there. US Marines ignored the protests of the neutral Spanish and hauled up the Stars and Stripes instead. Guam was barely defended by the Spanish who had no desire to go to war, so no one attempted to stop the US Marines under the command of one George Armstrong Custer. The island peacefully fell into the hands of the United States and this was far from Dewey's final target.

What the US Navy was doing was laying down a path across the Pacific Ocean setting up one coaling station after another and all at very little cost. It was Roosevelt's desire that when the war was over with the US would have its own way to China and not have to rely on the Russians in Alaska. It was a move that had been completely overlooked by the British and one that went almost completely unopposed until Dewey met up with the flotilla that had departed San Francisco about the same time he left Port Arthur. This second task force was nowhere near as strong as what Dewey brought to the table, but it did carry a larger contingent of soldiers and towed three Zeppelins along with them as well. They rendezvoused without incident just northwest of the island of Oahu in the Sandwich Islands.

Theoretically the nation that was called Hawaii by its residents was a sovereign and independent Kingdom. In reality its primary harbor, known as Pearl Harbor, was the single largest Royal Navy base in the central Pacific and this fact made the island nation just another possession of the British Empire. It was also the largest single threat to the US west coast and ships departing from Oahu had raided the California coastline on any number of occasions. Usually, these raids were confined to coastal shipping but with Vancouver out of the war, Pearl was now the only British base left that could allow them to do this. The base was also responsible for protecting shipping to Mexico, which had become far more valuable than in the prewar days.

US zeppelins were the first sign at Pearl Harbor that something was horribly wrong. The airships began by bombing the port facilities and managed to even critically damage a destroyer that was sitting in drydock and undergoing repairs. Then the airships went after the cruisers that were anchored in the narrow channels. This started a panic in the city of Honolulu since they had heard of the firebombing in Atlanta. They had no wish to see their city go up in flames and these protests reached as high as Hawaii's reigning monarch, Queen Liluokalani. She promptly protested to the British authorities and made it clear she wished for the Royal Navy to leave until they could defend against such attacks.

What kind of resistance that Liluokalani could have mounted is debatable but fortunately for her the British were already pulling up their anchors and fleeing the harbor, not wishing to be caught in such a narrow channel during another bombing raid. This was exactly what Dewey was hoping for. There has been a great deal of debate about whether or not the Royal Navy squadron had any alert as to Dewey's presence, but if they did then they did not act on it. It is entirely plausible that some of the sightings by local fishermen of American ships did get reported, but again the fact remains that the British either ignored them or never imagined a task force the size of Dewey's was possible in these waters.

Thanks to the reports from the US Air Corps, Dewey was sitting in the perfect position and ready to intercept the fleeing British squadron. The US Navy cut them to pieces in short order and with almost no losses in return. The simple fact was that most of the British ships were not even ready to fight nor did they expect this kind of battle would fall upon them. A few of the British ships would escape the trap and flee right back to Pearl. It would do them no good. General Custer's troops landed on the undefended beaches of Oahu's northern shores, marched over the hills in less than a day, and found an unprepared British garrison on the other side. Within three days, the Hawaiian Islands would be mostly in American hands, and at very little cost.

By the time that Moore received word of the disaster on Oahu it was too late for him to do anything about it. He did have one attractive option though. With the US task force elsewhere, he considered the option of raiding Port Arthur itself. He did have some support from Jackie Fisher but ultimately the plan was rejected in Plymouth and the main reason was that Dewey's offensive was far from the only one that the Royal Navy was dealing with. French cruisers had attacked several smaller ports on the Australian coast. US raiders had struck the Confederate base at Diego Garcia. Ships were being sunk along the Indian coastline and there was now even increased activity in the Mediterranean and Atlantic. Several US cruisers had even been spotted within a few miles of Gibraltar. All of this had put most of the Admiralty in the mindset of defense. They were not interested in hearing about the reckless adventures being proposed by their commanders on the spot.

All of it was also a ruse. The main effort, the real objective of all these far-flung attacks, was not even thought of by the Admiralty because the main objective was not really their problem. Two days after Dewey left Port Arthur, Admiral Sampson departed Boston and New York with the larger portion of the US Atlantic fleet. He was protecting a large number of transports that were loaded with the bulk of a US Army Corps that was recently released from duty in Canada and the newly formed US 3rd Marine Division. They met up with a smaller but similar French convoy off the coast of Africa. Their transports were full of Foreign Legionnaires and Algerian Infantry. There were also a small number of Italian vessels as well as some mountain troops from the Italian

Alpini Division. It was one of the very first modern international forces to be assembled and it was a big one. This taskforce loaded down their bunkers with coal at Dakar and then sailed south for their ultimate objective.

Cape Town

It's hard to imagine that the Royal Navy would have missed a taskforce of the size and threat that the Entente assembled in September. The simple fact was that they did not. They were very aware that something big was about to happen but here the Royal Navy suffered from the same problem that Moore encountered in the Pacific. Strategically speaking the Royal Navy had been largely on the defensive since the start of the war. They had failed to overcome the enemy fleet or manage to gain a definitive superiority on any body of water. They did manage to prevent their enemies from doing this but when you are as spread out as they were, having to defend far flung sea lanes, this cannot hold forever.

When it was clear that the USN was on the move, just like with Moore in Hong Kong,

Plymouth was flooded with demands for increased protection from nearly everywhere they maintained patrols. Even Balfour took time out of his schedule to visit the First Lord of the Admiralty and discuss the possibility of a Franco-American strike on Britain itself. For whatever reason, no one in London seemed to consider that South Africa was exposed to such a danger or for that matter even worthy of such an attack. After all, the canal was still open and far more efficient at moving goods back and forth to India. It was certainly not in danger of being attacked and due to this fact, the Cape seemed almost irrelevant.

Unfortunately, this was not exactly the case and while the number crunchers at Plymouth were well aware of this fact, the idea did not seem to have filtered up the chain of command just yet. Again, men like Balfour and Chamberlin were still thinking very much under the delusions of pre-war standards. The loss of Canada had yet to figure in their strategic concepts nor had the true impact of exactly how much merchant shipping had been sunk. While it was true that the Suez allowed for the more direct passage over water that was far safer weather wise than the routes around the cape, the fact was that Britain still depended heavily on those secondary routes.

There was also the factor that only the fastest merchants were being allowed to make the run from Suez to Gibraltar, a fact that was made even more critical by the increased numbers of French airships that were now patrolling the Western Mediterranean. Many of the slower freighters were now having to use the west African route simply because technology was now rendering them obsolete. The possibility of replacing these aging merchant ships in the time allotted was nearly impossible, nor could these ships simply be retired since every ton of shipping that could be put afloat was now being required. It made Cape Town a necessary port for this trade route, critical even, and that was even if London had not quite come to terms with that just yet.

It does not seem if anyone in London had quite thought this matter over until the very first cable reached 10 Downing that an Entente fleet was engaging coastal batteries in the Cape Town region. At first, there was not a great deal of alarm since such reports had been coming in from all over the world for over a week. Chamberlin even wrote down his initial impressions and he most definitely thought this was just another harassment. This may go a long way towards explaining why nothing was done early on and how confusion reigned for the first few critical days of the attack.

In South Africa, Grey was not as confused but he had more than a few other concerns, some of which he was the direct cause of. No sooner had word of the arrival of the Franco-American fleet reached the Boers and their Zulu allies, when both stepped up their operations in an attempt to tie down as many Allied troops as possible. While this met with some success, the most important effect came from Grey's refusal and inability to protect the considerable black populations under his authority. Hunger combined with a fear of the Zulu and it was the last straw for many who were tired of suffering. Apparently, the idea began spreading that the Americans would be much easier to deal with than the British, and when your only other consideration is being gutted by a large spear, such ideas are powerful ones. The black population in South Africa rose up against their British overlords and many garrisons would not fall from the enemy outside their wires, but rather they would be overrun by the very people they were supposed to be protecting.

Despite the rapidly deteriorating situation, Grey still managed to pull together a force and march on the besieged Cape Town. He had to navigate through the narrow valleys that block Cape Town from the regions to the north and it was in one of the larger valleys, near the newly minted municipal seat of Worcester, that Grey would find himself blocked by the French Foreign Legion who would soon be joined by US Marines. Grey also learned of an approaching Boer Commando from behind and of considerable size. It was being led by Jan Smuts.

After weeks of disintegrating supply lines, collapsing garrisons, and having to march due to destroyed rail lines, Grey's men had reached their limits. Their ammunition was in low supply and many of his soldiers had not eaten in days. The British attacked Entente lines anyway. They attempted to break out and reach the supposed safety of Cape Town, but each attack was beaten back with heavy losses and once Grey's ammunition was almost gone, he contacted Entente forces and requested a formal meeting in order to discuss his terms of surrender. The single largest field force in South Africa laid down their arms two days later. Three days after that, Cape Town surrendered as well. Before the beginning of November most of the major Allied garrisons would join them.

The sea lanes around the Cape were now effectively gone. All of the critical British trade goods that flowed to and from India were forced into a single conduit that was growing ever more dangerous. This would become even more critical when a sizable Franco US Squadron dropped anchor in a long-forgotten harbor called Casablanca. They were now in the perfect position to disrupt shipping that was passing through the straights of Gibraltar, something that was more than likely going to force the Royal Navy into a sea battle that they had been trying to avoid.

On the other side of the Mediterranean, yet another threat was starting to materialize. A revolt by the Arabs against their Turkish overlords had been started early in the war, ironically by the British. When Turkey switched sides, the British had all but abandoned the Arab rebels, even if they tried keeping them on the line by tempting them with promises that never materialized. British intelligence would learn of a visit to one of the Arab camps just outside Medina by several Frenchmen who promised the Arabs all the guns they wanted. While nothing had come of this yet, it was all too clear that soon the Entente would be in a position to threaten the canal as well.

When the disaster became fully realized in London, Balfour left for Germany and spent several days in consultations with Von Bulow. Upon his return to London, David Lloyd George was summoned to the Cabinet and given a series of letters. He promptly left for Geneva and a few days later they were in the hands of William Howard Taft. The contents of these letters were promptly wired to Washington. Roosevelt was not as happy with them as one might think.

In Richmond Joe Wheeler was even less delighted when he finally learned of the news. Confederate Naval Intelligence had not learned the complete substance of this proposed ceasefire between Great Britain and the United States but what little Wheeler did find out convinced him that Balfour might be willing to sacrifice the Confederacy if Britain got its peace settlement. As we now know this was far from the case, but the fact was that Balfour had not bothered to consult with either the Confederates or the Japanese and Wheeler took this as an ominous sign.

The situation was enough. Wheeler had been holding back on the CSA's response to the US firebombing raids on the Confederacy. He now saw that he had no choice in the matter but to authorize a retaliatory strike. Unlike Balfour, he did cable his allies and announce his intentions. London was not dead set against the idea, and they began to stall in Geneva.

This Confederate response was the real cause behind Wilson avoiding Taft. It was not because of any diplomatic reason but more due to internal Confederate politics. Wheeler saw no political way out of this war until the CSA had responded to the destruction of its cities. They had been working on just such an operation and now with the shift in the fortunes of war, it seemed to Richmond as if it was the only thing left to do. Wheeler personally contacted the commander of the Confederate Air Flotilla in Alabama and gave him the verbal authorization to proceed.

Substance Abuse

London's sudden change to stalling tactics was all that was required to set off alarm

419

bells in Washington. Someone who worked in the White House, and we are not certain who because the person changes with each retelling, tried to calm the situation down by claiming that this was somehow normal. We do know that this set Roosevelt off like a volcano. He then shut the person down by proclaiming, "They are the ones who sent us this proposal! The only reason they would back off now is if something has changed! That something would have to be big!"

When Roosevelt looked around, all he could see was the very thing that Washington insiders had been paranoid about for months. They were afraid the Confederates would suddenly have the ability to launch their own firebombing raids on the US. The military had quite confidently assured the White House that the CSA had insufficient quantities of the substances required to make firebombs. That is not to say that they lacked the resources entirely. What US intelligence was talking about was that the Confederates simply did not have enough to make the number of bombs that were required to create a firestorm of the type that had consumed Atlanta. It was estimated that it would take years before such a stockpile could be amassed. They were even more confident of this when their own program proved to be very slow in replacing their own pyrotechnics.

This might have reassured the military but most of the older politicians, some of whom had clear memories of the last war, never counted the Confederacy out so easy. Too many times in the past when it was thought the Confederates lacked something, they managed to find a way around the problem and as events would prove this time was no exception. It seemed only logical to many of these people, including Roosevelt, that sooner or later the CSA would attempt to do something. The real question for these men was could they deliver an equally devastating blow. Roosevelt was betting that they could not.

In Richmond, Joe Wheeler was aware of the same sets of figures that Roosevelt had in Washington. Just as many of the older politicians in Washington had feared, the Confederacy did come up with what they hoped was a workable solution. It was very true that the CSA lacked sufficient ingredients to turn out effective munitions of the types that were favored by the US but as one young staffer at Mechanics Hall pointed out, "We're only trying to start a fire, right? How hard can it be?" They quickly sought alternatives and found one flammable substance that their nation had in abundance, even if most of it was illegal in all but a few places in the Confederacy at the time. This substance was plain and simple alcohol.

Unlike the situation that occurred a decade after the war in the US, there were no national prohibitions against alcohol in the Confederate States. The very fundamentals of their government prevented such things from ever becoming law. With a few noted exceptions, most States in the CSA refused to pass such laws. This exact same situation would later be the primary cause of the Confederacy becoming the center of one of the biggest drug smuggling operations in the hemisphere, when other illicit substances such as marijuana would be outlawed in the US.

Despite the lack of any resolution at the national and state levels, this did not prevent counties and cities from going dry and in the CSA, there were many. Entire rural swatches became no alcohol zones, and it created some strange situations. When many of these prohibited counties suddenly noticed that a great deal of their money was migrating towards urban centers, mostly spent to wet the lips of thirsty drunks, they did their best to shut this down. It suddenly became illegal to transport alcohol in some areas and when this happened those who preferred a drink simply started making their own. Before long, their neighbors wanted a drink as well and these home manufacturing centers suddenly turned to selling their products. Some of these would grow into very monumental if not illegal operations that would not only rival legal alcohol sales but surpass them in many ways.

In 1901 this underground cottage industry, that was tolerated by all but a few, was the butt of many jokes, and even had become something of a cultural legend in many places. Now these men, who had been hunted by government authorities for years, were being asked by that government to step up and save their homeland. Many of these men would eagerly cooperate, although the quantities that had been collected and 'processed' by November were still not what Mechanics Hall had hoped for. When Wheeler ordered his Air Corps to put a priority on the operation and be ready by a deadline in early November, this caused some panic.

There were many in the Confederate Military that were of the opinion that the shortages were due to the reluctance of their illicit industry to give up their entire supply. This seemed logical enough since a good number of these men still had to make a living and no amount of patriotism will do you much good if you are starving to death. This might explain why a sensible commander like Manget decided not to lean too heavily on men who were already very good at hiding things. Instead, he began rounding up stocks of legal liquors. Surprisingly, the owners of these operations were just as eager to support the war effort as were their outlaw counterparts.

The real problem did not come from the alcohol manufacturers at all but from the very county governments who had outlawed the substances in the first place. It did not help that the main Confederate airbase was located in a dry county. When the local Sheriff became aware of what was being transported in his jurisdiction, he showed up at the front gate with several deputies and announced he was confiscating the supplies. The Confederate soldiers, that outnumbered law enforcement on a scale of over ten to one, disagreed and the Sheriff was forced to back down. This did not hamper attempts to stop the transport of alcohol and Manget was forced to put guards on most of his shipments. It would also not be his only source of trouble.

The single largest stockpile of alcohol that Manget could reach was sitting in Tennessee. It all belonged to the maker and supplier of a bourbon that was heavily exported and known worldwide. In peace time it was the single largest employer in the county where it was located, and oddly enough, it was also illegal to sell in that very same county. The owners of the operation were more than happy to donate some of their stockpiles to the military, and in fact it was a considerable supply. The problem came when the army tried to remove the casks from the dark and damp store houses where the liquid was aged.

County officials showed up and tried to prevent the soldiers from doing their jobs. The officials were followed by a sizable group of deputized citizens who were all heavily armed. The soldiers pointed out their orders, signed by the President of the Confederacy, to confiscate the liquor. The county officials refused to recognize the authority of the President. They thought that to do such a thing was immoral and went even further by stating that no one had even voted for Joe Wheeler in their county anyway. The officer in charge, a young lieutenant, was arrested and thrown in jail. His men were sent back emptyhanded.

Manget did not react to this matter with any great emotion. He simply picked up the phone and reported the situation to Richmond. Wheeler was informed of the incident in less than an hour and he reacted with great resolve. The Confederate Army detailed an entire battalion to literally invade the county and confiscate the alcohol. They went further than the agreed amount and just took everything instead. This entire incident would remain controversial for years and would later wind up in the Supreme Court where the government was forced to pay an undisclosed amount for damages. That would be much later, but for the time being the situation was resolved. Manget suddenly had what he needed to manufacture the required number of bombs. Most of the ordinance would wind up being armed with grade A expensive Tennessee sipping bourbon.

The Confederate bomb was far less hi-tech than its US counterpart. You simply filled a container with alcohol. The finished product was very heavy and cumbersome, and as the case would prove it was also extremely delicate. You then attached a fuse to the side, and this was in direct contrast to the explosive itself.

While the bombs were primitive the detonator was actually very hi-tech in that it was filled with a mixture of chemicals that would combust at high temperatures once exposed to air. Many war projects came to a complete stop in order to make the required number of these devices that required some very hi-tech machine tools for that time. Fortunately for the Confederates, these devices were only needed to spark the fuel so the amount of needed industrial grade chemicals was small. It was usually less than a thimble full per device.

The job of making the detonators was miraculously completed showing what can happen when people are properly motivated by the fear of a foreign invader, and enough were delivered in time for Manget's people to attach them to the makeshift collection of bomb casings they had assembled. The idea behind the weapon was simple: you drop the bomb, it shatters on impact releasing the alcohol, and the detonators cause a spark that is hot enough to set off the fumes. In theory, if you drop enough of these you should be able to get a large enough fire that would begin to spread on its own.

A variety of cases were used, and they only really had two qualifying factors. One was that they could contain no less than fifty gallons of liquid and the other was that they broke on impact after being dropped from a few thousand feet. The original idea was to use wooden caskets, of the kind that were made for storing alcohol, but these proved to be inadequate in supply. That was why many of the bombs wound up in flimsy metal drums and they eventually ran out of those as well. This caused Manget to have to sit back and dream up an entirely new weapon on the spot. That's how they came up with the idea for the 'bomblet." What they did have an almost unlimited supply of were five-gallon jugs made of either glass or ceramics. They did not have enough detonators for all of these, but it was pointed out, they didn't need them. All that was required was to drop enough of the smaller bomblets on the target with a detonator on only one in ten. If they used these after the big bombs, there should be more than enough heat to combust all of the alcohol.

It was not a perfect solution but ultimately Manget found that he had little choice but to try it. The unrealistic deadline was moved up once again and this time Manget also received his target along with his orders. The entire Confederate Air Flotilla was going to New York City.

The secret Confederate weapon proved to be not so much of a secret. The clamor that Manget had caused in collecting his alcohol had been more than enough to alert US intelligence to the danger. It did not take them long to figure out why the Confederacy wanted so much alcohol and this news was presented to the President not long after word had been received about the victory in South Africa. Roosevelt was livid about what he exclaimed to be a conspiracy by his own military to hide relevant information, but it does not appear that any such conspiracy existed. The President had to be updated on so much every day it was virtually impossible for many of the intelligence analysts to know what was important and what was not. It was only after a retaliation for the firebombings seemed likely that some mid-level officer at Fort Lincoln decided the information was important enough to forward.

Very few at Fort Lincoln were aware that their own military was working on a counter to the Zeppelin raids. This would go a long way towards explaining why some at Fort Lincoln were almost ignoring the warning signs they were getting. They had no idea that the US was not only going to attempt to use a groundbreaking new weapon but had already done so. This was ironic in that most of the counterparts of the US intelligence officers down in Richmond already knew all about the US airplane. They had received multiple reports from the air flotilla about this new weapon. The CS officers were not impressed.

The Langley project in Wichita had found that building a working model was only the first of many steps required. Despite their success, they soon discovered that getting one of their planes off the ground was only the start of that process. Turning that vehicle into a workable weapons system was an entirely different matter and it was also one that they had given almost no thought to at all.

The first true combat aircraft in world history primarily the Wright Flyers models six and seven, suffered from any number of deficiencies. When compared to the capabilities of the Sky Trains, they were decidedly inferior. Zeppelins had now reached the point of almost intercontinental flight. Their ceilings were growing with every new model that came out of the factories, as were their bombload capacities. Many of them were also being equipped with machine guns in order to defend themselves against the chance encounter with an enemy Zeppelin although none had been needed as of that time.

In comparison, the very first combat airplanes had almost no real range. They also had problems just getting off the ground. Most of the six and seven models were launched from catapults that had to be transported and built on sight. In a moving war this is very much a disadvantage that will sink your attempts before you even get started. The airplanes also could never hope to match the altitudes of the Zeppelins. The dual engines were not powerful enough, the frames were too delicate, and the pilots were limited to altitudes where there was enough oxygen to breath. At the time this was seen as irrelevant because they all knew that the six and seven models would never get that high anyway. Even if they could it would take too long, and the Zeppelin would be gone long before the plane reached its target altitude.

While the CSA had yet to build a zeppelin that could reach the altitudes where a breathing apparatus was required for the crew, the Germans already had, and it was only a matter of time before the CSA would follow suit. Even so in November of 1901 the primary concern was with speed. The Germans had also built Zeppelins that were fast enough to outrun the top speeds of the WF-07. Fortunately, the US planes were not going up against the Germans but even so some of the newer Confederate Zeppelins were fast enough to narrow the window required for a successful interception. This was a serious factor but so was the fact that once you reached the enemy airship, you had to be able to damage it enough to bring it down. There did not seem to be a way to do this.

Oddly enough, the solution would come from the most unexpected of sources and this was once again, Woodbury Cane. He had no knowledge of the airplane project, but he was in constant communications with Theodore Roosevelt who did. Cane wrote extensively of John Browning and his revolutionary rifle. Roosevelt was impressed that Cane was impressed and so the President actually ordered some of his Secret Service men to track Browning down. As it turned out the man had set up a shop in Connecticut and had already hand produced nearly thirty weapons. That was roughly the number of planes that had been built and Roosevelt saw this as almost divine providence. Then he ran into his usual problems.

As it turned out, there were many inside the US War Department that knew all about Browning. This included Roosevelt's new Secretary of War, William McKinley, who had more than a few suspicions about Browning because the man was a Mormon. This little faction had friends in congress and every time Roosevelt tried to appropriate the funding to employ Browning and build these new rifles, he was met with one roadblock after another. Roosevelt finally gave up and employed the tactic he was coming to like; he ignored these men. Roosevelt was not trying to equip a division with these rifles and as he realized he only needed the ones that already existed, he paid for them out of his own pocket.

The weapons were delivered to Wichita and Browning came with them. He trained the men who would use them, and every weapon was field tested. Since they were all handmade prototypes, they all worked beautifully and seemed to be exactly what was needed. They were relatively lightweight, put out a lot of firepower and were easily re-loaded. It did not take long for Langley's people to figure out how to mount them on the frames of their vehicles. It was also one of the easier problems they had to deal with. Marksmen were a dime a dozen and easy to find. The WF-06 and 07 were two-man vehicles and the guy who would shoot was only half the crew. It was the other half of the team that was the true problem.

To say that Langley had a shortage of pilots was an understatement. The airplane was brand new and there simply were no pilots at all. To make matters worse there was almost no one who would volunteer to be one either. Still, in a nation with a population of the size of the US he was able to scrape together enough people who would give it a go. I say people here and not men because nearly half of those who volunteered were women. Five of them would eventually fly combat missions. Four of them would die in the process while the last one would go on to become famous.

After Langley had his pilots, he had the problem of training them, although strangely enough this would be much less of a problem than in later years of air warfare. The fact was that if you do not have any pilots to begin with you are also lacking for people to teach them as well. The entire pilot training program, personally overseen by the Wright Brothers, barely deserved the name. They made it up as they went and a lot of what the pilots eventually wound up doing were techniques they developed on the job while being shot at.

Luckily for the US about the only real skill these first pilots required was being brave enough, or foolish as some have claimed, to go up in these machines in the first place. Despite the popular images conjured up in movies that were filmed decades after the event, these early attempts in air-to-air combat were more akin to a slow speed police chase as compared to some daring war of fancy acrobatics. Most of the pilots only needed to do one maneuver and that was climb as fast as they could. The first attempt at an interception was in late August.

Given the lack of interception and the disposition of anti-aircraft artillery, Confederate zeppelins followed very predictable flight paths and usually at the same altitudes. The raids on Chicago were picked for a test and for no other reason than its proximity to Wichita. It was known that the Confederates were using the junction of the Ohio and Mississippi rivers as a navigational point and were usually quite low when then they did. The ramps for ten of the WF-06's were built in the area and then, they waited for the next raid to materialize. The results would be almost comical if it were not for the loss of life.

As it turned out, the single most dangerous element to the attempted interception was after the combat part was over. Half of the deployed aircraft were destroyed trying to land. Two of the aircrews were killed and almost all of them were injured, including several who landed their planes successfully. For the bill, they accomplished very little. The Confederate Zeppelins did the US Air Force one favor in that they were loitering in the area waiting for other airships when the attack occurred. The airplanes did nothing to encourage them to leave and according to at least one log the Confederate air crews found the entire thing amusing.

Most of the aircraft never reached their targets. We now know that one plane did manage to get in range of an airship and did hit its target. At the time it was thought otherwise but Confederate records clearly indicate that they found multiple bullet holes in the airframe. Had anyone in the US known this at the time it is possible they would have abandoned the entire project. They scored a direct hit, and nothing happened as a result. Still Langley had obviously considered this possibility because even before the first attempt he was inquiring about special munitions of the type used by anti-aircraft. These were the new hi-tech tracer rounds. Due to Roosevelt's efforts, Langley did eventually get a few cases, and this would prove to be fortunate.

The fledgling US Air Force would also get several more opportunities to prove its worth. The pilots were gaining some experience and subsequent interception attempts would produce fewer casualties of both aircraft and crew. They would also fail completely in stopping Confederate bombers. The Confederate aircrews took to calling the US planes 'gnats,' which was a completely annoying but otherwise harmless insect that was common in the deep south. That was pretty much their attitude about this airplane. They seemed to be completely harmless and most of the time the Confederates did not even bother shooting at them. The best defense the Zeppelins had was simply to fly higher and this seemed to eliminate any potential threat.

The new fire raids aimed at New York proved to be an unexpected blessing in disguise. Roosevelt was already feeling the heat over the airplane. The multiple attempts at stopping the zeppelins had been a very expensive disaster and many were using this to counter the influence that Roosevelt had enjoyed ever since he moved into the White House. These were closed door discussions, however. The public had yet to really hear about this but all of that would change when the first Confederate fire raid dropped its load on downtown Manhattan.

Lakehurst

New York City had been no stranger to the bombing campaign being waged by the Confederate Air Flotilla. This is perhaps the reason that most of its residents had become so accustomed to seeing the cigar shaped bombers that they paid them almost no mind at all. They would seek shelter but any real panic and urgency to do so was long gone by 1901. It would seem that the residents of Manhattan had some solid reasons for taking the bombings with a grain of salt. Despite the increased tonnage, they were simply not doing that much damage and for most of the residents the disruptions to their lives became little more than an annoyance. The government actually sided with this attitude because as the bombing campaign continued it was realized that the work stoppages created by air raid warnings were actually doing more damage than the bombs.

The attacks on New York were logical from the point of view of Richmond. While the size of the United States might hide this fact, the simple matter is that New York city is largely the whole of the US economy. Even large cities such as Chicago only grew to their metropolitan status because of a need to feed New York. Cities like San Francisco were large due to a gold strike but where did this gold get traded? It was in New York. Until the mid-twentieth century when industrial centers and major organizations became more diversified, New York City's supremacy was very much the case. If the US lost NYC it would be a handicap on the magnitude of Britain losing the Suez Canal.

By November, the Allies were growing desperate and Joe Wheeler seemed to offer them a way by which they could negotiate from a position of strength. Given that it was unlikely that Roosevelt would have accepted the terms that were being discussed in London, it is likely that a successful firebombing of New York would have prolonged the war for at least another year and quite possibly even longer. As events would prove the forces that were about to butt heads were largely bluffs but of the kind that cannot be ignored. They would also impact the future in many significant ways.

The actions around New York City in the late fall of 1901 have been portrayed in an overly dramatic fashion ever since they happened. For those who were actually involved it is hardly a stretch to believe that they thought this anything but high drama. It is most certainly true that none of them even realized the strange turn of events that would lead to this chapter of the war's ultimate conclusion. It is also highly unlikely than any of these people, only a hand full at best, realized that the fates of countless millions rested on everything that they were doing.

This was particularly true of the US warplane crews who had become somewhat frustrated with the results of their efforts. Had this been any other type of project it is likely that the entire thing would have already been scrapped. The main reason this did not happen was because those that were involved were extraordinarily passionate about what they were doing. They saw this as the future. What their political patron, Theodore Roosevelt, saw this as was his political career that was very much hanging in the balance along with the fate of his nation.

There is little doubt, given the comments made by those around him, that Roosevelt was extraordinarily apprehensive when he ordered Langley to deploy his entire compliment of planes to the environs around New York. The Confederates had now tested their moonshine and it had started a considerable blaze in Central Park. The otherwise laconic residents of the city became almost panicked. Everyone knew what had happened to Atlanta and now it seemed that payback was on the way. There was a mass exodus from the city and nearly all the facets of normal life came to a complete standstill. That's when Roosevelt found that he had to gamble everything. He released the existence of his airplanes to the newspapers in an attempt to calm down the situation. It had very little effect and Roosevelt could see the sharks already gathering to pick his bones when Langley and the Wright Brothers failed.

What no one knew, and this included Roosevelt, was that several factors had combined to increase the effectiveness of their new weapon. The first of these was the new ammunition. The tracer rounds were about to get their first try in the Browning rifles. The second was the location that Langley picked to set up his catapults, that being a field just outside of Lakehurst, New Jersey. That November was a bit warmer than most and the area around Lakehurst was getting an almost constant breeze, most of which was causing a considerable updraft. The last factor, and quite possibly the most critical, had nothing to do with US efforts.

As noted before, the Confederate ordinance was excessively bulky and heavier than the usual loads they carried. The US had actually toyed with the idea of these alcohol bombs in the early stages of their own project. The idea had been rejected for the exact same reasons that the Confederates were now having problems with. The size of these caskets was much larger than regular bombs and this meant more flights. The weight caused considerable drag and that meant the engines had to work harder. It limited the range of the zeppelins and this meant in order to actually reach New York they would have to fly lower, where the air was thicker, requiring less fuel for the trip.

All of this added up to the airplanes being able to get higher faster, while the lumbering zeppelins would have to fly within their range and at much slower speeds. This would even prove to be less of a blessing than the main factor and that was the very nature of the ordinance to be delivered. When the very first zeppelin came within range of a catapult, Lucy Q. Jones and her gunner, Corporal Douglas H Parks, a black soldier from Iowa City, launched towards their target. This was their third combat mission, and it would be the first that they actually reached their target which was the CSS Chattahoochee.

Jones was actually able to get above the Zeppelin which apparently astonished her since this was the first time she had ever been able to accomplish such a feat. Normally the airships would start climbing no sooner than they spotted an approaching plane. It is now believed that the Chattahoochee was attempting to climb, and this explains what happened next. Parks got off a single burst from his Browning Automatic, and apparently hit the top of the frame but once again it appeared to have no effect. Then, as Jones reported, they almost had the first midair collision in history. This is where it seems that Chattahoochee was trying to get some more altitude.

The next move by the US airplane was also atypical of the pattern that had developed over the course of the past few months. Both pilot and gunner were in the prone position, laying along the axis of the central fuselage, and had very little to hold them into place. No one had thought that the WF-07 was capable of any significant turns anyway so no one had put much thought into it. As Lucy came down on the far side of the airship, she tried just such a move and almost lost control. Both her and Parks almost fell to their deaths as well. Then they encountered an even more serious problem.

When Jones managed to re-establish some semblance of level flight, something that modern experts believe was only by the virtue of pure luck, she also had to overcome a few moments of disorientation. By her own recollection, she did not even realize which way was up until they were about to fly right into the underside of the Chattahoochee. Jones quickly started to dive but not before Parks got off one last burst with his automatic rifle. There is no way to know for certain but what we believe happened was that Parks was lined up perfectly with the bomb bay. We also know that nearly half of Chattahoochee's load were the glass containers that had been termed 'bomblets.' It is believed he must have shattered enough of them causing the fuel to spray the gas bags and that some sort of spark, the kind that you get when firing pyrotechnic bullets into an enclosed space, set the alcohol off.

This was far from the only lucky break that the US caught on this day. Not only did the CSS Chattahoochee combust in midair and begin to fall to the ground as her skin burned away, but thanks to another technological innovation that we have already covered, the entire world would get to see this happen. Lakehurst is not very far from Menlo Park and when Thomas Edison heard the buzz concerning the activities there, he quickly dispatched a crew with a motion picture camera. Despite later claims, Edison was not present when the film was shot but he did recognize its importance and copies were being printed and distributed within days.

The US Air Force would also have its second kill later that afternoon and despite the fan fair surrounding Jones and Park, the second interception was actually far more important. The CSS War Cloud met a similar fate after the US pilots, based on the reports from Jones, figured out the weakness of their enemies. When Sergeants Leeland and Conklin intercepted the War Cloud they went right for the bomb bay doors and scored an immediate and critical hit. Now it was definitive that the first interception was no fluke. The US suddenly seemed to have a viable weapon, and thanks to Thomas Edison, it would not be long before the entire world could see this with their own eyes.

While it was very clear to the war planners and national leaders alike, and this included Roosevelt, that the airplane was not yet a viable weapon system they also realized that it did not have to be. Both sides were already teetering on the brink, the first overtures of peace had been made, and the airplane was simply what tipped the balance. What Balfour in London and Wheeler in Richmond both had to contend with was that the firebombing had failed, even if most of the bombers did reach their targets. They also had to realize that while the airplane was not that powerful in 1901 if they chose to continue the war that might not be the case in 1902. It was also a technology that they were lagging far behind in. The zeppelins came about from established and well understood technologies. The airplane was simply too revolutionary and not that simple to develop. The US lead would give then an undisputed edge and it was not the kind that could be easily ignored. The ultimate result would be that the US could stop raids while continuing their own.

This is why Wheeler telegraphed Balfour in London, and Wilson in Geneva. He outlined his own demands for a ceasefire and the negotiations to end the war began in earnest.

Only the Dead

While the war did not officially end until April 15th of 1903, the fact was that this went largely unnoticed by the world and has long since been forgotten. The date that everyone remembers is 11/11/01, the date of the general ceasefire that ended all of the fighting in Europe, North America, and Africa. The fighting in China would continue for some time but not between the forces of the former belligerents. The fighting in Alaska would take years before it finally settled down. That only happened after what was surely a simple attitude change. People there got tired of it and would no longer tolerate it.

The Alaskan situation was also a part of a larger problem in Imperial Russia. Czar Nicholas found himself with a civil war on his hands. Before the end of the fighting, it had only been civil unrest but when the Russian Army demobilized a good number of these hastily conscripted draftees took their weapons home with them. Many would join bands like those in Georgia while others would form their own. Russia would not know peace for some years to come.

France was also not out of the woods just yet. While the violence never reached the levels that it did in Russia, the fact was that her inner political turmoil would prove to handicap the nation in many ways for some years to come. France's turmoil would also pale in comparison to that of Italy and Austria-Hungary. They would both know ethnic strife and internal wrangling that would often grow violent and greatly weaken both nations. This was never clearer than in 1914 when the reinvigorated Serbian group, the Black Hand, would attempt to assassinate the son of Emperor Franz Joseph. The attempt was botched, the plan failed, but it almost led the Balkans into another war that would have been compounded by the intervention of several major powers. Fortunately, no one wanted a repeat of 1898. A conference was called in The Hague, and the matter was settled and quickly swept under the rug.

The problems in North America were not so easily disposed of. Even as the final peace treaty was signed, too many thought that it was led with contradictions and none of it good enough to settle any future disputes that were already brewing. The fact was that the war had only left tensions between the US and CS at an even higher level, despite the fact that for the first time since 1861, both nations were officially at peace. The Confederacy was forced to give up her claims on territories she lost in the American 61 but in the hearts and minds of most Confederate citizens this was not the case. The people in the US still felt as if the CSA had not been punished enough for their traitorous actions. This bitterness would linger for years to come.

Of course, of all the nations involved no one probably suffered more from the peace than did Great Britain. Her empire was shattered by the war and even though she made great progress at repairing the damage, the fact was it was too little too late. The Commonwealth was all but a memory by 1903.

The republic of Canada successfully learned to stand on its own two feet and without military expenditures, life for the average Canadian improved. Even US interference proved to be largely an empty threat. The very first time the US made demands of unarmed Canada, it suddenly found that the Canadians

449

still had a weapon. The US was told, "Go ahead and invade, we won't cooperate." To put into practical terms even passive resistance to such an invasion would have made the venture cost more than it was worth. The US went on to largely ignore Canada while the Canadians gave the US no reason to do much else. This suddenly gave Canada a freedom in her foreign policy that she had never enjoyed before.

South Africa also successfully managed to put an end to the constant interference of British Foreign Policy. Both the Cape Colony and Natal would find itself under US administration for years to come but would eventually go on to join the Boers and Zulu in forming the USSA, the United States of South Africa. Ironically, this nation functioned more like the Confederate States than it did the federalist system that was used by the US. It would also be largely successful and much of that has been accredited to the fact that no one wanted to relive the situation that occurred in the great war.

With the loss of key members of Britain's empire, and the others rapidly faltering, Britain found itself turning more and more towards one of the undisputed winners of the conflict. The UK and Imperial Germany came out of the war with an unshakable strategic partnership that both nations greatly benefited from, however as time went on it became more and more clear who the senior partner was, and this was not Britain. Even so, both nations would be major players in the post war world.

This world was also more and more becoming one that was bipolar in nature. If US power had been doubted before the conflict, Roosevelt went on to prove that after the war it could not be. The rivalry that was forming between the US and Germany would only grow. This would rear its head in many parts of the far-flung globe, most prominently in China and South America. Both nations would also find themselves confronted with the emerging entanglements of rising regional powers that went well beyond the Confederate States and Japan, both of whom became leaders in that community.

Brazil got the upper hand with Argentina, thanks largely to the disintegration of the former. Some of the divided states of China would emerge as local powers in their own rights. All of these regions would go on to influence the larger picture in many ways, but none would be as successful as Mexico. She came out of the war a creditor state mostly to the smaller nations just to her south. Mexico, with its growing industrial base, would soon come to dominate and then outright annex the entirety of the Central American isthmus. It would be Mexico who finally went on to build the canal across Panama and it would be Mexico who mostly profited from this.

The war had reshaped the world in many ways but in the end, it was the decentralization of power that was probably the most significant. Europe had dominated the planet for centuries and the war both weakened the great powers and transferred much of that to other corners of the globe. This would eventually come home to effect relations between ethnicities in every nation. This would be hard felt in nations like the Confederate States, a country that was born of an attempt to ignore the changes in the world around it. What this war showed the CSA was that the world would not ignore them. The war forced the CSA to throw its doors wide open and the changes this fostered would play themselves out over the next century with many interesting results.

The technologies introduced in this war are still with us today. Some of those early attempts seem almost comical to us now and many have been largely forgotten. Some of the inventions have become so commonplace to us that we take them for granted. Others have developed into more advanced machines that would look almost like magic to someone in the closing years of the nineteenth century. All of our wonders today had their genesis in that time period and that makes it important to understand.

We must not forget the lessons of this war. In understanding its origins, in how it was fought, in the legacy it left behind, we understand the world that we live in today. We must also remember the sacrifices of those who most likely did not even understand them at the time. Yet, that has been our real history. It is a story of average men and women, all doing little and seemingly unimportant things. All contributing to the larger picture that is shaped in such a way that no one even realizes it until long after the fact. If there is any lesson to be taken from all of this, that would most likely be the important one.

THE END

Made in the USA
Middletown, DE
16 August 2021

46117012R00255